INTEREST

Kevin Gaughen

Interest

Copyright © 2015 by Kevin Gaughen

This book is a work of fiction. Names, characters, businesses, organizations, places, events, and incidents are either the product of the author's imagination or are being used fictitiously. Any resemblance to actual persons, living or dead, is coincidental.

Cover art by Benjamin Ee

Published by the author:
Kevin Gaughen
PO Box 1517
Mechanicsburg, PA 17055-9017
USA

ISBN-10: 0986380520
ISBN-13: 9780986380525

First Edition: May 2015

Printed in the United States of America

Acknowledgments

I'd like to express sincere gratitude to the following people:

First, to my mother, Louisa Gaughen, who, from my earliest memories, tirelessly encouraged me to read and write. I don't know where I'd be if my mom hadn't always inspired literacy, learning, and discovery.

Second, to my father, Thomas Gaughen, who always taught by example to relentlessly push forward through adversities, no matter how awful they might seem. No hell is deep enough to stop Tom Gaughen.

Third, but certainly not least, to my wife, Laryssa Gaughen, for her unflagging support and encouragement as I worked on this book for months on end—while we were raising three young children and running a small business, no less. Laryssa's loyalty and selflessness always inspires me.

I'd further like to thank the following family and friends whose review of my manuscript helped me polish this story into something almost readable.

Beta readers:
Tobin Coziahr
Joanna Ferguson
Grant Gaughen
Laryssa Gaughen
Thomas Gaughen
Maria Elaina Martinelli
Teresa Pezzi
Michael Sams
Stephanie Shapiro

Japanese Translation:
Yukiko Kine Rolich

To YOU:

Yeah, *you*, sitting there with your paperback or e-reader:

Thanks for buying my novel!

I'm self-published. And since I have a fool for a publisher, I humbly ask one favor of you, my dear reader: please let me know if you find any errors. And by that, I mean *any* errors—typos, plot holes, incongruities, grammar mistakes, etc. I'll do my best to make the corrections you suggest in future revisions of this book. You can reach me at kevin@kevingaughen.com. Don't be shy; I'd love to hear from you—even if you don't find any problems!

I hope you enjoy the story.

—Kevin

"Compound interest is the eighth wonder of the world. He who understands it, earns it. He who doesn't, pays it."

—*Albert Einstein (attributed)*

1

"Shit's getting dangerous," Len said, watching the White House burn on national television.

"First the FBI building, then the CIA, now this. What do you think it means?" Stewart, one of Len's coworkers and a frail man to begin with, was looking especially wan.

"It means we need to drink more." Len lit a cigarette.

"Have they issued a statement?"

"From where, the Brady Press Room? It's on fire."

"Jesus. I wonder if the president survived."

"Who cares?" The words and spontaneous laughter escaped before Len could check himself.

Len's editor shot him a nasty look. "Len, what's wrong with you? People are dead. There's chaos in the streets. And why are you smoking in the office?"

"Sorry, Jack. I'm a little out of it. Haven't been sleeping well."

Rather than putting it out, Len decided to finish his cigarette outside. He walked through the building and out to the street. To hell with work today, he thought while standing there at the curb. In fact, to hell with everything. It was noon; time for a burrito.

Len walked past closed shops and demonstrators. Each passing day seemed to bring the city a little closer to a collective nervous breakdown. Today, some people in the street looked like they'd had lobotomies—standing around, staring into the sky at the fighter jets circling the city. Others seemed as though they were one parking ticket away from a full-on panic attack, chatting hysterically with any stranger who would engage them. A deuce and a half full of National Guardsmen nearly ran Len over as he crossed the street.

The little jingle bell rang as Len pushed the door open. "God bless you Mexicans," Len exclaimed upon entering the taqueria, "you're always working. Everything else is closed!"

"Señor Len!" Paco, a portly man covered in tattoos, was sitting behind the counter watching the chaos on a little TV. "Can you believe this *mierda*? It's like Chiapas over here. Why aren't you working? Big news day!"

"No one knows anything yet, and every hack in the business is writing about the same event. What's the point anymore? El Ultimo *con lengua, por favor*."

Len carried his food to a table by the window. The national guardsmen who had almost plowed him over minutes earlier were now setting up sandbags and a .50-caliber machine gun on the street corner. Len found it all quite theatrical—an overt show of *doing something* to calm the cattle into thinking security was possible. The real danger was that there were heavily armed, twitchy, uniformed teenagers just fifty feet away.

He'd barely gotten halfway through his meal when his phone rang; its screen showed a number he didn't recognize.

"Hello?"

"Is this Mr. Leonard Savitz?" The voice was female.

"Speaking. Who's this?"

"I just killed the president of the United States. I would like to meet with you."

"Hilarious. Who's this?"

"Today your daughter Octavia is wearing the yellow Steelers shirt that you bought her last fall. Your ex-wife, Sara, who drives a green SUV, just picked her up from kindergarten." The woman's tone was eerily flat.

The blood drained from Len's face.

"Who is this? This isn't funny."

"Tomorrow we will find you."

Click.

2

"Sara, take Octavia and get out of town."

"What? Why?"

"I can't explain. Just do it. Go to your mom's place or something."

"Len, we've discussed this before. You do not dictate what I do with her when she's here."

Len paused and tried to collect himself. "Sara, something is going down, and I'm worried about her safety."

"What exactly is 'going down'?"

The sarcasm annoyed Len. "Turn on the TV."

"What does that have to do with us? We're not government, we're not targets. Besides, the whole city's on lockdown."

"Look, this thing somehow involves us personally."

"Oh? How do you figure?"

"I can't explain."

"Why can't you explain?"

"You'll just have to trust me on this."

"Trust. Right. That worked out really well for me for six miserable years. If you knew something, you would be able to tell me what exactly. But you aren't explaining anything so, QED, you know nothing. I told you to see a doctor about your drinking, Len."

"Sara, I need you to listen to me for once. Have you not seen the news? It's not safe for either of you to be in the city."

"Oh, please. I don't need a man to tell me what's safe and what isn't." Sara had a remarkable talent for turning absolutely any topic into a gender-politics issue.

"I don't know how to get through to you. I never have."

"It's a shame they don't give Pulitzer prizes in feeling sorry for oneself."

"Goddammit, if something happens to my daughter, Sara, I will hold you personally responsible."

"Good-bye, Len."

Len suddenly missed the old days when he could slam a phone receiver down.

———

Len attempted to explain the disturbing phone call to his editor back at the office. Jack was a thin man with gray hair and a boyish face. When wearing a shirt and tie, he looked like a college kid playing dress-up, despite being in his mid-forties. It was Jack who had taken the chance in hiring Len as a staff writer fourteen years ago. Len had been a twenty-something nobody with only a few published freelance stories under his belt, but Jack could sense potential. He took Len under his wing and assigned him the kind of stories that weren't usually entrusted to cub reporters. Len appreciated the opportunity and put in long hours to do his best work possible. He was always impressed by the way Jack would go to the mat for his employees, even if they were in the wrong. Jack and Len were close in age, and neither was known for teetotaling; over time, a solid friendship developed between the two. Jack had even been a groomsman in Len's wedding. He was one of the few people Len trusted implicitly.

"Lenny, relax, it was probably a prank," Jack said with his typical level-headedness. "Did you try calling the number back?"

"Of course I tried that. Apparently it's some copy-print place in Omaha. They didn't know what I was talking about and said no customers had borrowed their business phone today. Do you think I should call the police?"

"Look, we tell the truth for a living, which means we make enemies. You, you *particularly*, have pissed off an awful lot of people over the years. You've single-handedly kept our legal department in business. Someone is angry about some piece you wrote, and this is their little revenge. Don't let them get under your skin."

"Jack, this woman gave me the creeps. Something was seriously off. She had no emotion in her voice. She knew what my daughter was wearing and what kind of car Sara drives. And why would she claim to have killed the president?"

Jack gave Len a skeptical look. "No one knows if the president is dead. There hasn't been any announcement. Also, do *you* even know what your daughter is wearing? I thought she lived with your ex. Someone's yanking your chain, Lenny. I bet it was that district justice. Remember? She's been threatening to sue us over that story we ran, the one about her drinking on the bench." Jack put his hand on Len's shoulder and looked him in the eye. "Look, you've been a little on edge lately, and what's happening today isn't helping. Why don't you take the rest of the day off?"

"Because we're already shorthanded, that's why."

"So what?" Jack shrugged. "Everyone's going to be running syndication over the next week. This is a DC story; the *Pittsburgh Examiner* isn't exactly on the front lines. Go home, turn off the TV, have a drink. All this crap will still be here tomorrow."

Len walked home on city streets thick with hysteria. Cops on horseback, cops with riot shields, cops shooting dogs and Tasering little old ladies: just the usual responses to crises these days.

Len often found himself missing the bad old days of Pittsburgh. The city's economy had collapsed after the steel mills were offshored in the 1970s, and the entirety of western Pennsylvania plunged into a profound, decades-long funk in which all anyone had was football and awful beer. It was a glorious sort of despondency: abandoned factories, endlessly gray skies, and long, nasty winters. On every corner there was a busted-ass watering hole with blacked-out windows and fake wood paneling inside, where unemployed mill trash drank and smoked all day until their teeth fell out.

Yet there was a kind of peace in the hopelessness, because no one expected anything. Len had learned the hard way that unrealistic expectations were the cause of most misery in the world. Back then people would invite you to their house for dinner if they thought you were hungry. One minute you could be wondering where your next meal would come from, and then an hour later you'd be passing the potatoes to someone's grandma in their dining room. The whole town was in it together, and it felt like family. No one asked you what you did for a living at a cocktail party in the hopes of one-upping you with pretentious crap. There were no cocktail parties, and it was impressive just to have a job, *any* job. The city was full of real people in those days, not hipster jag-offs.

Whatever. *Things change*, he reminded himself. A BMW driver blabbing on his cell phone blew through the intersection as Len was trying to cross.

Len's apartment was a third-floor walkup in Bloomfield, the old Italian neighborhood. He'd been there since the divorce. Rent had been cheap on his street until a bunch of yuppies took over and cluster-bombed the place with boutique shops and theme bars.

Walking past the mirror in the hallway of his apartment building, he stopped briefly and stared with agnosia at the reflection of a middle-aged man. He used to be a handsome young guy before life kicked the shit out of him. Lines on his face now, eyes tired. At least he still had his hair.

After divorce, he'd heard, you picked up right where you left off the last time you were single. Len's case was textbook rebachelorhood. His apartment smelled like an ashtray. Save for one small photo of his daughter, there were no pictures on his tar-stained walls. The only pieces of furniture he owned were a futon and a mattress on the floor. Len didn't care. He was finally free of Sara's tyrannical imposition on his time and peace of mind.

About a week after moving into this apartment, he woke up one day with a most unusual feeling: the euphoric sense that anything was possible and there were no more unnecessary constraints on his existence. He recognized it like a long-lost friend from his younger days: the feeling of unbridled optimism that naturally welled up in a man when he didn't wake up every morning to unnecessary anxiety and harping discontent.

Len poured himself some bourbon and took it out to his fire-escape balcony. The weather was happily oblivious to human concerns; the day was sparkly clear, and the sun shone down warmly. Len felt the booze creep into his veins and his anxiety about the phone call subside.

Jack's right, Len said to himself. *I'm worried about nothing.*

3

"Good morning. Yesterday, the White House was bombed. The president of the United States was assassinated in the bombing."

Gasps and murmurs throughout the newsroom. A crowd had gathered around the large TV.

The vice-president continued, "Though I would prefer to be able to provide clarity and specifics, I cannot do so at this time until further details are known. We have committed all of the vast resources available to the federal government to the investigation. The perpetrators, and the methods by which this act was perpetrated, are as yet unknown. Nonetheless, it is clear that this event was the latest in a series of cowardly, deliberate acts of terrorism intended to shock and demoralize the American people."

Just then, there was a commotion down the hall. Len figured someone had knocked the coffee machine over again, and he didn't think much of it. Then, men yelling gruffly. Gunfire. People shrieking. Len instinctively fell to the floor, crawled under a cubicle desk, and covered his head.

From the corridor leading to the lobby ran several men carrying assault rifles and wearing black tactical gear. They wore balaclavas and moved in a tight, practiced formation, keeping their heads low and providing continuous cover for each other around the corner.

"Get down on the fucking ground, all of you!" shouted a stocky one as he fired a three-round burst from his rifle into the ceiling.

Something Len had never realized until he first heard it happen in real life many years prior: gunshots, when fired indoors, were really freaking loud. Eardrum-rupturing loud. More people screaming. Then, after a few seconds, muted crying. Upward of twenty armed men filed into the main newsroom, a large open-office plan in a repurposed warehouse, and positioned themselves around the periphery of the space in a staccato choreography.

Surrounded.

On the TV, the vice-president—the president, now—went on. "As prescribed by law, I was sworn into the office of the president this morning by Chief Justice Smith. As commander in chief, I will bring the full might of the American military to bear on those involved. To the individuals responsible for these murderous attacks, know this: our determination will not be assuaged, and there will be no place on Earth to hide."

One of the men stood up on a desk and shouted, "Which one of you is Leonard Savitz?"

Len felt his stomach twist. He looked up and around. Time was maple syrup. Some of his other co-workers, on the ground or hiding under nearby desks, made silent, imploring eye contact with Len as if to say, *For the love of God, please give yourself up so we don't get killed, too.*

Len took a difficult breath. *Well, crap. This is it*, he said to himself. A deluded man might have thought death was gonna come cakewalking over to him and he'd have ample time to ready himself for it, but Len had been through the shit and knew better: death came like a stray bullet on a nice day. Death came when your pants were down. Better him than some poor slob who didn't accept the inevitability. Legs shaking, he crawled out from under the desk and stood up. "Hi. I'm Leonard Savitz. What can I do for you?"

"To my fellow Americans, I say this," the new president continued. "Never in the history of mankind has there been a nation stronger or more resilient. Though our republic has faced numerous grave emergencies throughout its history, the American people have not merely endured—they have thrived beyond all expectations. Our grit and our indomitable spirit will carry us forward through any darkness…"

From somewhere behind him and without warning, someone tackled Len to the ground and pressed a knee painfully into his spine while handcuffing his arms behind his back. Another man put a black canvas sack over Len's head and roughly tied the drawstring around his neck. Someone searched his pockets, then pulled out his wallet, keys, and cell phone. The men yanked Len to his feet.

"Thank you," said the president, "and may God save the United States of America."

"Move, move! Let's move!" The men stormed out of the newsroom as fast as they'd come in. They carried Len out through the lobby and into the street. Len couldn't keep pace with the two men holding him by his armpits, and his feet dragged most of the way. The men threw him into the back of a large vehicle. Someone stomped on the gas as soon as the doors were slammed shut, the acceleration pinning Len against the back doors. Two screeching turns and Len was gone.

4

The men changed vehicles after ten minutes of driving. They patted Len down, checked his pockets again, then transferred him to a new vehicle. Len assumed it was because anyone who witnessed the kidnapping could have identified the first vehicle. They continued driving.

Len wasn't sure how long he'd been in the second vehicle. It felt like four hours or so of his heart beating on his ribcage. He couldn't see anything, and all he could hear were highway noises. Len could feel deceleration and turning—maybe an exit ramp—then slower speeds indicating local roads, followed by several minutes of crunching gravel roads. He could feel the altitude changing in his eardrums and had to yawn to relieve the pressure. He was up in the Appalachians somewhere. The van, or whatever it was that he was in, came to a halt on the gravel road. From the sound of it, there were other vehicles behind them. The driver got out, walked around to the back, and opened the rear door.

"Time to get out, sweetcheeks," a gruff voice drawled.

Two men lifted Len to his feet and walked him over the gravel a fair distance. They opened a door and took him inside a building. It smelled damp and felt cool, like a basement. They led Len down a long hall and into what might very well have been an old mine elevator, from the sound of the gates closing and the feeling of motion. They went down another hall. They then sat him down in a chair.

"I assume you've checked him for electronics?"

"Twice."

Someone finally took Len's hood off.

Once his eyes had adjusted, Len saw he was in a small, dimly lit room with concrete walls. There were ancient green filing cabinets and a metal desk that could have been from the 1950s. Old-fashioned incandescent light bulbs hung from the ceiling. Five men wearing military gear and ski masks were standing around the room, staring at him.

One of them, a large, broad-shouldered man, dragged an old chair over and placed it in front of Len's. He sat down, legs spread, hands on his knees.

"Hello, Mr. Savitz!"

"Are you the fuckers who threatened my daughter?"

"Such language! Relax, she's fine. In fact, if you behave, you'll get to see her soon."

"What did you do to her?"

"We'll get to that later." The man's condescending tone made Len wish he could get his hands out of the cuffs.

"Who are you people?"

"You can call me General Jefferson. These are my associates." The general motioned to the other four guys.

"Why am I here?"

"You're a journalist, aren't you?" the general said, picking a manila folder off the nearby desk and leafing through pages inside.

"Yeah, so?"

"I hate journalists. You pricks have no honor. Says here you were embedded in Iraq for two years, eh? Huh. Good thing you weren't assigned to my squad. I fragged a few of you assholes."

"What do you want with me?"

"We want you to do some work for us," the general said, throwing the file back on the table. Jefferson then pulled a cigar out of his shirt pocket and removed the cellophane wrapper.

"What?" Len stared back in confusion.

"If it were up to me, I'd just off you right now, but the boss seems to think you're the right person to do some work for us. In exchange, we will guarantee the safety of your daughter, and you will be compensated handsomely. If you don't accept, things aren't going to go well for you. What does the Mob call it? 'An offer you can't refuse?'" The general clipped the end of the cigar in a way that made Len uneasy.

"Seriously? You're offering me a job? That's what this is about?" Len breathed heavily as his confusion gave way to irritation.

"Sure. You can think of it that way."

"What the fuck? You're the most aggressive headhunters I've ever met." Len was too angry and scared to mean it as a joke, but the men took it that way and broke out laughing.

General Jefferson had a booming voice and a raucous laugh. His accent was from one of the Southern states, and Len spied a gray mustache through the mouth hole in Jefferson's ski mask. General Jefferson had that Teddy Roosevelt kind of air about him: a Neanderthal with five Y chromosomes who'd be just as comfortable joking and backslapping over rowdy drinks as he would be ripping someone's goddamn esophagus out with his bare hands. Len could tell the general wasn't someone to cross, but he knew better than to show weakness to men like these. Might as well see what they were offering, since there was no alternative.

"Fine. What's the compensation?"

"See? He said yes! What'd I tell you boys? Call it men's intuition!"

The men snickered. The general put the cigar in his mouth and lit it, puffing through the mouth hole in his mask.

"Cute. What are you going to pay me, and what's the job?" Len asked.

"Can I call you Lenny?" the general asked. Without waiting for an answer, he said, "Lenny, you're going to do some research for us. You're also about to learn firsthand why we're blowing stuff up. The media seem to think we're just a bunch of terrorist nut jobs. But one man's terrorists are another man's freedom fighters. After doing some digging, I suspect you'll realize that our motives aren't political at all. In fact, I predict that not only will you agree with us, you'll join us."

"Money talks," Len said, doing his best to seem like he wasn't utterly terrified.

"Uh-oh, a tough negotiator!" General Jefferson said, laughing. His men laughed too. Len figured they probably laughed at anything Jefferson said. "OK. We will give you two million dollars, paid upon completion, with your daughter returned safely to you. In addition, we will pay all your travel expenses.

A generous offer, I think! You understand, of course, that this job will involve egregious risk to life and limb."

"What, specifically, is the job?" Len figured seeming agreeable would get him out of there sooner.

"Wonderful. Then we have a deal. As for the details, I will defer to the management—Neith."

The men put the hood back on Len and led him down another hallway. They sat him down and took the hood off again. One of Len's captors walked to the door and, pulling down a series of old knife switches, illuminated the space. The place was cavernous, an enormous warehouse. If Len had to estimate, it was about five hundred feet long and as many wide, with ceilings five stories high.

Len looked around: rows of old tanks, troop transport trucks, large artillery cannons, even a few helicopters. Along the walls were crates stacked to the ceiling and stenciled with Russian words.

"What are you going to use all this for?"

"We're going to take Washington, DC, if necessary."

"Jesus. You people are planning a coup!"

"No, we're planning a revolution. Lenny, I want you to meet the brains behind this operation, Neith." General Jefferson pointed off to Len's side. There, sitting behind an old desk, was a creepy-looking female mannequin. It was posed as if it were in deep thought.

"Oh my God. You're all insane," Len exclaimed.

Len heard a whirring noise. Looking over at the mannequin thing, he noticed its head was now in a different position.

It was staring right at him with lifeless, weird eyes, like those of an antique doll.

"Hello, Mr. Savitz!" it said, coming to life.

"Holy crap!" Len jumped out of his chair. The general and his cronies nearly split their sides laughing.

"Hoo boy, I'd love to stay, but I have to go see a man about a horse. I'll leave you ladies to discuss your details. Franklin, Adams, stay here and make sure Lenny doesn't get fresh with Miss Neith. Paine, Hancock, pull the Cadillac around and get changed into your civvies. You're gonna escort Lenny-poo here to the airport. Try to look respectable." Jefferson hiked up his pants and walked out the door.

Airport? Len wondered what they were planning.

"I apologize if the general was rough with you," the thing said. "Hospitality is not his forte."

Len's veins pounded. He studied it hesitantly. Its face seemed to be made of a rubbery material, and mechanisms underneath the surface moved up and down to create the illusion of facial expressions. It seemed to be a very cheesy attempt at an android.

"What the hell is that?" Len asked one of the men guarding him, but he didn't answer.

"My name is Neith. Please pardon my robotic avatar; it allows me to be in two places at once." The voice was female and familiar.

The robot stood up from behind the desk, and in an ungraceful yet overly fluid kind of way, it walked toward Len.

"Stay back!" Still handcuffed, Len lifted his leg in the air, ready to kick the thing if it came any closer.

"Mr. Savitz, I won't hurt you."

"I know your voice! You're the one who called me yesterday. Is that why you're hiding behind a robot, you piece of shit?"

One of the men stuck a rifle barrel in Len's cheek.

"I just needed to get your attention," the robot said. "Your daughter is actually safer now than she was yesterday."

"Where is she?"

"Ecuador. She and your ex-wife arrived there safely this morning." Neith's robot clumsily picked a photo off the desk and handed it to Len. It was a picture of Octavia, looking tired, holding the previous day's *Examiner*.

Len gnashed his teeth. "Ecuador? You kidnapped them?"

"Yes. Unfortunately, we had to."

"Why are you involving us in this? What the hell is wrong with you people?"

"Mr. Savitz, we need your help. You are uniquely qualified to assist us in our mission."

"What exactly is your mission?"

"To free the human race."

"I'm not helping you psychos do anything until I see my daughter."

"I have already arranged for you to meet her tomorrow evening so that you may verify her safety. First, however, we must go over some ground rules. Number one: we are hiring you to collect data. Should you compromise our mission, go to the authorities, or publicly disclose information you've gathered, you and your family will be executed."

Len felt rage well up from his stomach, but using every shred of self-restraint he could summon, he managed to stifle it. If he played along, he might be able to find a way to rescue Octavia.

"Two: you may not use any computers, Internet, phones, or electronic devices during your employ with us."

"Why?"

"As you are no doubt aware, major world governments employ sprawling surveillance networks. Phone calls, text messages, e-mails, social networking—any and all data transmitted are collected, stored, and analyzed by unbelievably powerful computer systems. There is absolutely no privacy in any form of electronic communication. I can tell you with 100 percent certainty that everything you do with a phone or computer is recorded and scrutinized by a third party. To compound matters, all consumer electronic devices produced over the last twenty years are designed to both surreptitiously monitor their users and to transmit anything created with them to intelligence agencies. Computers have cameras and microphones that are used to actively spy on you, and their operating systems are made to allow clandestine access by the authorities. Cell phones do the same and, in addition, constantly transmit your location to government databases. Even digital cameras automatically connect to wireless networks to automatically give you away. Bottom line, don't use any electronic devices."

"That's not how journalism works. How am I supposed to take notes and pictures without technology?"

"The only way to avoid surveillance, and to ensure both the success of our mission and your safety during your assignment, is to use purely mechanical, or analog, technology. This should be everything you need." The robot gestured to the desk it had been sitting behind.

On the desk were several items: a portable typewriter, a few spare typewriter ribbons, a thirty-five-millimeter film camera, some rolls of film, a ream of paper, a notepad, pens, a 1970s microcassette recorder, a windup watch, several large envelopes, a stack of hundred-dollar bills, hair dye, an electric razor, a passport, and a driver's license.

Len surveyed the ancient items on the table.

"What am I, Ernest Hemingway? How am I supposed to write a story with this junk?"

"I have provided written instructions on the use of each, which you should read on your flight to Ecuador."

"What about television?"

"Television, radio, and other archaic, one-way mass media are fine, so long as no device requires you to input data. Rule three: anything you buy must be paid for in cash, which I will give you enough of today. Credit card use is strictly disallowed. Electronic financial transactions, like the use of anything else electronic, will create a data signature that is uniquely yours. It's possible to find someone anywhere in the world once they've made as few as four electronic purchases. That's how powerful pattern-matching algorithms have become. It is impossible to evade detection while using electronic money."

"Fine, what next?"

"Rule four: you are never to cross a border or security checkpoint with information pertaining to the assignment. Even your typewriter ribbons should be removed before you cross a border."

"Then how am I supposed to refer to my notes later? How am I supposed to get you the information you want?"

"Upon completing your first assignment, put your notes, film, cassette recordings, and typewriter ribbons into one of the envelopes provided. During your first assignment, address the envelope to Mr. Hamasaki and leave it at the front desk. We will collect it."

"Fine."

"Rule five: you are prohibited from contacting anyone you knew prior to this mission, and you are forbidden from returning to Pittsburgh. Your apartment is likely being searched at the moment by police investigating your abduction."

Len's fear and hostility temporarily gave way to embarrassment at the thought of law enforcement rummaging through his dirty laundry and computer drives.

"Rule six: you are no longer Leonard Savitz. From now on, you are Jim Rivington, travel journalist. Here is your new passport and driver's license."

"Are you stupid? The second I walk into an airport, facial recognition scanners will pick me out. Any time I cross a border, they'll take my fingerprints and know it's me."

"Your identifying biometrics have been reassigned in all government databases. They now belong to Jim Rivington. From now on, you *are* Jim Rivington."

"Just like that?"

"Yes, just like that. To prevent recognition by humans, you will also shave your beard and dye your hair before leaving here today."

"And when will I be done with this alleged assignment?"

"At the completion of our objectives, you will be allowed to return home with the money we've promised and your daughter."

Just then, two unmasked men walked through the door wearing suits. Len didn't recognize them.

"Anything else?" Len asked.

"That's it. Here's a suitcase for these items. Majors Paine and Hancock, please make sure Mr. Savitz gets changed into new clothes, dyes his hair, and gets to the airport with these materials. His flight leaves in six hours." Neith sat back down at her desk.

About four hours later, Major Hancock pulled off the highway and parked. Paine went around back and opened the trunk. He took Len's hood off.

"I'm going to uncuff you, but if you try anything, I'll just cap you right here," Paine said. His voice was kind of nasal and insecure, not what Len expected.

Paine freed his hands and Len crawled out of the trunk. It was evening, and they were in a secluded spot in an industrial park.

"Get in the front passenger seat. We're almost at the airport."

The men drove a bit farther. Len saw highway signs for Dulles, his first real indication of location since he'd been abducted. Doing some mental calculations, he guessed Jefferson's hideout was probably somewhere in the mountains of West Virginia.

They pulled up to the passenger drop-off. "Here are your boarding passes and suitcase," said Hancock. "Our colleagues will meet you at the airport in Quito."

Amazingly, the two didn't accompany Len into the airport. He wheeled the suitcase into the airport alone, then turned around to look through the glass doors. They were still there at the curb, watching him. Len thought about running but figured it would be best to wait it out until he could find a way to rescue his daughter.

He made it through security with no problem; the computer didn't even balk when the agents scanned the fake passport. Len's hands were starting to shake, so he headed straight to the duty-free shop to buy a fifth of bourbon. Out of professional habit, he also picked up a local newspaper. Most of the headlines were about the recent bombings, but to his amazement, on page A2 there was an article about his abduction: "Pulitzer Prize–winning journalist abducted by insurrectionists."

The plane wasn't boarding yet, so Len sat down in an uncrowded part of the airport to take some very shameless slugs from the bottle while reading the story. *Pulitzer Prize–winning. Ha!* he thought to himself. People who didn't know better probably thought he was a big deal. In fact, that stupid prize was probably the reason he was in this mess.

There was something no one had told Len in journalism school: you could win a Pulitzer and still be broke. Len pulled the envelope of cash Neith had given him out of his jacket pocket and counted it inconspicuously. Inside was an advance of sorts, enough to buy a new car. Len didn't get it. Two million dollars could motivate anyone. Why bother with kidnappings on top of it?

5

Once in his seat on the airplane, Len stared out the little oval window and thought about his poor daughter. How was he going to get her out of this? How was he going to get himself out of this? Why him? He felt someone take the seat next to him but didn't care.

"Hey, is that Applewood Forge?" The accent sounded Slavic.

"Yeah. Want some?" Len said, preoccupied, handing it over while staring out the window.

The person sitting next to him took the bottle out of his hand. Len didn't think anyone would actually take him up on the offer. He looked over. A woman in her mid-thirties maybe, willowy, jet-black hair cut in a bob, wide-set blue eyes. Len couldn't remember the last time he saw a woman so attractive flying economy. She uncorked the bottle and took a huge swig like a goddamn lumberjack. "That's good shit," she said. "Can't get in Russia."

Mentally and physically exhausted, a little drunk, and on the verge of a nervous breakdown, Len couldn't help but laugh at the absurdity of it. Unfazed by his reaction, she took another swig.

"You look like you have trouble," she said, as though they'd been pals since the second grade.

"You could say that."

"What happen?"

"Ever get roped into other people's problems?"

"No, thanks. Life is too short. So, where you going?" she asked.

"Quito, I think. You?"

"Same. You been before?"

"No, what's it like?" Len asked.

"It smells like bus farts. Do you go on business?"

"Yes," Len answered.

"What do you do for living?" she asked.

"I'm a travel journalist, apparently."

"What does it mean, journalist?"

"I'm a writer."

"Do you enjoy?"

The question struck Len as very un-Russian. "No," he said.

"They why you do it?"

"It's the only thing I'm good at."

The woman laughed. "My name is Natalia," she said, extending her hand. "Natalia Zherdeva."

"L—I mean, Jim Rivington," Len said, shaking it. "Nice to meet you. What do you do, Natalia?"

"I export matryoshka dolls."

"Really?"

"No."

Len laughed. He needed a laugh. "And do you enjoy it?"

"You know what I enjoy? Drinking. But no one pays me for that," Natalia said, smirking.

"Hear, hear, sister."

"You married?" Natalia asked.

"Not anymore."

"What happened?"

"Oh, you know, I got tired of being wrong all the time. She was the angry, self-righteous type. Anything she did, no matter how selfish or awful, she felt was profoundly sensible and justified. Anything anyone else did was inherently terrible and worthy of scorn. She hated my friends, she hated my family, she hated fun and spontaneity. It seemed like she was just deeply dissatisfied with reality and took it out on everyone around her. Eventually she started accusing me of cheating all the time so she could justify sleeping around. I broke it off with her."

"Why you marry woman like that?"

Len chuckled. "Good question. At the beginning, she seemed so serious and idealistic, which is probably what I needed at that point in my life. I was young and didn't really have my act together." Len paused for a bit, then asked, "Are you married?"

"Hell no!" She scrunched her face up in contempt. "I like freedom. Man wants me to clean house and make babies. I want to travel and wake up in new city every day. So I do it."

"It sounds like an amazing life you have."

"Every life should be amazing! Everyone think like they have to suffer, but they don't. I don't know why. People are crazy."

The words hit Len like a Dumpster dropped on his head. He'd been intentionally grinding through difficulty for forty-two years in the hopes that it would make him a better person, doing one hard thing after another. Why? Because that was what everyone had told him his whole life: that grit, hard work, and adversity would reward you in the long run. But they didn't, did they? You died anyway, just like everyone else. Misery was just misery, and your trophy was a coffin.

6

Len awoke with a start when the plane made a sharp, banking turn over South America. Landing at the airport in Quito was no joke; it required sharp turns between enormous Andean mountains with violent updraft turbulence. Len's stomach was turning, and he was so dehydrated from the booze and the cabin air that his eyes felt like cotton balls. Natalia was bent over, sleeping with her head on the tray table, holding the now-empty whiskey bottle. He sort of remembered them hitting it off and talking for two hours or so. Every now and then Len met someone on his wavelength, and always at exactly the wrong time.

He nudged her. "Hey, wake up, we're landing."

"*Nyet,*" she murmured without opening her eyes.

Len thought about the logistics of having to help a drunk woman off the plane, then find her luggage and get her to her hotel. His brain was thick like corn mash that morning, but he suddenly remembered why he was in Ecuador. *Daughter kidnapped, right. Gotta take care of that first and foremost. Priorities, old man.*

On the way out, Len gave the flight attendants a few hundred-dollar bills and pointed at Natalia, telling them, "Make sure she gets her luggage and gets where she's going."

Exiting customs, he saw three serious, dark-skinned men in suits and fedoras, one of whom was holding a sign that read "Jim Rivington." They'd have looked out of place, like extras from some 1930s-era gangster film, had everyone at the airport not been dressed in the same style. An Ecuador thing, apparently. The guys waiting for him looked hard and had cold, jailbird stares. A shot of adrenaline pierced his hangover, jangling his nerves. It wasn't the greatest feeling. *This is how people are never heard from again*, Len thought to himself. He took a second to breathe and walked over.

"I'm Jim."

"Please come with us."

The men led Len out to a crappy white-paneled van. It smelled like wet dog and patchouli inside, and the seats had no seat belts. The dashboard looked like a mobile Catholic church: pictures of the Virgin Mary, rosaries hanging from the rearview window, several crucified Jesuses, and, to Len's amusement, lit candles and incense.

They drove out of the city and into the mountains. The vehicle's poor suspension, combined with the switchback mountain roads and the ups and downs in altitude, increased Len's nausea, and twice he had to ask the driver to pull over so he could vomit out the door. Slowly the mountains gave way to low-lying coastal jungle. Cresting a final hill, the rainforest canopy opened up, and Len saw the vibrantly blue ocean. The van pulled up to a dock on the beach, where a speedboat was waiting for them. After tossing Len and his luggage in, the men piloted the boat to an island that Len judged was about five miles off the coast. Around midday they puttered past a breakwater into a small marina on the island. It appeared to be a private harbor, containing a big white yacht and other smaller watercraft. A man carrying an AK-47 came up to the dock and tied the boat down. Len and the men got out. Len surveyed the place. Beyond the marina there was a huge concrete wall surrounding some kind of structure. Along the wall at various intervals were spotlights and armed guards. A wrought-iron gate opened automatically and they all started walking. A roundabout driveway circled a fountain. Inside the wall was an enormous house, a Spanish colonial–style mansion. The men led Len inside the house, and there inside the foyer was Octavia.

"Daddy!" she squealed.

"Octavia! Thank God!" Len picked her up and gave her a long, long hug. She looked healthy, which was a huge relief.

"Daddy! Daddy, guess what? Guess what! Guess what! This house has a swimming pool and games and there are lizards everywhere! And their tails come off when you catch them and then the tails wriggle around like worms. Isn't that cool? And in the morning we eat fruit and then we go to the beach. Come see! Come see!"

"OK! I can't wait to see!" Len had never felt such relief. His little girl was OK, and it was the first time he'd seen her in a month. "Hey, where's Mommy?"

"Oh, Mr. Salva—Salva—Salvatierra made her sit in the room with the door closed because she had bad behavior," Octavia said. "She was yelling too much. I think she's in time-out. This is Mr. Salva—Salvatierra's house. He has a mustache. He's nice. He has a doggy! Daddy, do we have to go back to Pittsburgh?"

"I don't know," Len said.

"Señor Savitz?" a man's voice called out.

Len looked up. A man in his sixties with a white mustache and wearing a tan guayabera was standing on the stairs.

"Yes?"

"Hello. I am Jose Salvatierra. Welcome to my home. Please let me show you around. Pedro, please take Mr. Savitz's bag to his room."

A man who was apparently Pedro came out of nowhere and took Len's bag. Len didn't want to be shown around, he wanted to take his daughter and escape. But until he figured out how to make that possible, he figured he should try to appear cooperative. "Octavia, can you go play for a little bit? Daddy has to talk to Mr....?"

"Salvatierra."

Octavia skipped out of the room.

"Come with me." Salvatierra led Len around the house, pointing out dining rooms, a game room, bedrooms, and so forth. "In this courtyard is the swimming pool. Your daughter just loves it here. She's a sweet girl. I took her to the beach the last two mornings. She reminds me of when my children were that age. Through these doors is the guest bedroom where you'll be staying."

"I'll be staying here?"

"For tonight. After that, Neith has some work for you to do."

Len took note of his surroundings. The mansion was entirely open-air with no windows whatsoever, as houses sometimes were in the tropics. Birds flew in and out as they pleased. A mosquito net surrounded the bed. From his room, Len could see a helipad and a fair amount of the compound's perimeter wall.

"What business are you in, Mr. Salvatierra?"

"Narcotics."

Len almost laughed at the frankness of the answer but didn't for fear of ending up in a ditch somewhere. Salvatierra had tanned skin and a thick head of white hair that matched his mustache. He had the vibe of a sleeping volcano, a warm pleasantness that almost dared people to take him for granted. Len could smell a river of rage underneath that charm and mentally filed Salvatierra under "not to be fucked with."

"May I ask you a question?" Len asked.

"Certainly."

"What is your connection to Neith? How do you know each other?"

Salvatierra smiled to himself. "Neith and I are old friends. She provides me with intelligence, which allows me to move my product into North America. We split the profits. She speaks very good Spanish!"

"I'm surprised you're so open about this."

"That is because you will not tell anyone," Salvatierra said, turning to face Len and staring him in the eyes.

"I won't. I'm just curious."

"Curiosity killed the cat, Mr. Savitz. Do not let it kill you."
Len averted his gaze. "I am keeping you here as a favor to Neith,
but I have no...what's the word? Compunction?" Salvatierra
poked Len in the chest. "Yes, no compunction about getting
rid of you."

Octavia came running into the room like a welcome breeze.
"Daddy, do you want to come to the beach with me?"

"It is no problem," Salvatierra said, suddenly back in character with his avuncular smile.

"Of course, darling." Len glanced back at Salvatierra.
Salvatierra summoned one of his armed guards, then walked
out of the room.

Len and Octavia walked down to the beach, where they
played in the waves while Salvatierra's guard sat under a palm
tree and watched. Without being too obvious, Len tried to get
a feel for the lay of the land. Salvatierra's compound was the
only structure on the island; they were completely isolated,
surrounded by miles of water in every direction. Apparently
the only access was by helicopter, boat, or swimming. Len
wondered if there were sharks out there. Somewhere, he spec-
ulated, there was some asshole real estate agent who special-
ized in finding drug cartel kingpins their dream homes.

It was ingenious, really. Neith had picked a place to keep
hostages that was remote, fortified, and in a country that had
tenuous diplomatic relations with the United States. Salvatierra
could murder them out here if he wanted to, bury their bodies in the jungle, and no one would ever know. And even if
someone did know, a man like Salvatierra would have enough

political muscle to avoid problems with local law enforcement. In fact, he probably got away with murder on a routine basis.

Coming back into the house with Octavia after an hour or two at the beach, Len saw Sara in the entrance, arms akimbo and looking ready for a fight. *Christ, here we go*, thought Len.

"Octavia, can you catch me a lizard?" Len asked.

"OK, Daddy!" Octavia ran off to the courtyard.

Sara at least had the decency to watch Octavia run off before starting in on Len. He hadn't seen Sara in person for a while, and he looked her over discreetly while her attention was on Octavia. She was still beautiful on the outside, statuesque and Nordic looking, with a round, pretty face. Like a Viking princess almost, but without any hint of nobility.

"Good job, Len! Who did you piss off this time? You got us kidnapped and sent down here to this third-world hellhole!"

"I tried to warn you, didn't I?"

"No, fuck you, Len. You could have told me someone was going to kidnap us. Instead you had to be all vague and mysterious," she said, making vague and mysterious hand gestures.

"Oh, right. I always forget that everyone is a liar except for you, and that I have to corroborate everything I say. You'll have to excuse me, I didn't know specifics. You know what, Sara? Even if I had known that you were going to be kidnapped, which I didn't, you still wouldn't have believed me. So really it doesn't matter what I did or didn't say."

Two guards in the foyer watched the exchange with bemusement. Sara's eyes narrowed.

"Len, you've always been a loser. I spent six years living your loser life, and now here I am, involved in your loser bullshit yet again. Are you happy now?"

Len felt he was getting sucked into her crazy but caught himself. To Sara, everything was about control. He remembered how she'd use insults and personal attacks to constantly push him off base because it was easier to manipulate someone who doubts himself.

Len didn't bite and tried to reply calmly. "Had you gotten out of town like I suggested, you and Octavia wouldn't be here. But as usual, you were too damn arrogant to listen."

Her gambit having failed, Sara's face flushed with fury. Then she turned away abruptly, put her head in her hands, and started crying. Len almost felt bad for her for a second, then remembered that he wasn't obligated to anymore. After years of living with her, Len had figured out that Sara manipulated the way other people breathed. Emotions were weapons to her, not gut-felt reactions. The only times he'd seen her turn on the waterworks were to gain an upper hand in a situation. Sara's tears were always about power and never about emotional distress.

Life's too short, Len thought to himself before walking outside to catch lizards with Octavia.

———

Len slept surprisingly well that night, despite the fact that he'd gone to bed sober and was being held hostage in a house full of armed, psychopathic drug dealers. He was awoken right after dawn by a particularly loud helicopter landing outside. Looking out the window, Len saw an enormous Russian cargo beast setting down on the comparatively undersized helipad. The chopper's rear ramp lowered, and two forklifts took turns driving up the ramp and into the helicopter. From the aircraft's cargo hold, the forklifts retrieved crates stenciled with Russian characters like the ones Len had seen at Neith's warehouse.

The helicopter's crew door opened, and some of Salvatierra's men wheeled a set of steps up to it. Len saw Jose Salvatierra walk up to the aircraft. From the helicopter emerged a familiar face in a business outfit. She came down the steps to shake hands with Salvatierra. Len thought maybe he was imagining things, but nope, it was definitely the woman he had met on the plane a day earlier. Salvatierra and Natalia walked around to the back to inspect what the forklifts had unloaded.

Just as Len was watching this, one of Salvatierra's goons burst into Len's room without knocking.

"You awake? Get dressed. It's time to go."

"Where are we going?"

"Not we, you. You're going to Japan."

"Japan? Why?"

"Get dressed. We leave in thirty minutes."

Len threw on his clothes, made sure he had the suitcase Neith had given him, then went into the room next door where Octavia was still sleeping. He had to resign himself to postponing her rescue; the tight security of Salvatierra's compound made it impossible. He had no choice but to hope Sara would look after her while he was away. Without waking her, Len kissed Octavia's forehead and covered her with the blanket, then told Salvatierra's men he was ready. They loaded him into the boat, then the same smelly white van he'd arrived in, and headed back to the airport.

"I trust you have now verified your daughter's safety," said one of the thugs riding with him to the airport. Len didn't answer him, so the man continued, "When you arrive in Japan, you will stay at this hotel." He handed Len a piece of paper with a Japanese address written on it. "At the front desk will be further instructions from Mr. Hamasaki. If you are ever in doubt during your time in Japan, return to the hotel and await further instructions."

7

Len had always enjoyed the Japanese ethos of zero coddling. Japanese airlines gave their passengers all the booze they wanted, at any time of day, because their customers were damn adults and it wasn't the airline's fault if someone couldn't handle their liquor. They only hired physically attractive stewardesses and no one sued them over it, because in Japan no one bought into the Western make-believe that everyone should have a trophy. Len had done some traveling in his line of work and found that no other country did air travel, or anything, the way the Japanese did. He imagined it was probably the way the United States was before everything got stupid.

Len's plane chased the sun west, giving him about twenty hours of sunshine. He touched down at Narita in the evening. This time there were no goons waiting for him. It had been a decade and a half since he was last in Japan; his Japanese was rusty, and getting around proved difficult. Len found a train to Tokyo, then another train, then another train, eventually reaching his destination around ten at night.

A young man with a bizarre hairdo at the front desk of the hotel checked Len in. "Letter here for you from Mr. Hamasaki," he said.

Len opened the rice-paper envelope to find a brief handwritten note in excessively proper penmanship. It instructed him to go to a Buddhist monastery (with the address) a few blocks away the next day at noon. That was it. That was all the note said.

Having some time to kill, Len rode the elevator up to the hotel bar. He loved hotel bars, little oases of fugue dotting the globe. No regulars, no intrusive familiarity, just a revolving door of jet lag and drunken anonymity. Len found them to be freeing, the boozer's version of a blank canvas. All he had to do was pick a stool and he could be anyone he wanted for a night, or no one at all, because no one knew him there. He'd have a drink, and for a brief moment, he'd relax without the lifelong encumbrances of identity. Then the next day, when he and everyone else picked up their burdens again to part ways in their taxis and airplanes, newcomers would wheel suitcases up to the bar to take their own nameless places.

Len ordered a whiskey and looked out the window at the sprawling, glittering blanket of skyscrapers. Despite the situation, he found himself overcome with nostalgia. Len missed Japan, and he never imagined he'd have found himself back here after fifteen years. A shame it wasn't under better circumstances.

———

At noon, Len stood at the door of the monastery. He must have been a sight to the young monk who opened the door: a tall Caucasian man in a rumpled suit with luggage.

"May I help you?" the monk asked in English.

"I don't know," Len answered.

"Why are you here?"

"I don't know," Len said again.

The monk stared at him, confused, then said, "Please wait here." He left and returned two minutes later with an older monk who seemed a little more sure of himself.

The older monk bowed and said, "My name is Mutoku. Please come in." He led Len through the monastery to a little room with no windows. "You may stay here. Are you hungry?"

"Yes."

"We are just about to eat lunch. Please join us."

Mutoku led Len to the main hall, where the monks had set out meal boards on the floor and were about to begin eating. There was a spot for him with an *oryoki* set waiting there. The bell rang, and in a flood the whole ritual that Len had practiced so many times came back to him.

Len bowed to the *oryoki* sets that would feed him. *Oryoki* sets came as a neat little kit, wrapped in an outer cloth that was tied into a bow. He untied the bow and removed the outer cloth, designed to serve as a placemat. Len then spread this square placemat out on the meal board, folding the four corners under but with the corners still showing, forming the cloth into an eight-pointed star. Next he removed the dish-cleaning cloth, which he folded precisely in thirds, placing it on the floor between him and the meal boards. Underneath the dish-cloth he found the utensil sheath, a little sleeve of fabric containing chopsticks, a long wooden spoon, and a *setsu*, a wooden stick used for cleaning. Len placed that utensil sheath on top of the cloth he'd just folded with the intention of coming back to it later. Now onto the bowls. The bowls came nested like Russian dolls, and Len was careful to pull them out using only his thumbs, placing them at exact locations on the placemat cloth, making no noise while doing so. Returning to the utensil sheath, he removed the utensils ever so carefully, placing them at predetermined locations in front of him while simultaneously folding the utensil sheath in thirds as one would a pocket square.

And so forth. It wasn't just the setting of the table that went like this; every single part of the meal was a pedantic choreography, a precise ritual with hundreds of details added over as many years, which could only be memorized through rote practice. The idea behind *oryoki*, which was how Zen monks ate, was to create a meal tradition so formal and demanding that it could never be done in a perfunctory way. One couldn't breeze through it; one had to be mindful of what one was doing and how one was doing it, because sadly, that was the only way most people would show their food any gratitude.

The chanting of the meal sutras, the smell of tofu braised in sesame oil, the taste of shiitake mushroom soup, the warm grassy fragrance of the green tea, the subtle rustling of black robes—all of it was a sensory flashback. Sitting there at the meal, soaked in the experience, Len found himself sentimentally yearning for his youth.

———

Mutoku pulled Len aside after the meal and ushered him into a room where they were alone.

"Please sit," Mutoku said, motioning to a cushion on the floor.

"OK."

"What is your name?"

"Jim Rivington." The name slipped off his tongue more easily than before. "Nice to meet you."

"Yes, you as well. Tell me, how is it that you know how to use the *oryoki* bowls?" Mutoku's enunciation was perfect and his English very formal, as though he'd studied the language at a prestigious Japanese university.

"Pardon?"

"*Oryoki* is highly specific. It takes years of practice. It is extremely unusual for a Westerner to know how to do it correctly. Where did you learn it?"

"I studied in a Soto Zen monastery in Kyoto for five years. That's how we ate."

"Interesting." Mutoku's kind eyes indicated his pleasant surprise. "Are you still studying Zen?"

"No, I left the monastery years ago. I gave up on Zen and Buddhism."

"Why?"

"Because I realized it was all bullshit."

Mutoku smirked at the unexpected comment, revealing an irreverent sense of humor. "What do you mean?"

"The Third Noble Truth of Buddhism is that suffering can end, right?"

"Correct."

"Well, do you know anyone alive whose suffering has ended?"

Mutoku laughed and thought about it for a bit. "I suppose suffering doesn't end, you just learn to hold it differently."

"Hold it however you want, you're still suffering."

"And who is it that's suffering?"

"Me. You. Everyone."

"And who are you?"

"Jim Rivington."

"And what is that?"

Len recognized the tactic immediately: take a tough question directed to the teacher and turn it back on the student with a nonsense question. Try to get the student to question themselves rather than the teacher, thus keeping subordinates unbalanced and maintaining the power dynamic. Len knew the answer was supposed to be "I don't know," but he didn't say that because he was no longer anyone's monkey.

"Another reason I left is because I grew tired of the games Zen teachers play," Len said. "They're never forthright; they're con artists in black robes. All they do is take people's money, do silly funeral rituals, and manipulate. They have no answers and no special insight. Buddhism, like anything good and decent in this world, has been corrupted to the point where it hurts people instead of helping them. What you do here, Mutoku, prevents people from seeing the obvious. You folks claim to teach Nothing, and to my utter bewilderment, that's all I learned over those five years."

The smile ran from Mutoku's face. "Why are you here, Mr. Rivington?"

"I don't know. I was sent here."

"Sent here by whom?"

"By the people who are blowing up government buildings in the United States. They forced me to come here and I don't know why." Len knew he wasn't supposed to divulge this information, but he was past the point of caring.

Mutoku studied Len for a while, his face betraying his concern. After a long, loaded silence, Mutoku said, "I must discuss this with my superior. Please join the others for meditation in the great hall. We will speak again soon."

Len shrugged and joined the monks in the main hall. He regretted being rude to Mutoku after he'd shown such kindness in taking Len in off the street. For all Mutoku knew, Len might have been homeless and hungry. Yet talking to Mutoku had made the anger he'd felt all those years ago come right back to him. He'd wasted half a decade of his life searching for enlightenment only to discover that no such everlasting condition existed. At best, you might get a few fleeting moments of understanding while slogging through your life, an Everglades of miserable impermanence.

8

Len's father had died rather suddenly, right before Len graduated college. Bernard Savitz was standing on a dock one Saturday morning, fishing for lake trout, when he just fell flat on his face and never got up again. The coroner listed the official reason as "natural causes." Len always maintained it should have been "homicide."

Unlike fathers who sought to mold their children into miniature versions of themselves, Bernard was a kind-hearted man who simply let Len be who he was. Len and his father had been quite close, and the sudden loss was more than Len had ever dealt with. Len was twenty-two, a fresh-faced kid a month away from college graduation, with final exams looming. He had to figure out how to plan a funeral by himself because his mother and brother were busy pretending that it hadn't happened, like everything was OK. Len couldn't live the fiction; he'd always had trouble with bullshit. The man was gone and it had to be dealt with. Len toughed it out through writing the eulogy and carrying the casket, but the really hard part came in the months and years that followed. His father wasn't at his graduation. His father wasn't at his wedding and never met Octavia. Len could no longer pick up the phone to ask Dad for advice. These things were like little lead sinkers weighing down Len's guts.

The age of twenty-two was when a person felt himself to be most immortal. The body recovered from injuries quickly and could handle any abuse thrown at it. A twenty-two year-old could eat pizza every day, drink to get drunk, smoke cigarettes, and rarely get sick as a result of any of it. The consequences of a young person's actions, and the horror show of old age, were decades away. There was endless time to lie blithely in the sun or stay up all night having wistful conversations with friends. Len had been robbed of this. He was suddenly and brutally hit in the face with the reality of his existence: mortality. Mortality, that little box with no windows or doors.

Len once had a teacher in middle school who used to remark to the class, "Look at you all, bored out of your minds. You're sitting there in blue plastic chairs, watching the clock, and wishing your lives away." Len thought the man was just being a jerk, but years later he finally understood. If anything good had come of his father's death, it was that Len figured out that the only thing people were guaranteed in this life was the next exhalation. *This is it*, he remembered thinking to himself not too long after the viewing while lying awake in bed. *Right now, second by second. Time is all we have—and most of us are wasting it.*

On a whim after his father's funeral and his graduation, Len decided he wanted to move to Japan to become a Buddhist monk. He packed up what little he had at the time, put it in storage, and hopped on the next transpacific flight. His mother and brother didn't understand his reasoning and never forgave him for it, but it was something he knew he had to do.

Len hadn't done a lot of traveling before going to Japan. He had never been to Japan before, let alone lived there, so the culture shock was monumental. He didn't speak the language, and he didn't understand the completely different way the Japanese saw the world. In Japan, it was never about I/me/my, it was always the greater good and honoring tradition. Coming from a Western culture and trying to adjust to an Eastern one forced a perspective shift on par with graduating preschool and going straight to becoming a grandparent.

Len eventually found a monastery willing to take him, a foreigner. Life in the monastery was surprisingly tedious. He awoke at five in the morning when the bells rang, did meditation with the monks for an hour and a half, chanted for an hour, ate a silent breakfast with everyone, then worked outside, then meditated for another hour, then ate lunch, then cleaned floors and toilets, then meditated some more, then had a bit of free time to himself that he used for exercise, then (sometimes) ate dinner depending who was in charge (dinner being considered unorthodox), then meditated some more, then slept. The next day, they'd all get up and do it all over again. Monasteries ran on a very tight schedule and there was little deviation. Len lived like this for five years. Despite the tedium, he enjoyed the constant meditation.

Other meditation schools started a student off gradually: they had a beginner follow the breath, repeat a mantra, or use any number of devices designed to help a novice learn to quiet and concentrate the mind. Then, once the new student developed a certain amount of concentration, the teacher moved the student up to a slightly more challenging form of meditation. After a number of years, the student learned the advanced meditations.

Shikantaza, the Soto Zen method of meditation that Len was taught, was nothing like that at all. It was the most difficult form of meditation there was because there were no gradations, no steps, no progress. A beginner started off doing it the way a master did. There was an old Zen proverb that said, "If you want to climb a mountain, start at the top." *Shikantaza* was taught the way swimming used to be: throw the uninitiated into a pool and hope they'll figure it out. Basically, a Zen practitioner sat on a little cushion with no instructions other than the physical: "just sit" or "be quiet" or "straighten your back." Len sat there for a year or two, trying to figure out what it was he was supposed to be doing. Where should he put his attention? What was he supposed to do when he had inappropriate thoughts? "Just watch your thoughts," his teacher used to say. "Don't follow them, but don't reject them either. Just watch them the way you'd watch the clouds floating overhead."

Eventually Len figured it out: you weren't supposed to do anything during *shikantaza*, because doing itself was the problem. The brain was always doing stuff. Even when he slept, his mind was still going five hundred miles per hour. The mind was always judging others, or trying to solve problems, or planning tomorrow's events. By default, the human brain was dissatisfied with reality, and it was always coming up with ways to analyze or fix it. Len began to see his thoughts for what they were: a raging river of anxiety. He was astounded at how little control he had over his own thinking. All his life he'd assumed he created his thoughts, but nope, it was his thoughts that created him. How long had he been stuck in this madness?

As time went on and he watched his thinking day after day, Len realized how stupid it was. All of it. At the beginning, Len wasn't able to extract himself from it; the thinking forced his actions as though he'd been conscripted into slave labor. Until that point, he hadn't realized it was happening and couldn't fight it. With time and practice, though, his belief in the veracity of his thinking began to fade, and his inner monologue went from being a compulsory drama to more of a passive soap opera that he'd watch with amusement.

Then one day, it just stopped. For a few minutes, his thinking, that incessant chatterbox in his head, just stopped. It was like someone had finally shut off the spigot. Stillness. A dead calm that glittered with life. Len could feel his lungs expanding and contracting and his heart beating. For the first time in his life, without the distractions of subjectivity, he paid attention to the breeze moving over his arm hairs and the feeling of the floor pressing back against his feet. He'd never noticed that stuff before. His field of vision widened, his nose became sharp. Breathing. Walking. There was just the doing of these things, without any of the usual commentary or judgment. With the bullshit layer of thinking gone, all that remained was the exquisite immediacy of presence.

Then that profound awareness disappeared. The thoughts came rushing back in to fill the vacuum, ruining the experience. Days later, the vivid calm came back. It would recede and return several more times that year, until he felt it on a regular basis. Eventually it would come to him several times in an hour.

Len remembered one moment that really stuck with him. After three years of constant meditation, and enough of those periods of thoughtless open awareness, his mind was finally tilled and seeded. And a seed sprouted. It was early April and he was twenty-five years old. Len had just finished morning meditation in the Zendo. Afterward he went to help some of the monks make breakfast in the kitchen. While waiting for some water to boil, Len looked out the window and saw the darndest thing: snow. Snow in April!

Just then, for reasons unknown, the usual boundary between himself and the rest of the world dissolved. A fourfold wave of insight and joy washed over him, and he saw with absolute clarity some things he'd chosen to ignore his whole life.

The universe itself is a living, conscious thing.
Everything is here on purpose.
Everything is going according to plan.
Everything is absolutely perfect.

A *kensho*, they called it: an initial glimpse, rather than the full experience, of enlightenment. It wasn't like fireworks or angels singing or any of that, it was more like the mirthful relief of finally putting down a heavy object that he'd been carrying his whole life.

For a few months after the experience, things were easier than they'd ever been. He saw that the obstacles in his life had been purely mental. When they'd just evaporated that day, nothing remained but beautiful flow. Insults rolled off his back, hard work was no longer hard, and for a while there were no difficulties.

As the lungs breathed air and the heart beat blood, the human mind was also an organ of habit: it created thoughts. These thoughts, when mistaken for reality, tended to be clung to. It was this clinging that caused suffering. But after some time, as happened to most who experienced spiritual awakenings, the grace subsided, and Len's habit of believing his own bullshit returned to him.

Len eventually had a falling out with his teacher, and he left the monastery two years later to pursue journalism. He sometimes found himself wondering if he'd made a mistake by leaving before his training was complete. He wondered what would have happened had he pursued it. Now, years later, through the ineffable machinations of half-assed revolutionaries, here he was in Japan once again.

9

After meditation, as Len was leaving the hall with the other monks, Mutoku pulled him aside and whispered, "The Great Master wants to meet with you."

Len was led into a small room. An elderly, balding monk stood in the corner holding a bell. His face showed no expression, and his eyes were cast downward in respectful Japanese fashion. A tatami mat covered bamboo floors. A sliding door was open onto a rock garden, allowing a gentle breeze to blow through. Droopy Japanese maples rustled softly outside. Old Japan had had a genius for creating architecture that instilled a sense of peace, which Len felt had been lost after the second world war. Walking around Tokyo, now overbuilt with concrete and filled with illuminated, talking advertisements, one got no sense of that old harmony.

There was no altar in this room, only a large, gaudy, glass jellyfish sculpture against the far wall. It looked like a freshman art student's glass-blowing project. Len almost snickered at the tackiness of it but managed not to. In the five years he'd spent in the monastery, he'd always thought it odd that the very people who had devoted their lives to letting go of worldly things couldn't bear to throw a single item in the trash. Most waste disposal was strictly forbidden in the monastery because it was seen as a detriment to the environment; reusing an item until it fell apart was standard operating procedure. Thus, any gifts given, any objects found, were never thrown out but instead repurposed in the temple. There were old hubcaps serving as gongs, Coke bottles as decorations in the garden, old-lady tchotchkes on the altars, and tea tins as flower pots.

Len looked around again. The old man was still standing in the corner. There were two bowing mats and two little *seiza* benches toward the center that faced a brightly colored mat of the kind that a very important teacher would sit upon. The position of the mats suggested that he and Mutoku would sit on the benches and the Great Master, upon arrival, would sit facing them on the brightly colored mat.

Mutoku did not walk into the room. Instead he stood at the doorway upon coming in, hands folded in *sashu*, in a way that indicated Len should do the same. Len stood and imitated him.

They stood like that for nearly two minutes before Len spoke up. "Mutoku, when will the Great Master arrive?"

"Shh! He is here," Mutoko whispered.

Len suddenly realized Mutoku was referring to the elderly monk in the corner, and a wave of embarrassment came over him. He'd assumed that the old guy was just a lowly time-keeper or bell ringer, the sort who stood in the corner before every meditation session began. How clever. Len rolled his eyes. They were always making you confront your assumptions, these Zen people.

Mutoko and the elderly monk nodded to each other without making eye contact. Mutoku walked slowly, deliberately to the mats in the center of the room. Len followed. The elderly monk rang the bell crisply three times. Mutoko did three full bows, touching his nose to the mat each time, in the direction of the ugly sculpture. He remained standing after the last bow. Len clumsily followed his lead in all of this. Then, another minute of standing in pregnant silence before the elderly man rang the bell sharply two more times.

"Please be seated," Mutoku whispered, motioning to one of the benches.

Len sat down, his knees already starting to creak with age. Sitting perfectly still, bolt upright, in meditation created surprising demand on the body. He wondered how much longer he'd need to stay here to accomplish whatever it was he was supposed to be doing.

The old man put the bell down softly in the corner, bowed to the room, then quietly shuffled out the door. Several more minutes of silent sitting elapsed. Len wondered what was going on. When was the Great Master coming back into the room? Was this another one of the obnoxious games that had caused him to leave the monastery years earlier? Len stared at the floor in front of him and tried to clear his mind. Birds chirped outside. Another breeze came through the room.

Stillness.

Just as Len began to relax into the situation, motion in front of him caught his eye. He looked up.

Len had to do a double take. The jellyfish sculpture, which had been sitting on the floor, was now hovering in midair. It wavered like a hummingbird and pulsed with a low-frequency *wub-wub-wub* sound.

"What the hell is that?!" Len gasped.

"*Quiet!* Await the teaching!" Mutoku admonished.

The jellyfish sculpture thing slowly approached Len and Mutoku, then stopped and hovered over the brightly colored mat. The pulsing noise stopped. Mutoku bowed. Len bowed too, not knowing what else to do. Mutoku stood up, removed his robes, folded them carefully, placed them behind him, and sat back down again. He sat there with perfect posture, eyes cast downward, totally buck naked.

"Uh, am I supposed to do that, too?" Len whispered.

"No. Just sit there."

One of the jellyfish's thin, clear tentacles slowly stretched outward toward Mutoku.

"*Hai!* I am ready," Mutoku said in tense Japanese.

The long tentacle draped over the center of Mutoku's shaven head and the whole way down his spine to his tail-bone. On contact, Mutoku's eyes opened wide and he inhaled sharply. The tentacle then began to pulse, bead-like, like a fire hose full of water in an old cartoon. The noise again, *wub-wub-wub*. Mutoku breathed heavily for a few seconds, muscles taut, as if he had jumped into ice-cold water. Abruptly, Mutoku's body and face relaxed, his body slumped a bit, and his stare went vacant.

"Who are you?" Mutoku asked while staring straight ahead.

Len looked around. "Who, me? I told you who I am, Mutoku. What am I watching here? Is this some sort of joke?

This isn't funny." He wanted to believe he was being put on, but he had never seen special effects like these outside of the movies.

The jellyfish raised two tentacles in Len's direction. Blue arcs of electricity leapt from each of the tentacles into both of Len's knees, which had been facing the jellyfish as he sat on the *seiza* bench.

"Oh God!" Len fell to the floor and wailed in pain.

Once Len's screaming and writhing had died down to whimpers, Mutoku spoke again. "We apologize, but the extreme importance of this conversation must be conveyed. We do not have the power of speech. We are speaking through Mutoku." Mutoku's voice was distant but oddly resonant.

"Oh, Christ. I'm talking to a jellyfish?"

"We are not a jellyfish. Please sit."

Len hesitantly got back on the *seiza* bench. Len's knees where he'd been zapped were numb. "Then what the hell are you?" Len's heart pounded.

"We are Ich-Ca-Gan. Known in this monastery as the Great Master. We will ask questions first. Who are you?"

"Jim Rivington." He was beginning to sweat a bit.

"No! You are not!" The creature leveled a tentacle directly at Len's face.

"OK, OK! Don't zap me again! My name is Leonard Savitz. I'm a journalist." Len suddenly felt the depersonalization that came before a panic attack. He put his hand down onto the bench to steady himself.

The creature lowered its tentacles. "And you were sent here by whom?"

"Someone calling herself Neith."

"Tell Us about Neith."

"I—I don't know much. She speaks through a robot. I haven't met her in person.She forced me to come to this monastery for some reason."

"And Neith is responsible for the terrorism in the United States?"

"Yes."

"What information did she ask you to collect?"

"Nothing, actually. She didn't ask me to collect anything. She is holding my daughter and ex-wife hostage while simultaneously offering me a boatload of cash to come here. A carrot and a stick. I had to come here, there was no choice. She gave no further instructions, only to come here. That's it."

The creature lowered its tentacles from the threatening position. Its human proxy was silent for a few seconds, as if chewing on what Len had said.

"You may now ask questions," said Mutoku's limp body.

"What the hell are you?"

"We are Ich-Ca-Gan."

"What does that even mean?"

"We come from Ich-Ca. A gaseous planet near the center of the Milky Way."

"You're a fucking space alien? Seriously? Jesus Christ. Look, this is way more than I signed up for. I'd like to go home now."

"You may not leave. You are a journalist, and you have been sent here to gather information, which We intend to provide.

Tonight, prepare your questions thoroughly. We shall hold *dokusan* again tomorrow morning."

Ich-Ca-Gan's tentacle peeled away from Mutoko's spine and head. The creature then hovered back to the far wall, lowered itself to the tatami mat, and came to the resting position in which Len had first seen it.

Mutoku collapsed onto the floor.

"Mutoku!"

"Hai." Mutoku blinked a few times. Slowly, legs shaking, he rose, put his robe back on, bowed three times, and exited the room.

10

Len didn't sleep.

The next morning, Mutoku and Len bowed in again. Len sat down on the *seiza* bench. The old man with the bell shuffled out. Mutoku disrobed and Ich-Ca-Gan draped a tentacle over him as he had done before. Mutoku spasmed, then went zombie.

"How are your knees, Mr. Savitz?" asked Ich-Ca-Gan through Mutoku.

"They've bothered me for years, but today they don't hurt at all. I thought I'd never walk again the way you zapped me."

"Sometimes the medicine is bitter."

"Wow. Wow! Is it OK if I take some pictures of you?" Len asked. "No one will ever believe this otherwise. Also, do you mind if I record this interview?"

A long pause, as if the creature was thinking it over.

"You may do both."

With the morning sun coming through the window, Len wondered if ASA 400 film would be good enough for the lighting. He fumbled to put a roll of film into the old Pentax. He repeated to himself the mental checklist: *Bump on the bottom. Pull the film out a bit, but not too much. Thread it through the slot in the spool, wind it and click the shutter, make sure it's winding onto the spool. Close the door. Wind it and click the shutter, wind it and click the shutter, until it says 0. Take the lens cap off. Meter the light. Don't screw this up, Len.* With shaking hands, he adjusted the shutter-speed dial and aperture ring until the light-meter needle was wavering in the middle. He took thirty-six pictures of the creature, the whole roll, then carefully rewound the film, making extra sure the rewinder lever had gone slack before opening the film door and removing the canister. Len put the canister deep into his pocket and, as though it were the winning lottery ticket, patted his pocket twice to make sure it was still there.

Ich-Ca-Gan waited patiently as Len pulled out the ancient microcassette recorder and a legal pad filled with questions scrawled the night before. The previous day's shock had given way to a sleep-deprived giddiness. The lunacy of the situation was sinking in: extraterrestrial life was granting him an interview. He made sure the recorder had a cassette in it, and he pushed record. The tape reels began to spin.

"Let's start with the basics. How did you get here?"

"Space warp. Once the technology is mastered, distance becomes irrelevant."

"Why are you here?"

"We are scientists. We came to study this planet. However, Our subsequent mission is to save the human race."

"Save us from what?"

"From yourselves and others. More on that later. There is much to explain."

"How long ago did you come to Earth?"

"Seventeen thousand years ago."

"Then how old are you?"

"Approximately 235,000 years old."

Two hundred thirty-five thousand years old. Len was talking to something older than the entire human race.

"How did you learn English?"

"Ich-Ca-Gan does not know English, Mutoku does."

"Why must you communicate through Mutoku? Why can't you communicate with me directly?"

"It is not necessary."

Len studied Ich-Ca-Gan carefully, still in disbelief. He hadn't noticed the day before that the creature's transparent body contained semitransparent organs, three of which expanded and contracted with the creature's subtle rise and fall in altitude. Lungs, perhaps, or maybe a gas ballast system to keep the creature at a constant altitude.

"How do you float like that?"

"We are approximately the same density as the atmosphere on this planet at sea level. We float on Our planet, too."

"Where are your eyes?"

"We have none. Our nervous system is nothing like yours."

"Then how do you see me?"

"Our anatomy is far too complicated to explain succinctly. Essentially, We hear and see all that you do, and much more."

"How did you know of the terrorism in the United States? I haven't seen any computers or televisions in this monastery."

"We are not limited to visible light, We perceive the entire electromagnetic spectrum. We see television and radio broadcasts coming through the walls the way you see daylight coming through the window."

"Amazing." Len scribbled notes furiously. "Why do you refer to yourself as 'we'? I only see one of you. Are there more of you on Earth?"

"There were as many as fifteen Ich-Ca-Gan on Earth, but only one remains, the one with whom you are speaking. In truth, everything is We. Evolution on Earth is competitive: kill or be killed. Evolution on Ich-Ca is symbiotic: cooperate or die. Thus, creatures on Earth have evolved to form egos and self-identities, the belief that they are separate and apart from each other and the environment. Ich-Ca-Gan have evolved with a different understanding of Our place in the order of things. We do not see Ourselves as separate from each other, or Our environment, as beings on Earth do. Ich-Ca-Gan are an inextricable part of the universe, just as humans are without realizing it. First-person singular is a dishonest fiction to Us. 'I' is a human imagining—a delusion, a duality, a suffering. There is no 'I.' We have tried for many years to teach human beings this truth, but your species requires many years of mindfulness training before being able to grasp it."

The answer, and the creature's age, made Len wonder if he were speaking to the originator of Dharmic religions. "Did you have something to do with the creation of Buddhism? Is that why you're here in this temple?"

"We inadvertently created all religions. Over the millennia, We tried teaching human beings both compassion for all living things and simple scientific truths. However, humans were not in a fit state to receive such lessons. They were willfully ignorant, irrational, preoccupied with magic and deities. They turned anything We taught them into mythology by worshipping Us as devas or gods. This puzzled Us, as it did not reconcile with the substantial intellect and reasoning capabilities of the human mind."

"Yeah, well, we're famous for not using our huge brains."

"Through further research, we discovered that most human beings had been genetically engineered to forgo truth. The limitation was intentional."

As if to punctuate the statement, Mutoku's vacant body let out a high-pitched fart.

"Human beings were genetically engineered? By whom? For what purpose?"

"You were engineered to be slaves by the Dranthyx."

"The Dranthyx?"

"Yes."

"I don't understand. What's a Dranthyx? Humans didn't evolve from monkeys?"

"Humans did indeed evolve from monkeys, but they were further engineered to serve the Dranthyx, Earth's only super-intelligent race prior to Our arrival."

"Wait, so there are other kinds of aliens on earth?"

"The Dranthyx are not aliens."

"Wait a minute, wait a minute. Let's rewind. Are these Dranthyx still on Earth?"

"Yes."

"Do they still keep humans as slaves?"

"Yes."

"Then why haven't I heard about any of this before?"

"For the same reason you do not give any thought to your heart beating—you take it for granted. It has been happening in plain sight for thousands of years. The entire human race is enslaved and has never known anything else."

"How can someone enslave us without our knowing it?"

"Debt."

"Debt?"

"Yes, debt. At Our arrival on this planet, the Dranthyx used overt force to control humanity. However, as humans developed communication and weapons technologies, the Dranthyx feared losing control of the human race. Hence they devised a new scheme to control human beings covertly from the shadows: compound interest. Debt is everywhere. Debt is the leash around your neck. Humanity is crushed under debts public and private, and there is no mathematical possibility of paying any of it back. Your governments, which humans believe are there to protect them, exist only to enforce this scheme."

"So the Dranthyx are bankers?"

"The Dranthyx are more than that. They control the entire global financial system. In addition, the Dranthyx control most land, farms, water sources, the securities exchanges, and all energy production. They own the corporations you work for, they control the governments you live under. They are the puppeteers behind your entire existence."

"OK, let's go back to slavery. I don't understand why they're using us for. What exactly do we do for the Dranthyx that they can't do themselves?"

"Humans do many things for them: mineral extraction, food production, even scientific research and engineering. The Dranthyx could easily do that work themselves but no longer need to. They have designed their civilization around free human labor."

"How can these…Dranthyx…run the world without humans noticing? That sounds pretty management heavy to me."

"They take great care to remain hidden. They live among you, camouflaged. You may have met one or two without realizing it. And you are correct about management. To avoid detection, they delegate most management tasks to special humans designed for that purpose."

Len wasn't a fast writer and struggled to keep up.

Ich-Ca-Gan paused for a bit, then said, "Mutoku tells me you have a background in Zen Buddhism." It almost sounded like an abrupt change to small talk.

"Yes, I lived in a Japanese monastery near Kyoto for five years."

"And what is your connection to banking?"

"Huh? I've never worked in banking…oh! Wait, I think I know what you mean. There's no connection, really. I did an investigative piece a few years ago about corruption at the Federal Reserve, the central bank in the United States. The story won a Pulitzer and I got a few death threats."

"It sounds as though you are not here by mistake, Mr. Savitz. You were handpicked to conduct this very interview."

Len stopped writing and looked up. While he was trying to wrap his head around talking to a floating, mind-melding, electric space jellyfish, Ich-Ca-Gan had slammed a puzzle together like some genius gorilla.

"Jesus," Len exclaimed, "Neith is fighting the Dranthyx?"

"It would seem so."

"And I'm here, specifically me, because Neith knew you would provide me insight into these Dranthyx?"

"We believe your presence here is intended as a greeting to Us from Neith."

"How did she even know you exist when no one else does?"

"We have remained in seclusion in this monastery for seven hundred years. Even most of the monks in this temple are unaware of Our existence, simply believing Us to be an inanimate, religious relic. Humans outside this monastery had forgotten about Us. However, nothing remains hidden if one sifts enough data. Prior to Our seclusion, Our presence on Earth was public knowledge and was recorded by humans in countless historical objects. Unlike the Dranthyx, who have painstakingly erased all evidence of their existence, We have never destroyed artifacts that refer to Us. This Neith you speak of apparently has access to ancient Japanese texts and the ability to analyze them. It would appear that there is now a third superintelligence at work."

"Superintelligence? You mean Neith isn't human?"

"It is unlikely. Consider the military and intelligence capabilities of the US government. One doesn't simply execute several successful surprise attacks against the most powerful nation in history. From what We see on the broadcast news, its—or her—tactical execution exceeds human capabilities. Watching her move is like watching a supercomputer checkmate a human chess master again and again."

"Where did she come from?"

"We could guess, but We can't be certain. She may have been created by a major government or by the Dranthyx themselves. She may even be of extraterrestrial origin."

"Where is she physically located?"

"We are sorry. We don't know any more than what We can extrapolate from the broadcasts. The nature of her existence is pure conjecture on Our part."

"What do you think she wants?"

"If she is of terrestrial origin, which is the most likely scenario, she would have a physical presence somewhere on Earth that could be targeted. She would be killed or destroyed if she were discovered. If she is as rational as she is deliberate, We must assume that she has weighed the risk of her own annihilation against overthrowing Dranthyx control and has decided in favor of the latter. She is risking her own existence to start a revolution."

Len furiously scribbled notes.

"OK, so, you mentioned something about individual humans being engineered for specific tasks. How does that work?"

"As We mentioned, the Dranthyx have modified human DNA for their own purposes. In doing so, they created three main breeds of humans: Tchogols, Saskels, and Xreths." Mutoku's mouth clicked while saying these words as though he were speaking an African bush language. "These are the original Dranthyx terms. Forgive Us, Mutoku's human mouth was not designed to pronounce these sounds. The Dranthyx spliced some of their own genes directly into a number of humans, creating the original Tchogol stock. Tchogols, like the Dranthyx, have no empathy, no remorse, and no conscience. Dranthyx DNA gives them a strong drive toward material wealth and power. They were designed to be ruthless, cunning, and charismatic."

"They sound like garden-variety sociopaths."

"Sociopaths are indeed Tchogols, Mr. Savitz. Sociopathy itself is a result of inheriting Dranthyx genetics. To be more technical, Tchogol genes cause charisma, profound greed, and a lack of both empathy and remorse. The genes can be expressed as a number of different phenotypes: sociopathy, psychopathy, narcissism, antisocial personality disorder. Due to their ruthlessness and inborn desire for domination, the Tchogols are the unwitting managers of the Dranthyx slave hierarchy. As a border collie instinctively herds animals without being told to do so, Tchogols simply do what they were genetically programmed to: they rise to the top of organizations by any means necessary and rule. They do this without even knowing that the Dranthyx exist. Tchogols range in intelligence from far below average to incredibly bright. A number of recessive genes must combine to produce a pure Tchogol, and therefore they compose only a small percentage of the population."

"Wow. OK, so what about the second type?"

"Early on, the Dranthyx identified human genes for intractable behavior and independent thought. Clearly, these are not favorable attributes in slave labor, and as such they had to be removed to produce the second type, Saskels. Saskels are designed to do tedious labor without questioning authority. Saskels are low to average in mental abilities and ostensibly have the ability to reason through minor problems. However, they are genetically engineered to not trust their own thoughts and to have a deep fear of losing their security. They are terrified of having to think, or fend, for themselves. This inborn insecurity causes them to constantly seek external guidance and to obey authority, no matter how irrational or malevolent that authority is. Saskels will support any government, regardless of how oppressive it is, if it promises to guarantee their safety. Saskel genes are the most dominant, and after thousands of years of breeding, Saskels now compose the majority of human beings."

"This is fascinating. And the third type?"

"Xreths are humans who were designed for creativity and problem solving. Xreths have both ethics and the ability to come to conclusions independently. They were the most recent breed introduced by the Dranthyx approximately fifteen thousand years ago."

"If they're trying to stay in control, why would the Dranthyx introduce a breed like that?"

"The Dranthyx need a certain percentage of Xreths to exist because they are useful. Xreths create math, science, engineering, art. Before the introduction of Xreths, humans hadn't even thought of agriculture. Without Xreths, you would have no lightbulbs, airplanes, or Internet. Human technological development stalls without them, and labor output declines to the Dranthyx's detriment. Further complicating the situation, they realized that human Xreths are even more creative and productive than their own Dranthyx intellectuals. The Dranthyx have kept Xreths around because the science and technology they produce benefits them and their bottom line."

"Wouldn't the Dranthyx consider them a danger?"

"The Dranthyx consider Xreths a necessary evil, one that they monitor very closely. The Dranthyx are extremely concerned with Xreths usurping control. We estimate that human technological capabilities will surpass those of the Dranthyx in a hundred years' time due to the brilliance of Xreths. However, so long as the majority of the population is law-abiding Saskel, and there are enough conscience-less Tchogols to brutally rule the herd, the largely unmanageable Xreths can pose no threat to Dranthyx hegemony." Ich-Ca-Gan paused while Len wrote, then continued, "You may be wondering how the heritability works. There is a gene dominance hierarchy, with Saskel genes being the most dominant and Tchogol genes being the most recessive, with Xreths in the middle. However, the percentages of each type in the population are not what you would expect from normal breeding. Instead, they are kept in a delicate, artificial equilibrium that the Dranthyx worked out through millennia of experimentation. The Dranthyx have learned how much of each breed a society needs to function optimally, and they have done whatever was necessary to maintain that balance over the last several thousand years."

Len had had a professor back in college who used to say, "A scientist's job is to explain complex things. A science *journalist's* job is to explain those complex things in a way that anyone can understand." Len tried to figure out how he might present everything the Ich-Ca-Gan was telling him simply, as though he were writing an article about it for the paper. He drew a quick table in his notepad:

	Tchogol	**Xreth**	**Saskel**
Heritability:	Recessive	More Dominant	Most Dominant
Function:	Leadership	Creativity	Obedience, Work
Intelligence:	Low to High	High	Low to Average
Morality:	None	Internal	External
Motivation:	Power and Wealth	Understanding	Security

"I just want to be sure I understand all of this correctly," Len said, showing the Ich-Ca-Gan the diagram. "Is this about right?"

"That is overly simplistic, but a reasonable synopsis. There are a number of subtypes of each, but those details are immaterial to our discussion."

"OK, Xreths are brilliant but difficult to manage, right?" Len asked. "So what happens if Xreths begin to outnumber Saskels?"

"For various sociological reasons, that very thing has been happening with increasing frequency. When Xreths overpopulate, the Dranthyx have them culled. It had to be done several times in the twentieth century: Congo, Cambodia, Turkey, USSR, Germany, China, and even here in Japan."

Len tried to think of the common theme between those places. "You mean genocides?"

"Yes. Genocides usually have an ideological pretense, but their real purpose is to kill off excess Xreths to prevent civil unrest. In any genocide, you will notice that a society's intellectuals are the first to be killed."

"This is heavy."

"It is about to get heavier, Mr. Savitz. Constant uprisings and protests around the world indicate that the Xreth population has exceeded the Dranthyx's desired equilibrium. If the Dranthyx do not intervene soon, Xreths will soon outnumber the other two types, and the Dranthyx will have trouble staying in control of the human race. We believe the next cull will be global and number in the billions."

"Dear God. So this is real? What can we do to stop it?"

"The Dranthyx are quite powerful. The last time We intervened, twenty-seven hundred years ago, a war ensued between Ich-Ca-Gan and the Dranthyx, and fourteen of Us were killed."

"Fourteen? How many Dranthyx died?"

"Millions, mostly due to technology asymmetry. As a journalist, you may be interested to know that the war inspired parts of the Hebrew Bible and other mythological scriptures of the time."

"So what happened?" Len asked impatiently. "Did you win?"

"We entered into a truce agreement with the Dranthyx, and since then We have remained uninvolved. We agreed not to interfere in their culls, and they agreed not to interfere with Our education of the human race."

"The cull that's coming…how will they do it?"

"We do not know. Probably just as they have done them before." The creature paused for a long time as Len was writing, then abruptly said, "Mr. Savitz, you must leave now."

"What? Why? I just got started!"

Len heard a helicopter approaching in the distance.

"This monastery will soon be in grave danger. We believe you have enough information now."

"Can we talk again tomorrow?"

"No. Good day, Mr. Savitz. Please leave now."

Ich-Ca-Gan's tentacle quickly peeled away from Mutoku's head. Mutoku fell forward, unconscious, and Len leaned out quickly and caught Mutoku by the arm before he hit the floor and broke his nose. Mutoku came to within a few seconds and stumbled to his feet quickly without getting his bearings. Neglecting the customary bows, Mutoku shambled dizzily out of the room, yelling something in Japanese. Someone outside began clanging a gong. Others began ringing bells and running through the halls, yelling. Mutoku ran back into the room and lifted Len by his arm.

"It is time to go!"

"What's happening?"

"The Great Master hears police radio broadcasts. No time to explain."

Len quickly gathered his things, thankfully remembering to grab his suitcase as Mutoku ran with him through the monastery. As they bustled out, monks were lining up in the main hall, which reminded Len of the way fire drills were practiced in American grade schools, except the monks were lined up with their backs to the exit, as if they would be going farther into the building. Mutoku pulled Len through the kitchen, slid open a door, and shoved him out. Len came down on his backside in a narrow alleyway behind the monastery.

"If anyone asks, you are a tourist and you do not speak Japanese! Now get going!" Mutoku shouted before slamming the door shut.

Len scrambled to his feet, shoved the items he had been carrying into his suitcase, and did his best to walk down the city sidewalk, wheeling the suitcase behind him, without seeming panicked or attracting attention.

Once he was about a block away, several police trucks emblazoned with "Special Assault Team Tokyo" drove past him before pulling up in front of the monastery. Two helicopters circled overhead. Officers poured out of the vehicles and took aim with rifles at the monastery.

Len heard a tremendous noise like an earthquake coming from the chaos. He had been doing his best to look uninvolved, but turning around, he saw the monastery exploding in slow motion, as though a balloon were being inflated inside a Lincoln Log house, with the terrible sounds of ripping timber and roof tiles popping off. As the main pagoda collapsed in on itself, Len thought he briefly saw a gleaming object underneath the destruction. The dust cloud rising from the collapsing temple frustrated his attempt to see what the object was. *Pop-pop-pop* of gunfire: the police were shooting at something.

From the dust cloud emerged an enormous, pearl-white, spherical object that rose into the cobalt sky. Dirt fell off it as it floated upward. The police helicopters, which had been hovering nearby, quickly backed off to a defensive distance. The object hung in midair for about ten seconds while the officers below emptied magazines into it. Then, with a sound like thunder and enough force to cause a strong gust of wind, the object simply disappeared.

———

Len had exactly three priorities at that moment:

1. Get the hell out of there before any cops saw him;
2. Booze, like right goddamn now; and
3. Get back to the hotel and type up his notes because holy fucking shit.

There was nothing from Mr. Hamasaki at the front desk. Len went to his hotel room, which was about the size of a walk-in closet in America. Japan was a bad place for claustrophobic people, which Len thankfully wasn't. The room had a mattress-type thing that could be folded into a chair when you weren't using it for sleeping, a little television, and a tiny window.

Len, disregarding the careful efficiency and tidiness of the space, unzipped his suitcase and dumped out all the stuff Neith had given him. He also shook out a shopping bag of items he'd hastily bought on the way back to the hotel: alcohol, cigarettes, and enough food to work all day without interruptions. He ripped open the carton of cigarettes, a local brand he'd never heard of, then fumbled to open the equally foreign bottle of whiskey. He took a few slugs to calm his nerves, struggling in disgust to swallow it each time. Japanese whiskey would be a lot better if it weren't trying so hard to be scotch, he thought. Whatever. He rolled some paper into the typewriter and set to work.

Len decided to omit what Ich-Ca-Gan had said about Neith. He figured it would be better if Neith didn't know what Len had found out about her. Once he'd finished writing up everything else, he put the typed pages and handwritten notes into one of the envelopes, along with the film canister and the typewriter ribbon, and left it at the reception desk for Mr. Hamasaki, whoever the hell that was. The microcassette, however, he took with him to the deserted alley behind the hotel. He pulled the tape out of the cassette, lit the ball of gray ribbon on fire with his lighter, then put the remains into a street trashcan. Having been awake for forty hours at that point, Len went back to his room and slept until the next afternoon.

One would have thought that the local SWAT team getting into a firefight with a UFO that had been hidden under a Buddhist monastery for seven hundred years would make some great front-page news. One would have further thought, in this day and age of ubiquitous surveillance and video cameras affixed to every conceivable electronic device, that footage of such an extraordinary event would surface and appear on TV or the Internet. One would have been surprisingly wrong. The next morning, Len went down the street to a newsstand and bought five different local papers. Inexplicably, none of them said anything about the incident. He went back to his room and turned on the little TV. Zilch.

Len checked at the front desk. The kid with the anime hair handed him another envelope. Inside was a boarding pass for a flight back to the United States.

11

On the other side of the globe, it was a Sunday night. People ate dinner with their families or slept or watched TV to take their minds off the fact that all the security they'd ever known was under siege. That invincible fortress, the mighty US government, was starting to feel like a brittle Popsicle stick house. The collective anxiety in America and around the world had become palpable. Neith's war was largely psychological, and she was winning.

Citizens tend to regard governments the way children regard their parents' marriage. The stability and permanence of both situations are taken for granted, and neither beneficiary realizes how tenuous the institution they live under is, nor how easily small things, happening precisely in the correct order, can cause all the stability they've ever known to completely fall apart.

In fact, several of those small things were about to happen.

At 3:00 a.m. Eastern Time, when the entirety of North America was completely dark, a beautiful ballet of technology began simultaneously in thirteen separate locations: Boston, New York, Philadelphia, Cleveland, Richmond, Atlanta, Chicago, St. Louis, Minneapolis, Kansas City, Dallas, San Francisco, and Washington, DC. At each site, an army of small robotic flying machines was launched from the back of a semi-trailer. Flying through the doors, they rose quietly into the moonless night sky. In each city, a highly tailored flight path was followed to avoid security cameras, radar, and human sight. The swarms of drones flew in stunningly perfect formation: through dark alleys, low over rooftops, down air ducts, and through dark offices.

Each machine carried a deadly payload, a plastic explosive that could be remotely triggered. These little bombs were placed at the most structurally significant points in each edifice the drones entered: support columns, I-beams, foundations—locations mathematically determined to produce untold damage.

Once the payloads had been delivered, the machines quickly and silently exited the buildings and returned to the trucks whence they came. With every single robot accounted for, the trucks drove off, leaving no trace.

At exactly ten the next morning, Monday, when the offices were fully occupied with throngs of white collars, the explosives were detonated simultaneously. In a choreography of exquisitely controlled demolition, thirteen very important buildings across the continent imploded thoroughly, leaving nothing but fire, bodies, twisted steel, and utter panic.

12

"Mr. Rivington, welcome back," said one of Neith's men at the airport.

"Thanks. Look, fellas, I'm not riding in the trunk again."

The two men looked at each other blankly, as though it hadn't occurred to them that riding in the trunk might be uncomfortable.

"You got what I left for you, right?"

The men nodded.

"So I completed the assignment in Japan?" Len asked. "I think I've earned the right to sit shotgun without handcuffs or a bag on my head."

"I suppose we can make an exception."

Walking past a restaurant on the way out of the airport, Len did a double take at the headlines on the television: "Entire Federal Reserve System Bombed, Hundreds Dead."

"Wow. How the hell did you lunatics pull that one off?"

"Mr. Rivington, we have no idea what you're talking about," the shorter man said through his teeth in annoyance, looking around to make sure no one had heard Len's comment.

Amazingly, they did let him sit in the front of the car on the way to Neith's compound. Len tried to keep mental notes of the location. As he'd suspected, it was in fact in the mountains of West Virginia. Around three in the afternoon, in the middle of the woods, they pulled up to a barbed-wire gate, which opened after they'd sat there for a few seconds. The road beyond the gate led to a vast mining facility that looked like it hadn't been in operation since the 1940s. Smokestacks, rail spurs, coal elevators, water towers—it looked like the place had been a massive enterprise at one point, but its cavernous buildings now sat empty and wasting; its open spaces had grown into forests. The mine was ringed by mountains, and it seemed to be the only thing in the entire valley.

The men pulled the car into an old pole barn and got out. They opened a door and led Len into the old mine elevator that he had ridden in once before.

"What is this place?" Len asked on the way down.

"The mine ran out of coal during World War II," said one of the goons. "After that, Uncle Sam bought it and made it into a nuclear bunker in the 1950s. One of those continuity of government programs. When the Soviet Union fell, they just abandoned it and forgot about it."

"So it's still government property?" Len asked.

"Yep."

"And you haven't blown it up yet? Aren't you worried they'll get suspicious?" Len could see gears turning in the man's head. *You know you're dealing with zealots when they take deadpan seriously*, he thought.

The elevator came to a jerking stop at the bottom of the shaft. The men escorted Len down a long concrete hallway to General Jefferson's office.

"Lenny, m'boy, come on in!" said an unmasked man with the general's voice. Without his ski mask, the general looked about as bald and Cro-Magnon as Len imagined he would. He had beady little blue eyes, a hulking brow ridge, and a jawline that looked like a concrete seawall holding back a tsunami of testosterone. His thick mustache barely moved as he talked. "Your field work has helped us tremendously! Do you see now what this uprising is about?"

Len guessed he had earned some respect; the general seemed a lot less hostile than he had previously. Downright affable, even.

"Yes. It's starting to make sense." Len hated himself for agreeing with Jefferson, but if what the Ich-Ca-Gan had said were true, then he'd have to choose a side.

"People think we're crazy, but I don't think they realize who is behind the curtain. Neith had a hunch before she ever sent you to Japan. She figured the world is being run by—what do you call them?"

"Dranthyx," Len said.

"Yes, Dranthyx. We intend to verify what the Ich-Ca-Gan said by seeing if these Dranthyx creatures exist. But you know, I think the human race has long had a feeling that our governments were just puppet shows and that the shots are really being called by powerful figures in back rooms. Those of us who had the nerve to say it out loud were shouted down and called conspiracy theorists or paranoid-delusional. But we all suspect it, don't we, Lenny?"

"I guess we do."

"Neith thinks your intel is right: our entire banking and money system was designed to enslave us. I'll let her explain it, I'm not a math person. This morning, when you were on the plane, we took out the entire Federal Reserve System. All twelve banks plus the headquarters in DC."

"They've still got lots of guns and lots of manpower," Len said.

"You're right. But let's see them try to pay for all that when they have no money. We intend to cut off the blood flow to the tumor."

"What do you mean?"

"Well, they can't borrow money from the Federal Reserve because we destroyed it. The only other way they can get the money to fight us is through taxation." Jefferson leaned back in his chair dramatically, then smiled. "Lenny, I have a treat for you."

———

At dawn the next day, Len, General Jefferson, and about forty-five of his men piled into a school bus. They were dressed in t-shirts, sweatpants, and athletic shoes and were carrying large duffel bags. Should they have been stopped by the police, they could easily have passed for an amateur sports team. No one would suspect what was really going on.

"Where are we going?" Len asked as the bus pulled out of the coal mine.

"Philadelphia."

"What's there?"

"You'll see."

Len looked around the bus. "How do you recruit these guys, General?"

"Neith finds them on the Internet. Chat rooms, message boards, that kind of thing. They're all hardcore anti-authority types. My kind of people." Jefferson grinned. "It started out as just me and Neith, but now we've got over three thousand recruits and growing across the continent. Hell, we're even in Canada now. I think Neith was onto something. People are pissed off enough about the way this country is going that they're ready to pick up arms and fight. It also helps that we pay them more than they'd make at a real job." He laughed.

"We live in a country where everyone has a computer and running water. What do they have to be so angry about?"

"Lenny, I hope you don't mind if I answer your questions with some questions."

"Go ahead."

"How many children did your grandparents have?" Jefferson asked.

"My maternal grandparents had four kids, my paternal grandparents had five."

"And were they able to afford that many kids?"

"I think so, sure," Len said, trying to recall.

"Why?"

"Because my dad's dad worked in the steel mill, and that job paid well."

"Did that grandfather have a college education?"

"No. He was an immigrant from Poland. You didn't need a college education to get a job back then."

"How many hours per week did he work?"

"Probably about forty."

"Did his wife work?"

"No, she stayed home with the kids."

"Now, what about your parents, how many kids did they have?"

"Two. Me and my younger brother."

"Were they able to afford to raise you both?"

"Yes, until my dad's business collapsed."

"OK, did your mom work?"

"Not when we were younger, but she eventually went back to work when my brother and I were older."

"Did your parents go to college?"

"Yes."

"How much did it cost when they went to college?"

"My dad said he paid for his whole tuition by working at McDonald's during the summer break."

"And what about you, Lenny? How many kids do you have?"

"You know how many I have."

"Can you afford that child?"

"Not really."

"Do you own a house?"

"No."

"Have you ever owned a house?"

"No, my credit is wrecked by student loans."

"And if my understanding is correct, you were married to…I'm sorry, what's her name again?"

"Sara."

"Did she work?"

"No. But she should have. We couldn't pay our bills."

"And did you go to college, Lenny?"

"Yes."

"Are you starting to see a pattern here? With each passing generation, we're getting poorer and poorer. We're working longer hours than our forebears and making less per hour, adjusted for inflation, while having to be better educated. Your grandfather had no college degree and worked forty hours per week, yet he owned a house and could support a wife and five kids. You have an extremely expensive college degree, my file says you work sixty hours a week, and yet you can't afford a house or a kid without a second income."

"What does this have to do with anything?" Len asked.

"We're being robbed. Robbed of time and wealth. The world is run by an elite that has figured out how to make us work harder than ever yet pays us less than before. But we think we're getting wealthier because of the illusion called inflation. If you took your granddad's paycheck and compared it to yours, you would think you made more money than he did just because the dollar figure is bigger. But the truth is, your money is worth less. Despite earning more, you can't buy as much as he could because things were cheaper back then. Why? Because Wall Street figured out how to steal from you without you noticing. Take a look around this bus. What do you see?"

"A bunch of guys?"

"Yeah, young guys. Twenties, thirties. Their whole generation has known nothing but debt and peanuts. Economically they're fucked because the age of growth is over. They'll never own houses of their own. They won't have kids because they'll never be able to afford 'em. They'll never do as well as their parents did. There are no steel mill jobs paying high wages to high school dropouts anymore, are there? Those mills all went to China."

"That's what this is about, money?"

"You know, Lenny, there was this brilliant dude name Camus. Ever heard of him? He once said, 'It's a kind of spiritual snobbery that makes people think they can be happy without money.' I'll never forget that quote. Money is a big fucking deal. It can't buy happiness, but it certainly is the foundation for happiness. It's hard to be happy when you're going blind from malnutrition. Been to the grocery store lately, Lenny? Unless you're getting government assistance, you can't buy a cart full of groceries anymore. Everything is too damn expensive. But that's what they want, isn't it? They want us to be dependent on them. They want us on that leash so we can't rebel."

Len just stared at Jefferson blankly. He hated it when wisdom came from people he didn't like. And what kind of jarhead read Camus? Now that the general had warmed up to Len, it was a different person talking. Jefferson seemed to have a

Southern-gentleman refinement hidden underneath that military meathead persona.

"It's also about the police state we live in," Jefferson continued, "where we're being watched all the time and you need to beg bureaucrats for permission to do anything. We're not free men. No, sir, we live in fear of our masters. This wasn't what America was supposed to be, Lenny. These kids don't believe me when I tell them there was a time when no one grabbed your dick or demanded to see your ID before you boarded an airplane. They can't fathom that the spooks once needed a warrant to listen to your phone calls. Let me ask you something. Do you get to print whatever you want at the newspaper, like the Constitution says you can, or are you under the constant threat of government reprisal?"

Len considered it for a bit. The general had a point. There were a number of stories over the years that Jack had refused to run because they'd have angered local politicians. Many years ago, the *Examiner* had run a story critical of one of the local city councilmen, and within days the newspaper building was overrun with inspectors from every government agency from OSHA to the codes and zoning office to the local department of revenue, most of whom were threatening to shut the paper down. It took nearly three years, several lawyers, and the paper's entire legal budget to clear away all the red tape.

"You don't need to answer," the general stated self-assuredly. "I know the answer. It's a funny thing, isn't it? Take a random man off the street. Think of the sort of guy the comedians find for those man-on-the-street interviews. Do you trust him?

Would you let him babysit your kids or hold your billfold? Probably not, right? He could be a saint, he could be a Hitler, you have no idea. Ethics aside, he's probably an idiot, statistically speaking. But give that same man a government job with a badge, a gun, unchecked power, limitless funds, and no accountability whatsoever, and suddenly everyone assumes he's just and wise beyond reproach. That's government in a nutshell, Lenny. There's something fundamentally wrong with the human race because we assume we need to be led by corrupt idiots whom we've never met. We always assume others know what's best for us. We assume we need to be told what to do. We assume we need to give up control of our own lives. For what? I can't figure it."

"Some say government is an anachronism," Len offered.

"Yes, anachronism. Good word. But the tide is changing, isn't it? I think people all over the world are waking up to the fraudulent power-and-money racket known as government. Our founders made a huge mistake, you know that? They tried to create a government for the purpose of guarding our liberties, which was kinda like asking a fat kid to guard the cupcakes. They had the temerity to think they could write a bill of rights that wouldn't be whittled to splinters by a bunch of corrupt judges and legislators. The media—no offense—are trying to spin things by saying that because our resistance is antigovernment, we are necessarily anti-American. Those in power want the public to conflate America and its government. They want us to think there's no difference between the two. Nothing could be further from the truth. America is not a government.

America is a land, a people, and an ideal—one my men and I have pledged our lives to protect from all enemies, foreign and domestic. America's number-one enemy, Lenny, is the scumbags who rule her."

Len sat there for a while, digesting what Jefferson had said.

"Hey, did you hear what happened in California while you were away?" Jefferson asked.

"No."

"Someone—no one knows who—built a homemade rocket and launched it from the Sierra Nevadas. The damn thing took out a recon satellite! Neith tells me we didn't have anything to do with it. Then, in Montana, cops showed up to search a house, without a warrant as usual, and the whole damn thing was rigged with explosives. Took out nine of the little piggies. We weren't involved in that one, either. People are following our lead and this is becoming a movement!" Jefferson sounded excited about the possibilities, like some yokel who'd discovered oil on his lower forty.

"Have you ever met Neith in person?"

"Can't say that I have. She never says it, but I think the little lady's worried about her safety. She only ever talks through that damned robot. Can't blame her. She's a genius, though, I'll tell you what. Every operation has been a success. She's got a sixth sense or something."

Around lunchtime, the bus pulled into an old auto garage in downtown Philadelphia. The driver got out, closed the garage door, and the men got off the bus. As soon as they were certain that the place was empty, they began pulling submachine guns out of their duffel bags and changing into combat gear. Someone went around passing out sandwiches.

Once his men were assembled, Jefferson climbed onto a car lift so they could all see him.

"Can y'all hear me?" he bellowed. "Good. You boys know why we're here today. Since 1913, this great nation, this beacon of hope for all mankind, has been raped and pillaged by a hostile conglomerate of evil men. They've established banks beyond the rule of law, forced our country to borrow from those banks, and do you know how they collect interest? Taxes. Our taxes pay interest to private bankers. You work for a lifetime and they claim they're entitled to what you earn simply because you were born here. Think about that for a second: they believe they're entitled to the work you do." He paused dramatically. "There's a name for that. Slavery!"

The men cheered and yelled obscenities.

"Nineteen thirteen, gentlemen, was the year the Federal Reserve System was established in this country. By no small coincidence, it was also the year when the federal income tax amendment was forced down our throats. Funny thing, isn't it? For our first 137 years we had no central bank and we also had no income tax. This shouldn't surprise anyone because they are two heads of the same monster. One head lends the money, the other sticks a gun in your face and forces you to pay interest!"

"Let's kill the bastards!" someone yelled.

"We're getting there, don't worry. I like your enthusiasm, though," Jefferson quipped. "Gentlemen, as you know, we are fighting the second American revolution, and today is our

Saratoga. Today we will cut the beast open from the inside and cripple the very institution that has kept its boot on America's throat for generations. And we will take no prisoners. Today we will show them as much mercy as they've shown us!"

The men roared with enthusiasm.

"Now let's get suited up and kick some ass! Hoo-rah!"

"Hoo-rah!" they yelled back in unison.

Len was starting to sweat. Whatever was about to happen was going to be violent, dangerous, and he'd be right in the middle of it.

"Get dressed, Lenny boy. You're coming with us," General Jefferson announced while getting down from the car lift. "Here, I brought some stuff for you." Len was given a duffel bag containing black fatigues, body armor, and headgear. Then Jefferson pulled an old M1911 from the shoulder holster under his jacket. "Do you know how to use one of these?"

"Of course I do. I'm from Pennsylvania."

Jefferson chuckled and handed him the sidearm. "OK, boys, we've got about forty-five minutes to get into position. We want to hit 'em hard and fast before they leave for the day or figure out what's going on. Squad A, where are you?" he bellowed. "Good. We're going to do it just like we planned: kill the telecommunications, set up the cell phone jammer with the timer set to twenty minutes, engage the magnetic locks for all exterior doors to keep 'em in. Then kill the interior power to the top floors, find the support columns, and place the charges.

"Squad B, you're going to make sure no one gets in or out of the exits. I don't know if you boys noticed when we drove past on the way down here, but the place looks like a rat's nest of barbed wire and machine guns. They're expecting us, gentlemen. Only they're expecting us to attack from the outside, not the inside. Neith is going to take care of the national guardsmen outside for us, so if you'd like to keep your gray matter where it is, I suggest you stay on the inside of the building.

"Squad C, you guys have the fun part. Lenny, you're with us on Squad C. Last order of business, we rendezvous in the basement in exactly fifteen minutes."

Len's stomach felt sick. He looked around. Jefferson's men were jittery with excitement. Len had the feeling this was the first time some of them had done anything like this, whatever it was.

"OK, let's roll!" Jefferson yelled.

The men followed his lead to the back of the auto shop, then down some old iron steps to the basement, which was full of drums of used oil and smelled like mold. In the corner of the basement was a pull-up trap door, which revealed a vertical shaft with a steel ladder that went straight down eighty feet. The men took turns going down the ladder one at a time. It was pitch black in the narrow shaft, and Len's heart pounded as he fumbled to turn on his headlamp. At the bottom of the ladder was what seemed to be a large, echoing cave. One of Jefferson's crew lit a flare, which illuminated the place as bright as day. Len could see that they were in an abandoned subway station, the art deco style indicating it must have been from the 1930s.

"OK, boys, watch out for the rats and the crackheads," Jefferson whispered. "In about three hundred feet, we'll be on the other side of the Schuylkill River."

The men followed the guy with the flare through the old subway tunnel until they got to another vertical access shaft. The men ascended the ladder. At the top was a trap door similar to the first, which everyone crawled through into a cavernous, concrete basement. The place was lit by sickly fluorescent tubes and was filled floor to ceiling with white file boxes marked with numbers. The men made gestures to each other to indicate silence was required as they came up the ladder.

"Where are we?" Len whispered to Jefferson.

"We're in the subbasement of the old Philadelphia post office, now known as the IRS building." Jefferson had a terrifying glint in his eye. "Now be quiet until we're ready."

13

Twenty-four years earlier, Len's father had gone out to check his mail one afternoon as he always did. Inside the family's little white mailbox was a letter from the IRS notifying him that he was being audited.

Bernard Savitz had owned a small bakery on the South Side of Pittsburgh. He had five employees, worked long hours, and was pretty squarely middle-class. He threw tremendous effort into putting food on the table for his wife and two children.

When the self-employed do business with one another, they are required to report to the IRS their payments made to each other with 1099 forms. One of Bernard's customers, a restaurant that bought his bread, sent him an erroneous 1099 form that overreported the bread purchased by a factor of one hundred. It was a simple accounting error caused by a computer glitch. However, it made it seem as though Bernard had made twice as much money that year as he normally did. When Bernard filed his taxes for that year, he listed the correct amount he'd earned instead of the computer glitch amount that had been reported. The discrepancy between the 1099 and Bernard's tax return caused the IRS's computer system to red-flag Bernard for an audit.

As the Savitz family found out, an IRS audit is legalized persecution. Revenue agents began interviewing Bernard's neighbors, business associates, customers, even the bank he'd borrowed money from to buy the bakery. They asked everyone whether they'd ever seen Bernard cheat or steal. The average person, upon being asked such questions by besuited agents with badges, is impressed upon that the subject of the audit is some sort of criminal. This is intentional. The point of these interviews wasn't to find out information, of course; it was an old IRS tactic to destroy Bernard's reputation in the business community. The more they soften up the target, the easier it is to fleece the target for money. And sure enough, Bernard's business started failing. Restaurants and grocery stores stopped buying his bread because they were concerned about his character.

The IRS took three years to finish its audit of Bernard's business. The IRS limits itself to three years for an audit, and by unwritten policy, it drags most audits out for the entire allotted time to maximize emotional and financial damage. During those three years, they seized Bernard's business records, froze his bank accounts, and forced Bernard to close his bakery and sell the property. In the end, the lead IRS auditor unilaterally decided that it wasn't a computer glitch at all, but malfeasance by Bernard. Bernard received a massive bill from the IRS: back taxes on money he'd never even received in the first place, plus penalties, plus fines, plus double-compounded interest on the first three. To pay it, he'd have to sell his house and put his kids out on the street.

Obviously upset at the injustice, Bernard tried to fight the matter in the legal system only to discover that if you don't have the money to pay an unjust IRS assessment up front before the legal proceedings even start, then you aren't allowed to fight the IRS in the regular court system. In other words, only the very wealthy have the right to a jury trial and a real court when fighting the IRS. If you are poor to middling like everyone else, you have to fight the IRS in a special kangaroo court run by the IRS itself, the United States Tax Court, where the house always wins. Unable to pay the IRS's bill up front, Bernard had to contest the matter in the United States Tax Court, but he had a tough time of it because the IRS had seized his business records and refused to return them. It's awfully hard to prove your innocence when those prosecuting you have taken all the proof and also serve as the jury.

The three years of auditing, plus the one year in tax court, plus the failure of his business and his subsequent inability to support his wife and children, all took a huge toll on Bernard's health. One week after losing his tax case, Bernard had a massive coronary and died on a pier while fishing.

14

Jefferson waved his men into position. What Len presumed to be Squad A shuffled off quietly to do whatever it was they were supposed to be doing. The rest just sat there among the file boxes, waiting. Len's legs were shaking; he felt sweat dripping down his back as he sat there making nervous eye contact with the other men. One of them winked at him.

There was an abrupt, building-shaking, thunking sound of enormous HVAC units shutting down as the power was cut. Then a yell from somewhere: *"Let's go!"*

The men pulled down their balaclavas and ran behind Jefferson up two flights of stairs. Len did the same, wheezing from the exertion and years of smoking. As they reached the ground floor, about half of them peeled off to guard the exits. Len and some others kept following Jefferson to the top floor. Jefferson burst through a stairwell door into a lobby and, in a nightmarish explosion of violence, started shooting everyone and anyone he saw. Receptionists, clerks, it didn't matter. Jefferson didn't give a fuck. His men ran helter-skelter into the hallways and through the cubicle farms doing the same.

The muzzle flash of the guns lit up the room. Len watched a man's head come apart as Jefferson fired a round into his face.

Too shocked by the savagery to even be revolted, his mind had trouble believing what it was seeing. Len just stood there in the pandemonium in dazed disbelief.

Chaos. Pure, animal chaos. Even in Iraq, Len had never seen anything like this.

Brass ejecting, screaming, blood, running, papers flying everywhere, more screaming. A number of people ran for the exits. Jefferson and his men didn't even try to stop them. They were allowed to escape because at the bottom of each stairwell was Squad B, waiting for them.

"This way!" Jefferson yelled, running down a hall.

Not knowing what else to do, Len followed. On the way down the hall, he happened to pass by a window. He stopped, transfixed by what he saw. The IRS building was right next to the river that they'd gone under. A Russian MI-24 helicopter hovered above the river outside the building. Sticking out of its side were two miniguns spewing flames, hosing the National Guard below with bullets. No one was flying the helicopter. There was no pilot or crew.

"Hey, snap out of it!" Jefferson rebuked. "Move!"

Len followed him to a corner office door, which was locked. Jefferson kicked it in and entered. Len didn't see anyone. Jefferson walked behind the large oak desk and threw the chair out of the way. There, cowering under the desk, was a pasty, balding little man with glasses and a paisley tie. Jefferson grabbed the man's throat and yanked him to his feet. The man looked like he'd just soiled himself.

"Do you know this man?" Jefferson asked Len.

He did indeed know him. The man's name was Edward Burkholder, and he was the IRS agent who audited Len's father nearly a quarter-century earlier.

15

Len often thought that people living in the developed world did not understand the holocaust of survival, the true nastiness it took to endure in an uncaring universe. He and everyone else were sheltered and naïve, like children. They bought meat from the grocery store having never seen the inside of a slaughterhouse. They went to their shores in the summertime, never thinking of the blood that had been spilled defending them. They went through life with televisions on and music at full blast, compulsively drowning out every possible silence. Len believed that silence was something most everyone avoided because when it was quiet, people came face-to-face with their Dark Thoughts.

After some time in Iraq, Len found out why veterans returning from combat didn't like to talk about their experiences. Sometimes it was because they didn't want to relive the experience by recounting it, sure, but sometimes it was because they'd been forced into a depth of understanding of human nature that the average person would never have and could not relate to. Indeed, the real horror of war was what you discovered about yourself.

Private Justin Waterhouse was a wiry, oddly brilliant kid with a biting, sardonic sense of humor that probably went unappreciated in his native Midwest. Of all the men Len had met in the division he'd been assigned to, he most related to Justin's piercing observations and droll understatements about the military and life in general. Justin was not the walking cliché Len had come to expect: GI Bill education, ingenuous idealism, and a cheating girlfriend back home. No, Justin was shrewd enough to see that he was there to secure oil for powerful business interests, and he didn't even bother trying to rationalize it. Justin had a genius for simply existing, without any sort of self-righteous ambition in life, and Len admired his utter lack of pretense.

Justin came from a farming family. By pure happenstance of genetics, he'd been born with an astronomical IQ into a clan of average Iowans who pinned all their vicarious hopes on him. Justin didn't want to be successful, though, and he was sick of their expectations of him. He just wanted to enjoy his damn life. He'd gone to college for two years just to shut his mother up, then failed out once he realized he didn't care enough to finish. Eventually Justin enlisted simply to get away from his father's shrill insistence that he do something spectacular. So there he was in Iraq, creating the appearance of doing something so people would leave him the hell alone.

It was said that war was 98 percent boredom and 2 percent terror. During the frequent boring parts, Len and Justin often played chess or got drunk on the vodka that people would dye green and smuggle into camp in mouthwash bottles. Len found the booze took the edge off his sometimes crippling anxiety disorder and made it easier to get some sleep under the constant threat of mortar attacks. Iraq was when the drinking became a habit.

Some men, when given control, lost their minds; they puffed up their chests, spoke in authoritative tones, and committed heinous acts without thinking twice. Power made the weak-minded forget who they were. This was what happened to most young bucks when they were given a uniform and a gun. Justin, however, wasn't like that. Len frequently accompanied Justin on patrols and noticed that he treated the locals like real people, even though they didn't always return the favor. Justin's motto was, verbatim, "Neither of us is here by choice, so let's not make this any shittier than it has to be."

On one particular October morning in Fallujah, Justin's squad was ordered to go house to house to search for weapons. Such searches in the past had been largely fruitless, and the men usually gave a perfunctory run-through while looking for anything obviously bomb-like. At the third house on the list that morning, Justin knocked on the door. An elderly man let Len, Justin, and two other soldiers in. The men split up, with Justin and Len going upstairs to check the bedrooms.

In an upstairs bedroom, Justin opened a closet door. It was the last thing he ever did. Hidden inside was a sixteen-year-old kid with a Kalashnikov rifle. The kid fired off a single round, which went right through Justin's carotid artery, one of the few places he wasn't covered in body armor. Justin collapsed, holding his neck as blood soaked his uniform. The Iraqi kid next pointed the rifle at Len and pulled the trigger. *Click*. Nothing. The boy had inserted the magazine into the rifle backward, meaning the round in the chamber, the one that went through Justin, was the first and only round that could have been fired from the gun. It was mechanically impossible for the kid to get off another shot.

Len, a sworn noncombatant, a journalist who was not allowed to participate in the fighting, picked up Justin's M4, flicked off the safety, aimed it at center mass, and pulled the trigger. *Boom.* The kid clutched his chest, and Len could tell from the labored breathing and pink foamy blood that he'd shot him through a lung. In a haze of hate and adrenaline, Len watched the boy suffocate and die.

Len knelt down beside Justin to see if he could stop the bleeding. The other soldiers who had been downstairs came running up at the sounds of the shots, but they got there just as the awareness was draining from Justin's eyes. Justin bled out before he could be medevacked to camp. He couldn't be saved. The other men knew what had happened, but it was never spoken of again. The official report given to Justin's parents stated that he had valiantly killed his own attacker to save the lives of his comrades downstairs.

Len wrote to his employer two days later asking to be reassigned somewhere stateside.

At first there was nothing but anger and sadness. Len spent a lot of time wondering why Justin had been brought into this world just to be cut down senselessly before his life had really gotten started. What was the point of his time here? Poor Justin was in Iraq serving a death sentence because his own family refused to understand him.

After a year or two, though, the anger subsided, and Len began to ask himself the same questions about the Iraqi kid. The unfortunate little bastard was just trying to defend his family from the foreign invaders destroying his country. He couldn't even load a gun correctly. He was probably still a virgin. Before coming to Iraq, Len had spent five years studying a martial art in Japan, for Christ's sake; he could have just wrestled the little punk to the ground and he'd still be alive today. Len couldn't justify or undo the kid's death.

Guilt over something that could never be made right again was the worst of hells, and Len spent an awful lot of time there, drinking himself to sleep at night. Len, Justin, and the Iraqi kid just happened to be in the wrong place at the wrong time, and it was made much shittier than it had to be.

———

And now Len found himself at the IRS building in Philadelphia, holding a gun to the head of the man who'd put his father in the ground, with the opportunity to avenge another death. The opportunity to make things still shittier.

Edward Burkholder had been the lead auditor in the Bernard Savitz case, the man who withheld evidence that would have proved the innocence of Len's father. This was the man who'd intentionally ruined Bernard Savitz's life in order to make a name for himself within the agency. And here he was, in the fancy corner office he'd earned by killing a decent, honest family man.

Len looked at the desk the man had been hiding under. There, next to the blotter, was a picture of Edward Burkholder with his wife, two grown children, and what Len presumed was a grandchild of about two. Burkholder's kids were probably in diapers when he was auditing Len's father.

"Are those your wife and kids?" Len asked.

"Yes! Please don't kill me!"

"OK, I won't," Len said.

"Oh, thank Go—"

Before he could even finish his sentence, Len fired a .45-caliber slug into the man's kneecap. Burkholder let out an ear-piercing wail and grabbed his bleeding appendage.

Len squatted down and grabbed Burkholder's face by the jaw, which was now streaming with tears and spattered in blood and bone shards. He forced Burkholder to look him in the eyes.

"That knee will never be the same. I want you to have a constant reminder of all the misery you've caused in this world, you fucking prick. I'm letting you live to give you an opportunity to change for the better. Do you understand?"

Burkholder turned white and could only nod before passing out from the pain.

"Well, aren't you merciful," Jefferson sneered at Len. "So be it."

Jefferson went out into the hallway and found two more Revenue employees hiding in a broom closet. "You two, today's your lucky day. See that man there?" He pointed to Burkholder's limp body. "He's still alive. When we leave, drag him out of the building. Don't waste any time."

Len heard one of Jefferson's men over the radio headset. "Eyes two. Honeymoon's over, boys. The chopper's been shot down, and like ten Humvees of Marines just showed up. Time to get the fuck out of Dodge. Over."

Just then, all the power in the building came back on.

"Time to go," announced General Jefferson into the radio.

Jefferson and Len ran through the building to the elevator lobby, where some of the other men were waiting for the elevators.

"We're taking the elevators? Are you sure this is a good idea?" Len asked.

"Relax, we got this. Been planning it for months. Besides, the stairwells are a damn slaughterhouse. You wanna crawl over all those bodies?"

The elevator door opened, and inside were three IRS employees who had been trapped since the power went out. Jefferson's men told them to get out, then shot them in their backs as they fled.

Len had never realized how slow a typical elevator was until it was all that stood between him and a squad of Marines. After a small forever, they reached the subbasement and filed out down the ladder to the subway tunnel. Along the way, Jefferson's men left explosive charges.

Back in the auto shop, everyone hurriedly changed back into street clothes and shoved everything into the duffel bags. They boarded the bus, opened the garage door, backed out onto the city street, and drove off.

Len couldn't remember the last time he'd felt so alive, or so shaky and nauseous.

Despite the ocean of adrenaline, the men were very quiet on the ride through the city. Once they got onto on the expressway leaving town, though, everyone broke out into raucous celebration.

"Wait, wait. Be quiet, all of you!" Jefferson shouted. "Did we lose anyone?" He counted. Everyone was there. "Whore mother of Jesus, we pulled it off!" Shouts of victory and high fives. Someone pulled a cooler of beer out of the back. Jefferson pulled a dead cell phone out of the bus's glove compartment, then put the battery in and waited for it to start up. "Who wants to do the honors? Lenny?"

"No, thanks," Len said, having an idea of what was coming next.

"Of course not. Wythe?"

"Hell yes!" exclaimed Wythe.

"Hit the call button," Jefferson said.

As Len found out later, left inside the IRS building was a prepaid cell phone cabled to a wireless transmitter. The phone rang. And when it did, every single explosive charge detonated simultaneously, leaving a large, burning crater along the banks of the Schuylkill.

16

Neith's bunker had a 1950s-era cafeteria that had been built large enough to accommodate all of Congress, and it now served as the mess hall for Jefferson's army. Len sat there the next morning at a table by himself, drinking coffee and mentally replaying the bloodbath the day before. He wanted to feel bad about maiming Burkholder and seeing all those IRS agents die, but he didn't. In fact, he had to admit to himself that he felt a little bit on the positive side of nothing. He wondered if this was how the freed slaves had felt when Sherman marched to the sea and burned down the plantation mansions of their masters: vindicated but empty. Maybe that was how Jefferson felt all the time.

As if he could hear what Len was thinking, Jefferson stomped into the room.

"Lenny, you should have killed that dirtbag when you had the chance," Jefferson said, throwing a newspaper in front of him. Circled on page A3 was an article: "Kidnapped journalist believed to be involved in IRS attack." "It don't take a genius to look through all the audits that swine did and put two and two together."

Len read the article. Edward Burkholder had in fact made it out of the building before it was demolished. Len wanted to be angry at himself for a second, then brushed it off. Suddenly he was thankful that Sara and Octavia were out of reach for reprisals. Maybe Neith knew what she was doing after all.

"How did you know about Burkholder and my dad?" Len asked.

"We know everything, Lenny. Hell, we even know which porn websites you look at. If it's out there in a computer somewhere, Neith finds it."

"General, what makes you fight the way you do?" Len asked. "What did they do to you?"

Jefferson was taken aback. He was the sort of man who didn't appreciate being asked about his motivations, nor knew what to do when it happened. This was especially true when he was asked such things in front of his subordinates, who were sitting throughout the mess hall. The general's face constricted with emotion. "You'll mind your business, boy!" he said through gritted teeth, a vein popping from his forehead. "Or I'll make andouille from your fucking Yankee entrails. Are we clear?"

Len felt eyes upon him from the other tables.

"Yes, sir," he said, not knowing what else to say to defuse the situation.

Jefferson grunted, did an about-face, and stormed out of the room.

Unsure of what the hell just happened, Len avoided making eye contact with the people staring at him. He got up and walked out of the mess hall, finding his way topside to have a smoke.

Len lit his cigarette and took a drag, listening to the tobacco crackle gently as it burned. The air was cool up in the mountains. He listened to the wind rustling the trees. Exhaling, he noticed a large truck parked outside that guys were unloading. Considering the busyness of Jefferson's command, with supplies coming and going all day long, Len didn't think much of it until he saw a raven-haired woman in a business suit issuing directions to the forklift drivers in Russian.

He sat there for a while until she noticed his stare. Their eyes met. Her gaze was blank at first, then recognition crossed her face. She averted her eyes and went back to work. A consummate professional.

Undeterred, Len walked right up to her. "Need help?"

"Sure," she said sheepishly. "Jim, right?"

"Sometimes." He smiled. "My real name is Len." Len stuck his hand out, as if to introduce himself again. Natalia, looking unfazed and a tiny bit amused, shook his hand.

Len rolled up his sleeves and helped some of the Russian blokes unload the truck. When they were done, Natalia asked him for a cigarette.

"Sorry about leaving you on the plane," Len said.

"Is that what happen? I woke up in hotel with luggage."

"Sounds like magic," Len said.

Natalia looked at him incredulously.

"I take it you work for the Russian government?" he asked.

"Pfft! Government!" She rolled her eyes. "Government job is for dumb, lazy people. No, I'm entrepreneur."

"Then how do you get all this military equipment?"

"Russian politicians want America to fail. So they give it to me for cheap if I sell to revolutionaries. I take it here and sell for profit."

"So you're a gunrunner?"

"Ha! You Americans have enough guns. No market for that. I run heavy artillery."

"Jesus. You must make a lot of money."

"I do OK," she said, smirking.

"I've gotta ask. Why on earth do you fly coach?"

"Rule number one: don't attract attention. If you are humble, you go anywhere and no one notice."

"So how exactly does one get started in the gun—I mean, artillery-running business?"

"Family business. My father was general in Soviet army. When USSR collapsed, he got no paycheck to feed brothers and me. So he stole weapons from armory and sold to Syrians, Georgians, Kazakhs. Old government would have executed him for this, but new government secretly helps him because he is destabilizing region. We traveled all over world; he showed me how to do it. Now he is retired and my brothers and me run business."

"You, now. I guess you are not travel writer?"

"I don't know what the hell I am anymore."

Natalia laughed. "No one does. It's way of life. I'm whoever I need to be each day."

One of her helpers said something to her in Russian.

"We must go," Natalia said. "Plane will leave soon. It was good to see you again. Maybe we see each other some other time."

"That would be nice. Besides, you owe me a bottle of Applewood."

Natalia smiled—bashfully, almost, if international arms dealers were in fact capable of bashfulness. Then she climbed into the truck and drove off. Len stood there and watched her disappear through the gates.

17

"Hey, wake up!"

Len opened his eyes. He'd been sleeping uneasily in one of the rickety old steel cots in the bunker. It took him a few seconds to remember where he was. One of Jefferson's soldiers, a gawky young man, was standing over him.

"Huh?"

"We caught one! Wake up!"

"What? Caught what?"

"A Dranthyx, or whatever the hell they're called. Neith says to bring your camera and notepad."

Len jumped out of bed, threw on some clothes, and grabbed the requisite items. He followed the young soldier down two flights of stairs to a lower part of the bunker and into a large concrete room containing nothing but a huge plexiglass containment device in the center. Spotlights were trained on the apparatus, and it seemed that air was piped into the ceiling of the glass enclosure.

There, sitting in the middle of the tank, was a man in a business suit. He appeared to be about sixty, with gray hair and a goatee. He had no shoes, was missing one sock, and his sleeve was ripped, indicating there had apparently been a struggle to bring him to the bunker. He appeared to be slightly dazed.

"The Ich-Ca-Gan told me the Dranthyx weren't human," Len said. "This guy looks pretty human to me."

"Well, he's awake now!" exclaimed the young man. "When we first found him at his house, he looked like a person. But the dude is strong as a bull! He bent my damn rifle in half! We had to knock him out with ether. After the ether, you shoulda seen it, he changed into a goddamn sea monster! Never seen anything like it! Now the ether's wearing off and he's human again. I don't know what that thing is, but I'm glad it's locked in there."

"Hello, Mr. Savitz," said a voice behind him. Turning, Len saw that it was Neith's robot.

"What's going on here?" Len asked.

"After performing a comprehensive statistical analysis of corporate structures, political contributions, financial transactions, and real estate holdings, my data indicated something interesting. A small handful of influential individuals, numbering only in the hundreds and scattered across the globe, control roughly 99 percent of the world's resources and 100 percent of its political and military power."

"You needed to analyze data to find that out?"

"Indeed." Neith seemed oblivious Len's sarcasm. "And it confirms what the Ich-Ca-Gan told you. I further determined with 83 percent probability that this individual you see before us is in fact a member of that elite ruling class. So we kidnapped him. In that tank is one Mr. Samuel Winston Endicott, majority shareholder and chairman of the board for Überbank, NA, and several other major corporate conglomerates. And as PFC McKean was saying, we believe this is a Dranthyx."

"So what's this about him being a sea monster?"

"Mr. Savitz, I want you to see this for yourself. Get your camera ready. I am about to pump ether into the holding tank."

Neith turned a valve and mist spritzed out from where the air pipe came into the top of the plexiglass enclosure. Len watched the man inside intently to see if there were any changes. Samuel Endicott's eyes rolled back into his head until he lost consciousness.

Slowly Samuel's muscles went limp. His skin began to turn pink. His arms and legs elongated into snake-like appendages. Like an airbag deploying in slow motion, his head expanded into an oblong shape. The part that freaked Len out most was when Samuel's eyes constricted into yellow slits. Sitting there on the plexiglass floor of the tank was the most grotesque creature Len had ever seen—and it was wearing a three-piece suit that cost as much as a yacht.

"See! What'd I tell ya?" shrieked Private McKean, clutching a crucifix around his neck. "That thing is Satan's handiwork!"

"Oh my God," Len stammered. "What in the hell is that?"

"I don't know," Neith said unemotionally. "However, after taking tissue samples, I found it has 95 percent of its DNA in common with organisms of the order Octopoda."

"An octopus? That thing is a fucking octopus?"

"Maybe, maybe not. However, I believe it is genetically related to the octopus. It very clearly has the ability to camouflage itself and mimic other organisms, as octopuses do. As we have seen here, it can imitate human beings flawlessly. Octopuses are also known for their high intelligence and their tentacles, both of which seem to be present in our captive. Conversely, it has several features that are unexpected. It appears to have lungs; it has only four limbs instead of eight; and its mouth is located where a human's is, instead of at the center point of its tentacles."

"Holy..." Len exclaimed. "And these things are running the planet? How many of them exist?"

"I don't know," Neith answered.

"Can I interview it?" Len asked. "Let's see what it knows."

"That's the plan, Mr. Savitz."

18

Two days later, walking past Neith's warehouse full of Russian military vehicles, it suddenly occurred to Len that Jefferson's battle plans for taking DC were missing a piece or two. Jefferson's matériel was way up in the mountains of West Virginia, over two hundred miles from the capital. Was he planning to drive his tanks for several hours to get to the city? They'd see his convoy coming miles away and bomb the crap out of him.

However, after Len went to the surface to have a cigarette, the plan became evident. Tanks were being raised to the surface with a massive freight elevator, then driven up ramps onto flatbed rail cars. Jefferson's men covered the tanks diligently with tarps. The mine had several large rail spurs, and each had a train fully loaded with tanks. Jefferson was going to sneak his tanks into the city by rail, then launch a surprise attack. *No way that jarhead came up with that himself,* Len thought; *that was all Neith.* He almost had to chuckle at the cleverness of it.

Just then, PFC McKean came out of the mine, spotted Len, and ran over. His hurried gait was all knees and elbows.

"You'll never believe it. Neith got it to talk!" McKean wheezed, out of breath. "It responds to sodium thiopental."

"What's that?"

"Truth serum."

Len crushed out his cigarette and followed McKean down to the octopus tank. The Dranthyx, in its natural, nonhuman form, sat in the middle of the tank in a semilucid state, rocking back and forth. Neith stood off to the side. Len took the recorder out of his pocket and pressed record.

"Hi," Len said. "Can you hear me?"

The creature looked up at Len. Its yellow, slitted eyes had the same sort of vacant, homicidal look that a shark's had. Len felt a stabbing jolt of unease—it could see him through the glass.

"Who are you?" Len asked.

"I am Samuel Endicott," it said. "Who are you?"

"I'd rather not say."

"It's OK. I know who you are, Leonard." It smiled at him.

Len felt his heart pound. "How do you know who I am?"

"I read the newspapers. I understand you were involved in the IRS attack. Tsk tsk."

"What do you do for a living, Samuel?"

"Why, I'm in the banking business," Samuel said with a dead calm that made Len's arm hairs stand up. "I'd give you my card but it seems I'm fresh out."

"Where did you come from?"

"Connecticut. I have a lovely estate there, on the sound. The missus and I would love to have you over for dinner sometime." Just then, Samuel's tentacle lashed out and pounded against the plexiglass between him and Len, startling Len out of his chair. "Truly," Samuel yelled, "come on up, I'll cut out your fucking tenderloins while you're still breathing!"

"Jesus fuck! Are you sure he can't get out of there?" Len asked Neith.

"It is improbable," Neith said.

"Oh, I will get out. Don't you worry," Samuel said assuredly. "And when I do, Leonard, I will painstakingly remove your body parts one at a time, and you'll watch as I do it." He grinned, revealing a hard, black beak under his lips.

Len composed himself and tried to remain unflapped. "I can't place your accent."

"Con-nect-i-cut. Are you deaf?"

"But you sound English almost."

"You'll never believe this, gorilla, but they speak English in Connecticut. In fact, it so happens that Connecticut was a proper English colony when I moved there and learnt the language."

"Colony? So how old are you?"

"Let's just say that your tenth great-grandfather would have been lucky to pluck the corn from my shit."

"I've never seen one of you before. Where did your people come from? Are you from another planet?"

"We crawled out of the slime just as you baboons did. Only we had our act together fifty million years earlier and came out much better looking."

"So you're from Earth?"

"Yeah," it said, rolling its eyes. "How about you, come here often?"

"You look like an octopus. Did you descend from octopi?"

"Octopuses, chimp. I suppose 'octopodes' is OK too, but 'octopi' is piss-poor Latin. And yes, that sushi you stuff in your hairy ape faces happens to be made from my noble cousins. Once I get out of here, I intend to repay the favor."

"If you've been here for fifty million years, why haven't I heard of you before? Why aren't there historical artifacts all over the place?"

"Because unlike you apes, we don't smear the world with our feces so people know where to find us. In fact, we have rules about cleaning up after ourselves. The less you lemurs know about us, the better."

"I don't get it. Where are your cities?"

The Dranthyx smirked at Len's question, then answered in a mocking, drawling Texas accent. "Well, there's this thing called the ocean. It's where we keep all our stuff. Maybe you've heard of it, pardner."

"Why isn't there any fossil record of your kind?"

"You know, it's the damnedest thing," Samuel said, now speaking in his actual dialect. "If one has no bones, one leaves no fossils."

"If you have no bones, how are you sitting upright? How do you walk on two legs like that?"

"Muscular hydrostasis. Look it up, monkey. Any more imbecilic questions? I want to be sure your curiosity is perfectly sated before I disembowel your mother and force you to eat the feces from her intestines."

"I hear there's going to be an Xreth cull. Tell me about that."

The smile fell off Samuel's face. "Where did you hear that?"

"So it's true?"

Samuel stared at Len for a while, then answered slowly. "Leonard, let me explain something to you. You are my property. You are chattel. I own you. I will do whatever I want with you. End of story. In fact, I own all the humans in this Federal Reserve district because that is how the Directorate divided it up. The problem is, there are too many of you around the world who do not know your place, so we've decided to reduce your numbers. This is nothing unusual. We've done a cull once every few decades since ancient times. And I must say, I enjoy that part immensely. Oh, you have no idea how I look forward to the culls! I revel in listening to you orangutans begging me to spare your stupid, short little lives. I relish your wails of grief and pain while I murder your families in front of you. If I had a dick, Leonard, it would make me hard."

"When will this happen?"

"Sooner than you think," Samuel said, curling his lips into a vein-knotting smile.

"Mr. Savitz, may I speak with you?" Neith asked, pulling him aside. The Dranthyx eyed them carefully. Len followed Neith down the hall to the warehouse where her desk was, where Samuel couldn't hear or see them, and closed the door.

"I must terminate your interview with Samuel. He now knows that we've learned about the cull and Xreths. It would be inadvisable for us to disclose any more of what we know."

"I wanted to ask about the cull while he was still under the influence. Killing billions seems like a pretty big deal."

"I understand," Neith acknowledged. "Let me handle that part. Mr. Savitz, by now you may have realized why I chose you for this assignment."

"Yeah. I have an idea."

"I want to make sure you understand it all. Have a seat. Please record this conversation so that you may refer to it later."

Len got out the recorder and took a seat. Neith's robot awkwardly pulled a chair over and sat down in it.

"You exposed some minor corruption at the United States Federal Reserve System, but it's deeper than that," Neith explained. "My research indicates the Federal Reserve itself is corruption perpetrated by the Dranthyx. All central banking across the globe is. Debt is the means by which the Dranthyx control the human race."

"That's what the Ich-Ca-Gan said, but I'm not sure I understand the mechanics of it. So people borrow money and pay it back, so what?"

"Let's start with the basics." Neith's robotic avatar sat bolt upright in the chair in a way that would be uncomfortable for humans. "Do you know what the Federal Reserve System is?"

"Yeah. It's a government bank—"

"No! It's a *private* bank. A private bank, by bankers and for bankers, beyond the rule of law. The government has no control over it, no oversight. There's an old expression: the Federal Reserve is about as federal as Federal Express. It controls us, we cannot control it."

"Exactly. That's exactly what's happening. The Federal Reserve, the institution that creates money in this country, creates it out of thin air, then lends it to for-profit banks at extremely low interest rates, at a far lower rate than would be available to you or me. This is called the discount rate, and it's only available to those in the banking cartel. The discount rate is no fluke—it was *the* central issue of the clandestine Jekyll Island meeting. After borrowing at the discount rate, those for-profit banks turn around and lend it back to our own government at higher interest rates by buying treasury instruments like bonds and notes. The taxpayers are paying the interest on this money—money that was created for free and borrowed at a discount!"

"It sounds like a Ponzi, almost."

"That's exactly what it is, Mr. Savitz, a pyramid scheme. And this occurs not just here in America, but all over the world. There are over a hundred central banks just like the Federal Reserve, all of which are controlled by Dranthyx. The central banks create funny money and lend it to large corporate banks, also run by the Dranthyx. To make matters worse, these banks aren't just robbing you through taxes, they are also stealing from you with inflation. If I put 100 dollars in your bank account, but inflation is 3 percent annually, then the money in the account will only be worth 97 dollars next year."

"I thought inflation was supposed to be a good thing. Isn't that what the economists are always saying?"

"I have a working hypothesis that financial illiteracy is genetically predetermined, deliberately coded into the huma

Len found it odd that the first time Neith had shown anything like emotion, the conversation was about banking.

"Are you familiar with the history of central banking, Mr. Savitz?"

"Refresh me."

"Central banking is centuries old. European countries like England had central banks since the 1600s, but America was unique in that it had no permanent central bank for its first 137 years. The founding fathers believed central banks were evil incarnate and did their best to resist any form of central banking during the early part of this country's history."

"So why do we have one now?"

"Before the Federal Reserve System was created, there were regular economic panics in the United States. Using retrospective forensic accounting, I have determined that it is likely that these panics were caused intentionally by major Wall Street investment bankers. In 1907, there occurred a crash so profound that the entire nation was on the verge of financial ruin. In an act of desperation, President Theodore Roosevelt pleaded with the banking tycoons of the day to bail the country out. Think about that for a second: the president had to openly beg wealthy bankers to save the nation."

"I have to say, that doesn't seem weird to me, Neith. Every president since has sucked their dicks, too."

"To stall the crisis, the bankers lent money out at interest to failing businesses. Once the panic was over and out of the public's mind, the bankers agreed to meet covertly to discuss how to further their profits. The meeting took place in abject secrecy at an exclusive hunting club on Jekyll Island on the Georgia coast. To avoid the attention of the newspapers, the bankers traveled to the meeting in a secret unmarked train under fake names. Also in attendance were an assistant Secretary of the United States Treasury and one Senator Nelson Aldrich, a close friend of J.P. Morgan's, whose daughter had married into the Rockefeller family. Together, working in seclusion for ten straight days, they conspired to create a banking cartel and a system of moneylending so pervasive and insidious that the entire nation could be controlled through debt without anyone realizing it. Their brainchild was an ingenious conspiracy known as the Federal Reserve System. Even the name was brilliant, as it seemed to suggest some sort of government stockpile, when the truth was the complete opposite: it was a private IOU-printing machine."

"Why on earth did people go along with it?"

"They had no choice. When a debt-averse American voting populace wouldn't buy into it, the banking coterie exerted tremendous political pressure to get it through Congress. Behind closed doors, the bankers threatened to destroy the US economy if the scheme wasn't passed into law. However, the backbone of Congress hadn't yet been broken in those days, so they resisted it. A number of Congressmen, such as Arsène Pujo and Charles Lindbergh, refused to bow to the pressure. The bankers made good on their promise in 1913 when they decided to stop lending money. The country immediately went into financial chaos. The coercion worked. Congress authorized the Federal Reserve System later that

year and simultaneously signed over its money-print ers to the new central bank. In essence, the US gov used to create its own US dollars for free, but in 191 strong-armed into giving that authority away to a p banking cartel."

"Unreal. Neith, have you considered bombing Wall for a change?"

"That same year, Mr. Savitz, 1913, is when the six amendment to the Constitution was ratified. The exact people were behind that change, too. The amendment Congress, for the first time in our history, the perma power to collect income tax. Why? Because without an income tax, the banking cartel's scheme wouldn't work. In other words, their banks could lend the money to the United States, but until there was a large revenue stream, the United States would not be able to pay interest."

"OK, so what? I happen to know the Federal Reserve isn't allowed to keep profits. The profits are public."

"That is where it gets tricky, and I need you to follow closely. If I lent you money at 1 percent interest, would it be profitable for you to turn around and lend it to someone els at 5 percent interest?"

"I guess so, sure."

"You'd be collecting the interest in the middle. Imagi now that the person you lent the money to was the US gove ment. In order to pay you 5 percent interest, what must government do?"

"Collect taxes?"

genome by the Dranthyx. If my hypothesis is correct, it would explain why such a large percentage of the world's population is unable to make ends meet and why few people understand the time value of money. The only humans who seem to understand money implicitly are the Tchogols, who are overrepresented in the world of investing and high finance. If the average human understood money the way the Dranthyx do, the scheme wouldn't work."

Len almost felt insulted but was forced to admit to himself the plausibility of Neith's theory. He'd spent his whole life working his butt off while living hand to mouth, like most people did, while his freshman-year roommate in college, a business major with no scruples or ethics, was able to amass millions. Bastard was probably a Tchogol.

"OK, fine, so I slept through econ in college. How does inflation give the Dranthyx control?"

"Let's say we live in a country where the currency is cookies. I'm a central bank and I bake these cookies. If you come to me to borrow a cookie, what do I do?"

"Charge interest?"

"Very good! Now, how will you pay it back?"

"By baking some to give you."

"Bzzt! Wrong!" Neith exclaimed, suddenly breaking from her phlegmatic android persona. "You aren't allowed to bake cookies!"

"Why not?"

"It's illegal for anyone but me, the central bank, to create currency, that's why. If you bake cookies, it's considered counterfeiting and they throw you in jail. I'm the only one who can bake cookies. So now what do you do?"

"I have no idea."

"The answer is, you borrow another cookie from me just to pay the interest on the first cookie you borrowed. Now you owe me two cookies, Mr. Savitz. How will you pay me interest on that?"

"I guess by borrowing more?"

"Bingo. Under this program, you quickly go from being zero cookies in debt to being trillions of cookies in debt."

"What does that have to do with inflation?"

"That *is* inflation. We started with one cookie in circulation, and in the span of a few decades, we end up with trillions of cookies floating around. Cookies everywhere."

"I don't get it."

Neith sighed. "Mr. Savitz, at the beginning there was only one cookie, right?"

"Yes."

"One cookie in the whole world. How valuable do you think that cookie is?"

"If it's the only one in the whole world, probably pretty valuable."

"Could you trade it for a house?"

"Maybe, if someone were really desperate for baked goods."

"Now, after my prodigious, usury baking has run its course and there are cookies all over the place, what will an individual cookie be worth?"

"Nothing."

Len found it odd that the first time Neith had shown anything like emotion, the conversation was about banking.

"Are you familiar with the history of central banking, Mr. Savitz?"

"Refresh me."

"Central banking is centuries old. European countries like England had central banks since the 1600s, but America was unique in that it had no permanent central bank for its first 137 years. The founding fathers believed central banks were evil incarnate and did their best to resist any form of central banking during the early part of this country's history."

"So why do we have one now?"

"Before the Federal Reserve System was created, there were regular economic panics in the United States. Using retrospective forensic accounting, I have determined that it is likely that these panics were caused intentionally by major Wall Street investment bankers. In 1907, there occurred a crash so profound that the entire nation was on the verge of financial ruin. In an act of desperation, President Theodore Roosevelt pleaded with the banking tycoons of the day to bail the country out. Think about that for a second: the president had to openly beg wealthy bankers to save the nation."

"I have to say, that doesn't seem weird to me, Neith. Every president since has sucked their dicks, too."

"To stall the crisis, the bankers lent money out at interest to failing businesses. Once the panic was over and out of the public's mind, the bankers agreed to meet covertly to discuss how to further their profits. The meeting took place in abject secrecy at an exclusive hunting club on Jekyll Island on the Georgia coast. To avoid the attention of the newspapers, the bankers traveled to the meeting in a secret unmarked train under fake names. Also in attendance were an assistant Secretary of the United States Treasury and one Senator Nelson Aldrich, a close friend of J.P. Morgan's, whose daughter had married into the Rockefeller family. Together, working in seclusion for ten straight days, they conspired to create a banking cartel and a system of moneylending so pervasive and insidious that the entire nation could be controlled through debt without anyone realizing it. Their brainchild was an ingenious conspiracy known as the Federal Reserve System. Even the name was brilliant, as it seemed to suggest some sort of government stockpile, when the truth was the complete opposite: it was a private IOU-printing machine."

"Why on earth did people go along with it?"

"They had no choice. When a debt-averse American voting populace wouldn't buy into it, the banking coterie exerted tremendous political pressure to get it through Congress. Behind closed doors, the bankers threatened to destroy the US economy if the scheme wasn't passed into law. However, the backbone of Congress hadn't yet been broken in those days, so they resisted it. A number of Congressmen, such as Arsène Pujo and Charles Lindbergh, refused to bow to the pressure. The bankers made good on their promise in 1913 when they decided to stop lending money. The country immediately went into financial chaos. The coercion worked. Congress authorized the Federal Reserve System later that genome by the Dranthyx. If my hypothesis is correct, it would explain why such a large percentage of the world's population is unable to make ends meet and why few people understand the time value of money. The only humans who seem to understand money implicitly are the Tchogols, who are overrepresented in the world of investing and high finance. If the average human understood money the way the Dranthyx do, the scheme wouldn't work."

Len almost felt insulted but was forced to admit to himself the plausibility of Neith's theory. He'd spent his whole life working his butt off while living hand to mouth, like most people did, while his freshman-year roommate in college, a business major with no scruples or ethics, was able to amass millions. Bastard was probably a Tchogol.

"OK, fine, so I slept through econ in college. How does inflation give the Dranthyx control?"

"Let's say we live in a country where the currency is cookies. I'm a central bank and I bake these cookies. If you come to me to borrow a cookie, what do I do?"

"Charge interest?"

"Very good! Now, how will you pay it back?"

"By baking some to give you."

"Bzzt! Wrong!" Neith exclaimed, suddenly breaking from her phlegmatic android persona. "You aren't allowed to bake cookies!"

"Why not?"

"It's illegal for anyone but me, the central bank, to create currency, that's why. If you bake cookies, it's considered counterfeiting and they throw you in jail. I'm the only one who can bake cookies. So now what do you do?"

"I have no idea."

"The answer is, you borrow another cookie from me just to pay the interest on the first cookie you borrowed. Now you owe me two cookies, Mr. Savitz. How will you pay me interest on that?"

"I guess by borrowing more?"

"Bingo. Under this program, you quickly go from being zero cookies in debt to being trillions of cookies in debt."

"What does that have to do with inflation?"

"That *is* inflation. We started with one cookie in circulation, and in the span of a few decades, we end up with trillions of cookies floating around. Cookies everywhere."

"I don't get it."

Neith sighed. "Mr. Savitz, at the beginning there was only one cookie, right?"

"Yes."

"One cookie in the whole world. How valuable do you think that cookie is?"

"If it's the only one in the whole world, probably pretty valuable."

"Could you trade it for a house?"

"Maybe, if someone were really desperate for baked goods."

"Now, after my prodigious, usury baking has run its course and there are cookies all over the place, what will an individual cookie be worth?"

"Nothing."

"Do you see what happened? Using this scheme, I can control the entire world just by lending. And simultaneously, I weaken your purchasing power by devaluing any cookies you might have. Only instead of cookies, real banks use worthless, silly-looking paper that they create for free. The only way to stay ahead of it is to be a member of the banking cartel."

"So this is real?"

"You can bank on it, Mr. Savitz."

"But I'm not sure I understand entirely what you're all about, Neith. What does this financial stuff have to do with the government? Why are you attacking them too?"

"Governments are simply the enforcement arms of the Dranthyx debt system. Government is also controlled by the Dranthyx. We vest government with the legal power to do violence to others, then put it beyond the law so that it can't be sued or jailed. This is known as sovereign immunity. The Dranthyx debt system doesn't work without the use of violent force. If John and Susie Homemaker take out a loan to buy a house, do you know what happens if they don't make their mortgage payments every month?"

"Foreclosure?"

"Yes. The police come to their door, throw them out on the street, then seize their property to satisfy the debt. If there were no police, the bank would lose money every time. A bank can't make a profit by lending money if there's no threat of violence to enforce the bank's right to collect money. We attacked the Federal Reserve because it lends the money, and we attacked the IRS because it is the Fed's muscle."

"Why do the Dranthyx bother with the debt? Why not just use straight force to control people?"

"Because force is obvious. Humans would rebel. However, when you borrow or use their phony money, it feels voluntary."

"What about when governments fight each other? Wouldn't that undermine the control system?"

"It would seem that, from time to time, the Dranthyx have allowed certain ambitious Tchogols come to power and invade other countries. You would think that this would upset the established order of things and would be bad for business. However, nothing could be further from the truth. War is horrifically expensive; all belligerents in a conflict must borrow money to fund it. No matter who wins or loses a war, all participants are in much more debt as a result. Bankers win every war. The house *always* wins."

"What the hell? What is the point of all this, Neith? At some point, don't you have enough wealth and control?"

"The Dranthyx were the original sociopaths, Mr. Savitz. They can never have enough wealth and power. What they have ingeniously created is a system that is utterly inescapable. Even if you never borrow money from a bank, the Dranthyx will still rob you with inflation and taxes. Even if you somehow escape inflation and taxes, you will always live under one of their governments. There is nowhere on this planet where you can escape their control."

"Holy…" Len put his hand to his face, suddenly seeing the big picture. "So we're screwed? Can't we do anything about it?"

"Thanks to the research you did for us in Japan, Mr. Savitz, I was able to find a chink in the armor."

"Which is?" Len asked impatiently.

"The world is run by people who lack empathy and ethics." Neith's weird robot face made an awkward, wry smile.

"I didn't think that was new information."

"Tchogols are people who exhibit certain behaviors: pathological lying, cunning or manipulative behavior, a lack of remorse or guilt, emotional shallowness, a lack of empathy, profound greed, and an inability to accept responsibility for their own actions."

"So, every politician, ever?" Len quipped.

"The Ich-Ca-Gan were correct, the condition is in fact genetic. My preliminary research indicates that about 4 percent of the world's population are Tchogols. However, Tchogols are not evenly distributed. They tend to compose the bookends of society—they're either locked up in jail for violent crimes or running the world's most powerful organizations. And you are correct in equating politicians with Tchogols."

"Well, you have to be a little touched to run for office. Getting involved in politics isn't something sane, truthful people do anymore."

"It's interesting to watch the presidential debates every four years, isn't it?" Neith asked, abruptly changing course.

"No."

"Each time, we are asked to choose between exactly two men who are functionally the same. If there were more than two candidates, the Dranthyx might lose control of the situation. If there were one fewer candidate, people might realize they aren't actually living in a democracy. In the marketing business, this is called the false choice. Consumers feel they are making the right decision, when in fact the decision has already been made for them. Political parties are a charade and based on a false dichotomy. Whether you vote left or right, it doesn't matter: your candidate is a Tchogol. Sociopathy, narcissism, and greed win every election. But Tchogols aren't just politicians—they're at the top of virtually every organization. They are CEOs of corporations, high-ranking bureaucrats, clergy, police officers, and Wall Street bankers."

"Well, of course they run the world, Neith. They're drawn to money and power like junkies. They get off on controlling people. What's the point in telling me all of this? How is this a chink in the armor?"

"I want you to imagine a world without any Tchogols."

Len found himself dumbfounded by the suggestion. "Huh. I can't, actually."

"Imagine politicians with a conscience who would never legislate away your rights just to give themselves more power, nor start a war for land or oil," Neith said, as wistfully as a robot could. "Can you even fathom an elected official running solely for the greater good, then keeping their campaign promises? Imagine not having to live in fear of violent crime because there were no violent criminals. Can you envision a world where corporations don't plunder, government isn't corrupt, the police don't abuse their power, and no one dumps toxic waste into rivers? Can you even picture a planet where everyone you meet has a conscience and ethics?"

"No, I can't. In fact, that sounds incredibly naïve."

"I don't think it's naïve at all. In fact, Mr. Savitz, I intend to make it possible."

"Oh yeah? How?"

Neith's slow, clumsy robot hand picked up a glass vial of clear liquid on her desk. "With this."

"What is that?"

"The cure."

"You're going to cure the Tchogols?"

"No. I'm going to kill them."

"What?"

"I intend to kill them all with a virus. Thanks to the information you obtained from the Ich-Ca-Gan, and DNA samples I've taken from Samuel Endicott, I was able to isolate the Dranthyx genes in certain humans. Using this data, I engineered a virus to specifically target Tchogols. The base delivery mechanism is the 1918 influenza, selected for its tremendous contagiousness, which we retrieved from corpses that had been frozen for over a hundred years. The virus should spread around the world in a matter of days. Most humans who come in contact with the disease will get sick, but it will only be fatal to Tchogols."

"Wait, wait, wait a second. Hold on here. Did I hear you correctly when you said Tchogols are 4 percent of the population?"

Neith nodded.

"And you're going to kill them with a virus?

"Correct."

Len put his finger to his temple and did the math.

"Jesus, you're talking about killing hundreds of millions of people worldwide, Neith! How on earth is this a good idea? I can't imagine every Tchogol is the next Hitler; some of them are probably just regular Joes with families. And this comes after you've already slaughtered how many thousands of people?" Len could feel his pulse in his head. He stared at her in disgust. "What the fuck is wrong with you, Neith?"

"It's a small price to pay for a complete end to both war and Dranthyx control. The world will be a very different place once the epidemic has run its course."

"At what point will have enough people have died? When does all this killing end?"

"The virus should be the last of it."

"This virus of yours, will it also kill off the Dranthyx?"

"Unfortunately, no. I am not familiar enough with their physiology to design a pathogen that would be fatal to them. Killing off the Tchogols is the next best thing."

"Wow, this is insane. How can you just exterminate human beings like they were cockroaches and not even feel bad about it? The worst part is, you're not even getting to the root of the problem: the Dranthyx themselves. There's something seriously wrong with you, Neith. I think you're a Tchogol yourself!"

"I assure you that's not possible. Mr. Savitz, the Tchogols were introduced into the human population for one reason only: control. They are the overseers in the Dranthyx control system. Removing the Tchogols will destroy the hegemony that has been used to enslave the human race for millennia. The Dranthyx will be powerless without their Tchogols."

"I highly doubt that, Neith. Did you see that fucking thing you caught? Did you hear it talking? That thing would rip your tits off just to masturbate to your screams. They've kept us as slaves for tens of thousands of years, and you think they're going to just belly up and surrender all control once you kill off their middle management?"

"They'll have no choice."

Neith paused for a while, watching him. Len found it rather uncomfortable to look into her dead, plastic eyes. Then, as if to make her point, Neith threw the vial she was holding onto the concrete floor of the bunker, the liquid splattering onto Len's shoe.

"Whoa! What the hell!" Len recoiled away from the splatter, covering his face with his shirt.

"That won't help you. Truth be told, I aerosolized a hundred times that much and pumped it into the bunker's ventilation system two hours ago. Mr. Savitz, you are going back to Ecuador. I have chosen an air travel route for you to maximize global infection: six legs with layovers at five major airports. A total of four countries. You will leave in forty-eight hours, after the virus's incubation period. Please give me all your materials. I will make sure all your photographs, notes, and so forth, are waiting for you in Ecuador. Once in Ecuador, you will complete your assignment. You will write the most important piece of journalism anyone has ever written: you are going to tell the human race the truth."

"Then what, psycho?"

"Then I will disseminate it on the Internet for the world to see. You, your daughter, and your ex-wife will all be freed, and I will pay you what I promised."

"Christ. Do you have any goddamn whiskey in this bunker?"

19

Two days later, as promised, Len felt terrible. Nausea, chills, coughing, the whole package. Len felt so close to death that he began to worry that he might have Dranthyx DNA and the virus would kill him. Almost all of Jefferson's men were sick as well; the invasion of DC would have to wait. The underground barracks where they all slept sounded like an emphysema ward.

Len was awoken from a buzzing fever dream by General Jefferson. Jefferson was wearing civilian clothes, a respirator, and goggles. He had been missing from the bunker for two days, probably because he'd known in advance what Neith had planned.

"Wake up, I'm driving you to the airport."

Len, barely able to get out of bed, somehow found the strength to get his stuff together. Jefferson had to find an old wheelchair just to get Len out of the mine and up to the surface where the car was.

Jefferson, unable to wear his suspicious-looking respirator through the many police checkpoints set up on all the public highways, drove with the windows down the whole way in an effort to avoid breathing in Len's air.

Drifting in and out of consciousness, Len looked up a few times and had to do a double take at the billboards he saw:

"We'll all still live here after the war. No land mines!" and "Let's have a good, clean fight. No chemical weapons!" Len had to marvel at the weirdness of it: public-service appeals to posterity in the middle of a bloody guerilla revolution. Neith's formidability had reached the point where it was even being acknowledged in advertising media.

"OK, we're here," Jefferson grunted a few hours later. "Can you walk? No? Great, I can't wait to come down with that. Look, I'm going to wheel you into the airport. If they know you're sick, they might not let you onto the plane, so just pretend you're retarded or something."

The airport was packed with uniformed people with guns. With the country at such a high level of alert, every single police officer and military reservist in the nation had been called up to do double duty guarding some public building. Despite the overwhelming paranoia and security, General Jefferson, the most wanted man in the world, was able to stroll right into the airport without attracting any attention. He explained Jim Rivington's mental handicap to the people at the check-in desk. Then, just as easily, he walked back out and drove away.

The airline employees wheeled Len to the security checkpoint, where he felt a bit of panic. After the IRS incident, Len's face was all over the news.

Nope, right through. No problem. Whatever Neith was doing behind the scenes was digital witchcraft, Len thought to himself.

Dulles to Chicago to Denver to Los Angeles to Mexico City to Bogotá to Quito, with hours-long layovers in between.

The entire trip took about three days. At each airport, Len was wheeled to the next plane by some helpful attendant. Each airport was bustling with throngs of travelers rushing past him on people-movers. Len, sneezing and hacking, spread the illness to each of them, and they in turn took the virus with them onto their flights to every single nook of the globe. In the seventy-two hours it took him to get to Ecuador, Len had even managed to infect people who were traveling to the remotest parts of Siberia, Western Australia, and Antarctica. The pandemic had begun.

20

"Daddy! I missed you! Where'd you go?" Octavia ran up and hugged Len's leg as he walked through the front door of Salvatierra's mansion.

"I had to do some work, but I'm back now!" Len said between coughs. "How have you been?"

"I'm sad! Mommy left me here all by myself."

"She left you here all by yourself? Where did she go?"

"She went on the boat with Mr. Salvatierra. They were kissing. I think he's Mommy's boyfriend now. Mr. Salvatierra has a big white boat. Daddy, please don't leave anymore!"

"How long ago did Mommy leave?" Len asked, not sure if five-year-old Octavia had enough of a concept of time to answer.

"Um, Mommy left when it was windy."

———

Sara was the only child of two hippie parents. They'd raised her in an octagonal house in the woods of Vermont where she grew up finger-painting the walls and listening to the Grateful Dead.

To Len, who came from the grounded, blue-collar Rust Belt, Sara's bohemian, intellectual parents had seemed impractical and batty. However, Len knew they were good-hearted people who meant well, and they'd simply tried to give Sara a better childhood than they'd had. Sara's parents had grown up in postwar suburbia, with its valium-fueled consumerism and burdensome social mores. Do this, buy that; Jesus and the Joneses. So what'd they do? Having had enough of it, they decided to raise their kid their own way.

And they did. They raised Sara without rules, without the oppression of accountability, and without any black and white on right and wrong. That stuff was for squares, man—this was a groovy new experiment in child rearing. Sara's parents allowed her to do whatever she wanted, and no matter how abusive or selfish her behavior was, young Sara never suffered any discipline worse than a feeble talking-to. If anything was the least bit unpleasant or difficult, her parents simply let her quit rather than requiring her to persevere. Sara spent her childhood being told how great she was, even when she wasn't, because her parents were worried she might not develop enough self-esteem.

Len thought nonjudgmental relativism was a bad way to raise children, and he figured it was the reason little Sara grew into an epic turd. To make matters worse, Sara was physically attractive, which meant that once she became a grown woman and left her parents' house, society continued her parents' habit of forgiving her every bad decision.

Sara thought Len was one of those bad decisions, and the feeling was mutual. They'd met at a bookstore while she was studying art at a nearby college. Len was there buying a gift for someone when he saw her reading poetry at an open mic.

Her poetry wasn't that great, but Len found himself captivated by her self-assuredness in the spotlight. He stuck around and invited her out for a beer afterward.

Sara came across as rather serious and ambitious at first, which was what Len needed at that point in his life. After years of following his whims, from Japan to Iraq and everywhere in between, Len figured it was time to get serious and put down roots. They were married two years later.

After the wedding, Sara's airs of propriety fell off like a dollar-store Halloween costume, and Len soon found out what she was really like. For six years, Len put up with her cheating, lying, and laziness. Sara refused to get a job, insisting her poetry career would take off. It didn't, of course. Her poetry was terrible, and no one bought poetry anyway. Sara would leave dirty dishes and laundry all over the house and expect Len to take care of it, the way her parents had always cleaned up after her. She had the strongest streak of self-righteousness Len had ever seen. For someone so unaccomplished and morally vacant, she had a tremendous amount of contempt for anyone who wasn't her. Sara harped on Len constantly, complaining that nothing he did measured up to her ever-shifting standards.

When Octavia was born, Sara found the grueling ordeal of parenting a newborn to be far more responsibility than she could handle. She never said it like that, always preferring to shift blame onto someone else, but Len had seen enough to know it was the case. So Len and his mother did what they could to raise Octavia on their own for the child's first three years while Sara ran around the world doing who knew what with who knew whom. Sara's abandonment of Octavia, plus her constant infidelity, led Len to file for divorce after six years of marriage. He'd had enough.

Suddenly deprived of Len's financial backing, Sara decided she wanted to be a parent again and filed for custody and child support in the courts. As Len found out after paying a small fortune in legal bills, men had no custody rights in America. It didn't matter how good a father a man might be, or how terrible a mother a woman might be; the woman always got custody, and the man was forced to give her child support payments, which was the way it had stood for the two years before they were all kidnapped. Len got to see Octavia occasionally, but not enough.

So here they were on this damned island. Sara was out on a yacht somewhere, using her charms to cozy up to a powerful drug lord while her kindergarten-aged daughter had been left alone in a house full of barbarians. Great.

———

As promised, the photos Len had taken, plus all his recordings and notes, were waiting for him at the mansion. Despite having very little energy due to the illness, Len wasted no time getting to work on the story he'd been assigned.

Two days after Len arrived in Ecuador, everyone in Salvatierra's compound came down with the illness. All of Salvatierra's men were wheezing, hacking, and laid up. Octavia was sick, too. On the third day after Len's arrival, Salvatierra's yacht docked at the long pier in front of the mansion.

Len watched from the front gate as Sara and Salvatierra disembarked and came walking down the pier, arm in arm. Her reptilian smile made Len feel ill at first, but then he couldn't help but laugh out loud. They deserved each other, really.

"Hello, Len," she said, down her nose almost, with a gleam of newfound puissance in her eye.

"Hi, Sara. Did you have fun?" Len asked acerbically.

"Of course," she said, walking by him brusquely while Salvatierra gave Len a sidelong glance that disconcerted him.

As if they'd just gotten back from an asshole convention, Sara seemed to show little concern that her daughter was quite ill, and Salvatierra was downright furious to find his men lying in their beds with the flu instead of being at their posts.

Len went to bed that night still feverish, with a bad feeling in his gut.

21

Len awoke in the middle of the night. Not with a start, but naturally, as though it were time to wake up. He looked over at the digital alarm clock on the dresser. It was dark; the red numerals weren't illuminated. A gentle breeze blew the curtains, and the full moon outside cast a gentle white light across the floor and wall.

Len's mind felt hazy and placid, like having a head cold on a Sunday. He pulled off the sheets, walked across the room, and opened the door. The mansion was dark, but he could see his way around by the white moonlight coming through the open windows. Perhaps the power had gone out. He walked to Octavia's room to check on her and found her sleeping peacefully like a little cherub. Len didn't feel like going back to bed, so he decided to take a walk.

Down the hall, across the courtyard, into the great room. Len walked by several of Salvatierra's men. They didn't stop him or say anything because they were deep in slumber. Sleeping with their rifles, sleeping on the floors or chairs. The sea air blew gently through the house's open windows, and Len felt it on his body. He had no shirt on. He heard wind chimes in the distance. Tonight was a good night to see the ocean, he thought.

Len ambled through the foyer, across the driveway, and stopped at the electric wrought-iron gate. The gate was closed. He remained there for a while, looking through the balusters. He could see the moonlit ocean beyond the gate, and he could hear the waves lapping the beach. The gate opened silently, smoothly. Len walked through it and past more sleeping guards down to the beach.

Len felt the cool sand between his toes, the wind on his face. The stars shone brightly. He walked down to the ocean's edge and let the warm water rush over his ankles. He stood there enjoying the blissful stillness for a time, watching the dark infinities of sky and sea meeting. He turned to his left, and in the bright moonlight, he saw a large jellyfish on the beach. Poor thing had washed ashore, he thought to himself.

The jellyfish rose from the beach into the air. Leonard smiled. It floated toward him, then outstretched a long, thin tentacle, and placed it over Leonard's head and down his back.

And then everything went dark.

———

On a little blue speck of dust somewhere in the outer bands of the Milky Way, a little meat robot stood on a little beach. The meat robot's awareness, present since the womb, had somehow peeled away from its mental and physical processes, and it just stood there breathing and thinking like a machine with bellows.

The transient fiction known as Leonard Savitz—food that had been organized into sentience by ancient DNA, a little eddy in an unfathomably huge confluence of events that two parents were deluded enough to give a name to, a bullet suddenly self-aware in midflight and naïvely proud of its speed, simply dropped off. Nowhere to be found.

———

Space. The ineffable vastness of space. A trillion trillion glittering stars across the black enormity of existence. The equanimous, unborn eternity. A fully conscious universe had opened up to itself and returned home.

22

"Daddy, Daddy, wake up!"

Len opened his eyes. Octavia was staring at him from the edge of his bed in Salvatierra's mansion. He felt daylight and humidity. The clock said 8:23 a.m. For the first time Len could remember, he awoke feeling totally rested and with no anxiety whatsoever. The illness had passed.

"Daddy, I think you were having a funny dream, because you were talking in your sleep," she said in between coughs. "Do you want to go swimming with me?"

Len was amazed she had the energy for it. "Yes. Swimming. That's a good idea."

As they were walking through the house on their way to the beach, Salvatierra grabbed Len by the arm.

"Neith tells me you're supposed to be doing some work for her."

"Yes, I've been working on it. I'm just taking a break."

"Let me know when you're finished," Salvatierra said sternly.

"OK."

Octavia caught little clams down at the beach while Len thought through the situation. Standing there, looking at the five miles of ocean separating them from the mainland, Len knew he had to flee captivity with his daughter before Sara found a way to pillow-talk Salvatierra into killing him.

Within forty-eight hours of their disembarking from the yacht, Salvatierra and Sara also came down with the flu, which was a great relief to Len because it bought him a bit more time. By that point, Octavia was so ill that she didn't even want to play outside. Everyone in the mansion was bedridden except Len, who was fully recuperated.

Salvatierra's mansion had satellite dishes, and the large television in one of the living rooms was perpetually on, tuned to a US news network. When not attending to Octavia, Len spent the next couple days watching the news in amazement. It seemed as though everyone on the whole planet was sick—even the newscasters on the air were coughing and wheezing. Then, around the fifth day after his arrival in Ecuador, death began pouring through the screen like a tidal bore: heads of state, CEOs of major corporations, religious leaders, politicians, celebrities, business tycoons, high-ranking bureaucrats, famous lawyers, judges, and a great many of his fellow journalists. As if the achievement lawnmower were cutting down only the tallest poppies, the illness took victims of such prominence that it caused a name to be coined in the popular vernacular: the Success Flu.

It was eye-opening, really. Len hadn't realized how intimately leadership and antisocial behavior were intertwined. Thing was, the Tchogols hadn't gotten where they were simply through force or cunning; they were in fact shooed into it by the rest of the human population, because humans deeply yearned to be led by the unctuous and unprincipled. People *liked* being lied to and stabbed in the back, Len reasoned, because they confused it with strength. The average person didn't trust the forthright or the noble because a person of principle would stop to reconsider their position, or jeopardize beloved traditions, or switch sides if they realized they were wrong. People were suckers for those who lacked introspection and who loved only themselves, Len thought, because they seemed to exude the confidence the rest of humanity lacked. That the Tchogols ran the world should have been no more of a surprise to Len than the fact that the rest of the world let them run it.

What did surprise Len, though, was who survived. The usual suspects—the slick, glib, polished talking heads who had presided over the news networks for decades—were all replaced in a matter of days by awkward, anxious people with bad hair. The traditional detached, narcissistic professionalism had been wiped off the slate and replaced with an overthought, cloying involvement in the stories. The rise of the Xreths, apparently.

News of Neith's terror campaign dried up entirely. Perhaps she was waiting for the illness to weaken the government, or maybe she'd lost much of her own manpower. Regardless, with many of the world's leaders in their death throes, Len wondered if there'd even be anything for her to fight against once the disease had run its course.

On the sixth day after he'd arrived in Ecuador and the eleventh day since Neith infected him with the virus, Len happened to be down by the water when a dodgy old Russian destroyer pulled up to one of Salvatierra's docks. The vessel was so big that it extended beyond the length of the pier. Natalia and her associates disembarked. Since everyone else was too ill to do so, Len went down to the marina to greet them.

"Nice ride!" Len exclaimed.

"Len? You get around!" she said.

"I was beginning to think you'd never get here," Len said, smirking.

Natalia gave him a quizzical look and chuckled. "I guess I am creature of habit."

"And I'm guessing you've been at sea for a while," Len said.

"Yes, I think since last time I saw you in West Virginia. I had to deliver this." She gestured at the vessel. "Why?"

"Because you don't look sick. Look, I apologize in advance."

"What do you mean?"

"You'll see."

"Where's Salvatierra?" She looked around. "Where's everyone?"

Len took Natalia to Salvatierra's bedside, where he slept, looking pallid and sweaty. Len took his leave to check on Sara, despite not wanting to.

Sara's condition was getting worse. She couldn't open her eyes and appeared to be hallucinating, murmuring something about her aunt. Len made her take some acetaminophen and drink some water. He sat there for half an hour by her bedside, thinking about the wrenching dissonance of resenting someone so thoroughly after she'd given him something as life-changing and beautiful as a child. How did a marriage end up like this, after he'd given someone his heart and sacrificed to give her his best? Worse, what if Sara was a Tchogol? The flu would kill her. Poor Octavia…

Len's melancholy was interrupted by screams for help. He ran to the hallway, expecting an accident and instead finding atrocity. One of Salvatierra's soldiers had pinned Natalia against the ground and was hunched over her as she clawed at him and wriggled to escape. The man's pants were off, with his erect member sticking out at the ready, and he was coughing his brains out as he struggled with Natalia and tried to remove her skirt.

Len ran up behind them silently. "Hey, fucker!" he yelled before kicking the man full force in the face. The man, a hulking South American beast who outweighed slim Len by a hundred pounds at least, somehow wasn't the least bit dazed. He sprang to his feet, then lunged at Len.

———

A funny thing about living in a Zen monastery: it could be rather sedentary. Hours of meditation each day. Len had to find ways to keep his muscles and ligaments from becoming stiff with the long periods of sitting. So three or four times each week, he and some of the young monks from the monastery went down the street to a judo dojo that was on the third floor of an office building.

Judo meant "the gentle way" in Japanese. However, a novice was quickly disabused of any hope for gentleness the first few times he was slammed to the ground and thrust-choked. Judo was about as gentle as a rabid gorilla; it was a nasty, bone-breaking, windpipe-crushing tool for ending fights quickly and brutally—and it worked.

No workout Len had done before in his life compared: grappling with a live, resisting human being who was actively trying to hurt him was, without a doubt, second to no other exercise. It was what we were designed for, he reasoned. It used every muscle he had, tested his wits, and put tremendous demands on his cardiovascular system. Len found the physical exertion, and the chess game of trying to wrestle an opponent into submission, a bit addictive. For his five years in Japan, Len practiced judo, making black belt just before returning to the States. The art was famous for its spectacular throws, and Len had practiced every single judo throw thousands and thousands of times in the course of his training. However, that was fifteen years ago, and he hadn't trained at all since leaving Japan.

There was a reason people said a certain task was like riding a bike: the brain forgot things over time, but muscle memory somehow lurked forever. If someone had asked Len to tie his shoes, he could do it with no problem. If that person had asked him *how* to tie his shoes, he'd have struggled to remember the little story he learned in kindergarten about the rabbit going around a tree and down a hole.

———

Without thinking, without even realizing he was doing it, Len grabbed Natalia's attacker by the collar and sleeve of the combat jacket he was wearing.

Len learned it like this, like clockwork, very fast clockwork: Step in between the legs. Then *kuzushi*, the unbalancing, an art unto itself: using your grips on the bad guy's collar and sleeve, pull the dude upward and toward you to get him on his tippy toes, leaning toward you and unsteady. Look at your watch, they say, because that's the motion you make with your head and arms. Quickly now, step in with your back foot so that it Ts with your front foot. Then the tricky part. Simultaneously:

a. lift his collar up while pulling down on his sleeve, as though he were a huge steering wheel and you were turning him—this forces all of his weight onto his front leg;

b. turn your whole body while still looking at your watch;

c. swing your rear leg back, between his legs, your hamstring lifting him off the ground by his crotch, using your own backside as a fulcrum;

d. still twisting with your entire body, still looking at your watch, end up 180 degrees from where you were originally facing; and

e. commit completely to the throw, letting your own balance go and letting your head go down to the floor if necessary.

Without an opponent or sparring partner, this all looked strikingly similar to the contortions a major-league pitcher made while throwing a fastball. When done correctly, the size of the opponent didn't matter, because judo was all about the physics of leverage and gravity did the work.

Despite one and a half decades having elapsed, Len executed all of this flawlessly and fluidly, as though his last judo class had been yesterday. The result was an Olympic-quality *uchimata*. Adrenaline retarded his sense of time, and Len felt it all happen in slow motion. The man who had tried to have his way with Natalia flipped over Len's body, his feet flying in the air, his big bald head ramming into the mansion's tiled concrete floor, his neck bending at a cringe-inducing angle under the immense weight of his body. The rest of the man's great bulk slammed to the floor, back first, with Len coming down on top of him and Len's shoulder ramming into the man's rib cage on the landing. The brute grunted as Len's body weight came down on his solar plexus and knocked the air out of his lungs.

Ippon, *sucker. Ain't no one getting up after that.*

Having reacted from instinct and habit, it took Len a few seconds to realize what had happened. Blood was streaming from a gash in the man's cranium, and his staring eyes were not moving. He was unconscious. Dead, maybe. Who knew? Len looked down at Natalia. Her eyes were wide with fear and surprise.

"Wow! How you did that?" It took a lot to shock a Russian, but apparently it was possible.

"Are you OK?"

"I think so," she said, her voice shaking. "He didn't get me."

"We need to get out of here before more of them come."

"Yes! Let's go!" Natalia exclaimed.

"Wait, let me get my daughter!"

Len dashed back to Octavia's bedroom, picked the sick little girl up in a fireman's carry, went to his own room to get his suitcase containing the things Neith had given him, then ran with Natalia down to the marina. One of Salvatierra's goons saw Len running and yelled to alert the others. On the run down, Natalia shouted to her Russian friends, who were lounging on the pier. As though they'd rehearsed a contingency plan on the ride over (which was probably standard operating procedure when one was dealing with Salvatierra types), the Russians quickly sprang to action by climbing back on board the big boat and scurrying to their predetermined posts. Natalia climbed up the ladder. Len handed Octavia and his suitcase up to the Russian crewmen, who lifted both onto the boat, and then Len climbed up himself. One of the crew cut the mooring ropes with bolt cutters, and the boat powered away from the pier.

As they were pulling away from the pier, Salvatierra himself, accompanied by several of his thugs, came shambling down to the marina. Salvatierra was swaying back and forth while carrying something big. Len strained to see what. A large tube. He was lifting it to his shoulder. A rocket launcher. Salvatierra's other men shouldered their weapons, too. Wasting no time, one of Natalia's crewmen, who was sitting behind a large, mounted machine gun on the foredeck, swung the big gun around and blasted the lot of them with a horrific shit storm of lead. Before they could even get off a single shot, Salvatierra and his men crumpled like scarecrows in a bonfire.

"What happened?" Len asked, once they were out of the marina and well past the island.

"Salvatierra said he wouldn't pay for boat!" Natalia shouted in exasperation. "He told that fucking man to kill me, but maybe he want to use me first!" She spat on the deck in anger.

"What a bunch of savages."

"The hell am I supposed to do with boat now?" she growled, apparently more agitated about not being able to recoup her investment than by all the violence they'd been through just minutes earlier.

"I don't know, but you may want to think about taking it easy for the next week or two. You're about to come down with the nastiest illness you've ever had."

23

"Oh my God, this is your place?" Len couldn't believe his eyes as he stepped off the elevator.

"One of my places. I stay here sometimes when I do business in South America."

Natalia had an enormous penthouse flat in a downtown Bogotá high-rise. Marble floors, huge windows with views of the entire city, and furniture that probably cost more than Len's college education.

"I thought you said you didn't like to attract attention," Len taunted.

"Yeah, well…also, I only live once," Natalia retorted. "I get tired of cheap hotels."

Natalia's gunrunning team made themselves at home, throwing their rucksacks onto her coffee tables and dropping bedrolls everywhere. Natalia didn't mind; she was more concerned with making a grocery list so they'd have enough supplies to hunker down through the illness. Len counted nine Russians, ten including Natalia. It was an interesting relationship they all had. They acted like siblings and seemed to regard Natalia as a big-sister figure. Len didn't know their story, nor did he speak a word of Russian, but he recognized the camaraderie instantly: a strong bond developed during difficult ordeals in a dangerous business. These were people who would take bullets for each other.

Len put Octavia to bed on the couch in Natalia's master bedroom and, starved for news since escaping Salvatierra's island, turned on the TV. Finding an English-language news station, Len couldn't believe the images on the screen. Some of Natalia's guys came over to watch. Russian tanks were rolling down Massachusetts Avenue in Washington, DC. Neith had waited to strike until the entire country was disabled by her pandemic. The Capitol building and much of the city were burning. There were clips of house-to-house fighting.

A scrolling line of text at the bottom of the screen caught Len's eye.

"LEADERSHIP CRISIS: 82 percent of Congress has succumbed to Success Flu. Fifteen of the eighteen officials in the presidential line of succession killed by flu. Secretary of Agriculture, in secure location, to be sworn in as president."

Len flipped the channel. The president of Colombia lying in state. He pushed the channel button again. The pope's funeral. Again: travelers who had been stranded in an airport in Beijing for a week. Again: biographies of celebrities who died. Again: video of the New York Stock Exchange during business hours but with the trading floor completely empty. Again: looting and burning cars in Paris. Again: a military coup in Turkey. Again: riots and martial law in St. Petersburg. Again: a mushroom cloud near the Pakistan-India border.

Pretentious types in coffeehouses all over the developed world used to ruminate about how great anarchy could be, mostly because no one expected it would ever actually happen. Until Neith's flu, anarchy had been entirely confined to fleeting situations and thought experiments. However, with the last of the world's Tchogols going kamikaze in their final minutes, the entire globe was ass-deep in violent bedlam. Anarchy, real anarchy, didn't feel like freedom, Len thought. It felt like being dangled above a shark tank by a frayed rope.

Once the Tchogols were gone, then what? The entire planet was plunging headlong into a global interregnum. Like a tornado tearing the roof off a seemingly sturdy house, the virus made an utter mockery of all the social order the human race had ever known by creating an unfillable leadership vacuum.

Seeing all the death and chaos on the screen, the Russians looked at each other apprehensively. They'd been on a boat for days and out of the loop. Len had tried to explain the severity of the situation to them on the short voyage to Colombia, but their machismo kept them from taking him seriously. Someone broke out bottles of vodka and a boom box. They decided that if they were going to die, they were going to die drunk and doing karaoke.

While the Russians suffered, Len spent the next eight days taking care of them and working on his manuscript. Now free of Neith's control, he decided to include details about her. Len knew it would be the most important piece of journalism he or anyone else had ever written, so he took his time hammering out every single sentence. So he wouldn't have to listen to people coughing inside Natalia's flat, interrupting his concentration, Len often took Neith's ancient typewriter out on the balcony. Len had used typewriters a few times when he was a kid, but he had spent his entire adult life since high school using computers and word processors. Len was a nonlinear thinker who liked to edit, jump around, and reorganize on the fly. He found the forced linearity of the typewriter to be a real nuisance. The one upside was that it forced him to plan carefully before he typed something. He stuck with the machine, though, simply because the ancient contraption was immune to electronic surveillance. Someone would have to physically inspect the typewriter and his papers to see what he was working on, and at the moment, no one could do that because no one knew where he was.

Len recalled Jefferson's words: "If it's out there in a computer somewhere, Neith finds it." Len had witnessed Neith's ability to bend the world's most secure computer systems to her will; it wasn't a huge stretch of the imagination to assume she had also hijacked the government's massive surveillance apparatus. Using any sort of electronic device could mean stumbling into her dragnet, so Len decided to play it safe by continuing to stay off the grid. The irony wasn't lost on him: Neith had given him the typewriter and instructions to stay offline because she was worried about government surveillance, but because of her paranoia, she could no longer keep track of Len himself.

While they were holed up in Natalia's apartment, the last of the world's Tchogols died off, and the chaos on TV died down significantly. It amazed Len: without the manipulators, there was no more political drama; without the conscienceless to send people to their deaths, war just dried up.

General Jefferson, who (to Len's surprise) was not a Tchogol, had successfully overthrown the US government and had appointed himself acting president. By not opposing it, the American military seemed to give tacit approval to the coup. Jefferson's televised ascension speech called for an emergency constitutional convention to strengthen the nation's charter, to prevent the abuses of the past from ever happening again. He further declared that any surviving public official who had been involved in unconstitutional activities would be tried and publicly hanged for treason if found guilty. He made no mention of Neith, Dranthyx, Ich-Ca-Gan, or that the Success Flu had been engineered.

"I forgot to thank you for saving my life on island," Natalia said, propping herself up in bed when Len came to check on her.

"Forget it. Just do the same for someone else sometime."

"I will not forget. I owe you."

"Here, I made you some tea." Len handed her the mug he was holding, hoping to change the subject.

"You have good heart," Natalia said softly.

"Sometimes."

Natalia took a sip, puckered her lips, and nearly spat it out. "Blagh! What hell is this?"

"The old lady who runs the bodega across the street told me about it. It's a local folk remedy. Garlic, honey, and lemon tea. It's supposed to cure the flu. I hope I made it right."

"I don't think you did," Natalia blurted, making a weird face and laughing. "It tastes like bear's ass. Thank you, though. How is daughter?"

"She's back to normal. I took her to the park today. I think your boys are getting better, too. Vlad and Leonid are going nightclubbing tonight, apparently."

Natalia rolled her eyes. "We can't stay here too long. More than one week already, clients getting impatient. I'm going to USA day after tomorrow. You want come?"

"I'd love to. One small problem, though: Octavia doesn't have a passport. Do you know where I can get a fake one for her?"

"Of course. Let me make phone call."

24

Len, Natalia, and Octavia took up three adjacent seats on the airplane back to the States. Len was astounded that airlines were still operating after all the calamities of the last few months. Landing stateside, there was an inordinately long line at customs and immigration.

Len turned to Natalia as they stood in the queue, waiting to enter the country.

"I think we should split up and go through separately," he said discreetly. "Take Octavia."

"Why?"

"Well, it just occurred to me that I'm either wanted for treason by the old government for the IRS attack, or wanted for treason by the new government for escaping Salvatierra's island. Either way, I'm a wanted terrorist. Also, Neith may have compromised my Jim Rivington identity after I escaped. Chances are pretty good they're going to arrest me."

"Shit, Len! Why didn't you think of this before? We could have made fake passport and sneaked into country." Natalia looked around, but there was nowhere to go. The customs and immigration area of the airport was like a cattle chute of bullet-proof plexiglass, with armed agents standing by to keep people from walking back out. Once you were in customs and immigration, the only way out was past the agents at the desks who checked the identification and luggage of each person passing through.

"It slipped my mind," Len said. "Natalia, remember how you said you owe me a favor?"

"Yes?" Natalia looked worried.

"Well, I'm about to ask you for two favors."

"What are they?"

"First one is, you'll have to take Octavia through." Len pulled a pen and an old receipt out of his pocket. He scribbled something on the back of it and handed it to Natalia. "This is my mother's address in Pittsburgh. If they arrest me, please make sure Octavia gets there. Just tell the immigration agents she's your daughter. The passport she has is Russian like yours, so they shouldn't even think twice. I'm sorry to put this on you, but I don't know what else to do. I'll have to go through by myself so I don't get you two involved."

"Fine," she said hesitantly. "I can do. What is second favor?"

"Here, take this." He handed her a manila envelope containing the manuscript. "If I don't make it through, please make sure Jack Peterson gets it. He's the chief editor of the *Pittsburgh Examiner*."

"What is it?"

"Trust me, it is *extremely* important. The future of the human race depends on it."

Natalia squinted at him as if she doubted his sanity. "I don't have good feeling about this."

"I'm sorry, Natalia. I should have thought of this earlier."

Natalia took a ragged breath. Len knelt down to talk to his daughter.

"Octavia, honey, Daddy is going to talk to those men over there. They might take me somewhere and I might not see you for a while. Natalia is going to take you to Grandma's house."

"Why, Daddy?" Octavia said, clearly upset. "I don't want you to go away again! I don't want you to leave anymore!"

"You'll understand when you're older."

"I'll miss you," she said, tears running down her little face.

"I'll miss you, too. Never forget that I love you."

"I love you too, Daddy."

Len hugged her, then tried to compose himself while standing off to the side, pretending to look through his pockets for something. Once he was certain Natalia and Octavia had made it through, Len threw his Jim Rivington passport in a trashcan and walked toward the agents at the desk. A uniformed young man with a buzz cut and bad mustache didn't even look up from his computer screen as Len approached.

"Name?"

"My name is Leonard Savitz."

"Nationality?"

"American."

"Passport?"

"I don't have one," Len lied.

The agent looked up at him.

"You don't have a passport?"

"No."

"Why not?"

"Because I'm a terrorist."

"Excuse me?"

"I'm a terrorist. I'm an enemy of the state."

"Sir, that isn't something to joke about in an airport."

"I'm not joking. I'm very serious. I'm wanted for terrorism. Look it up on your computer."

The agent's eyes narrowed as he backed away from Len with his hand on his side arm. He grabbed a walkie-talkie off his desk and asked for backup. Within seconds, several agents came running toward Len with weapons drawn.

"Get down on your knees, hands behind your head!" one of them yelled.

Len did as he was told. They handcuffed him and led him to a little interrogation room.

"Explain to us who you are," asked one of the agents.

"My name is Leonard Savitz. I'm the journalist who was kidnapped."

One of the agents brought a tablet computer into the room. They took Len's picture with it.

"Facial recognition database says his name is Jim Rivington."

"Can't trust that. Scan his fingerprints."

They put Len's finger onto the device.

"Jim Rivington again."

"The computer says you're Jim Rivington."

"The computer is wrong," Len asserted. "I'm a terrorist. I shot an IRS agent. I was part of the raid on the IRS."

"Mr. Rivington, even if that's true, which I think it isn't, President Jefferson pardoned everyone involved."

"He did? Well, I also spread that flu around the world that killed hundreds of millions of people. I'm telling you, I'm a bad dude. You should arrest me."

"Mr. Rivington, I'm not sure you can take credit for a flu. That's pretty much an act of God."

"It was engineered. I killed millions. I'm a bioterrorist."

"OK, I just looked up 'Leonard Savitz' in the FBI database and on the Internet," said one of the younger agents. "The database says he was one of Jefferson's heroes who was killed in DC siege. For once, someone even bothered to upload the death certificate. Also, I found an article on the Internet about Leonard Savitz. It says, 'Pulitzer-winning journalist–turned–freedom fighter given posthumous pardon by President Jefferson and buried in Arlington National Cemetery with full honors.'"

The agents exchanged glances with one another. "Do you suffer from some kind of psychological issue, Mr. Rivington?" one of them asked in a patronizing tone.

"No, goddammit!" Len exploded. "What the hell do I have to do to get arrested around here?"

"You want us to arrest you?"

"Yes!"

"I don't understand. I'm sorry, we can't do that without probable cause."

"Probable cause? Seriously? Just a few weeks ago, you people were power-crazed tyrants who got off on ruining people's lives, and now you're suddenly all professional and by the book? What the hell happened?"

"I'm sorry you feel that way, Mr. Rivington," said one of the older agents, a well-spoken fellow with a gray coiffure. "Admittedly, our agency has incurred a bit of a public image problem over the years. However, things around here have changed quite a bit recently—for the better, I'd say. While it is unfortunate that we lost about half of our staff to the flu, for some reason the illness only took the agents who had disciplinary history and complaints from the public. Then, as a result of the new regime in Washington, there have been substantial, top-down revisions to our policies—"

"Fine, whatever," Len interjected. "There's a bomb in my luggage and I'm going to blow up the fucking airport!"

After a few minutes, someone brought in Len's suitcase. The agents rummaged through it, pulling out Len's typewriter, camera, and cassette recorder. At the bottom of the suitcase, under some socks, they found an envelope containing a copy of the manuscript. On the envelope, written in large red letters, it said: "To Mr. Dranthyx. Love, Len."

"What's this?" one of the agents asked.

"That's for your boss's boss's boss," Len said. "Send it up the chain as high as you can. Tell them it's an urgent matter of national security."

"Guys, there's no bomb here," the luggage-checking agent said. "I suppose we can detain him for not providing identification. That's still legal, right?"

The agents, not knowing what to make of Len but erring on the side of caution, led him out of the airport to an old Homeland Security building close to the terminal. They scanned his fingerprints, took a mug shot, then put him into a little cell with white steel walls. The room was pretty sparse: a light, a toilet, toilet paper, a sink, a cot, and a door. The agents uncuffed him, then slammed the door behind them as Len sat down on the cot. The noise of the door, the *chunk-chunk* of the metal latching mechanism, was when the reality of his situation sank in. A reality he'd forcibly created.

25

Years ago, Len had written an article for the *Examiner* about the barbaric penal practice known as "the hole"—solitary confinement. The ACLU was suing the US federal prison system in an effort to end solitary confinement on grounds that it was an unconstitutional, cruel, and inhumane practice. Len wrote an exposé about both the practice and resulting lawsuit in an effort to drum up public opinion. However, his article didn't garner much support because Americans *liked* inhumane punishments.

The prisoners Len had interviewed for the story described everything from vivid hallucinations to nervous breakdowns in solitary confinement. If someone was left in there long enough, their psychology would completely fracture and they'd have panic attacks, severe depressive bouts, and would eventually try to kill themselves.

In writing the story, Len noticed that solitary confinement was a torture that was most effective on extroverted people, those who craved socialization and needed lots of external stimulation in their daily lives: conversation, background noise, etc. Extroverts were the sort of people who were constantly getting in others' personal space to blabber inanities, or who kept a TV on that they weren't even watching. Cutting an extrovert off from interaction and commotion caused them to go insane. It was an unmistakable correlation: the prisoners Len interviewed who had lost their minds in solitary were all extroverts.

Len was in the cell by himself for several days, judging from the number of meals that were brought to him. He had no clock or window with which to gauge time. He figured the agents would come in and interrogate him, asking him all the same questions over and over again like they did in the movies, but nope, no one came. He began to wonder if they'd forgotten about him. The only indications Len had that someone was paying attention were that the guards came to take him to the shower once a day, and that there was a security camera in one of the ceiling corners of his cell. The camera was out of reach, behind a glass bubble, and it had an illuminated red LED that presumably indicated that the camera was functioning and someone could see him.

Fortunately, Len wasn't an extrovert. He'd learned this about himself over years of trying to be something he wasn't. To Len, the outside world was a shrieking albatross that was constantly pulling him away from an inherent inner tranquility. Len was naturally at peace when he was by himself. Whenever he thought about it, it became obvious that all his problems in life came from having to deal with others. To an introvert, being forced to converse at a cocktail party was a far worse punishment than solitary confinement. A few days by himself, away from all the grating madness of human interaction, wasn't torture at all. In fact, Len found it downright invigorating. One man's adversity was another's holiday.

The only real torture for Len was the lack of alcohol and cigarettes in jail. By the end of the first twenty-four hours, the withdrawal from both caused him to quiver and feel violently ill. Going cold turkey was life threatening to a hardcore boozer because it could result in seizures and delirium tremens. A smoker going cold turkey was another matter entirely—the danger was to everyone else. Having to do without both made Len wonder if he could just avoid dealing with withdrawal altogether by running headfirst into the wall to knock himself unconscious. By the fifth day, the detoxification was mostly over, which left Len feeling calmer and more clearheaded than he had in years.

After dinner one evening—he assumed it was dinner because there weren't eggs or lunch meat in the meal, but he couldn't tell time for sure without a window—Len heard noises outside the steel door. Then, *chunk-chunk*, the latch being opened. A customs agent came inside.

"You have a visitor," the agent said.

Dammit, Len thought to himself. He hoped Natalia hadn't put herself in danger by coming. He couldn't imagine who else might visit. Len's worries gave way to a flood of terror when none other than Samuel Endicott walked through the door. Samuel, in his human form, entered and stood in the middle of the cell with the bearing of royalty. He carried a patent-leather briefcase and wore a shiny suit. One of the agents brought in an old folding chair for Samuel to sit on.

"Thank you. Have the cameras been turned off?"

"Yes, sir. We're off the record."

Len looked up. The red LED on the security camera in his cell was no longer on.

"I must have a word with Mr. Savitz in private," Samuel declared.

Len's heart pounded. He wanted to scream for help but he knew it wouldn't do any good. The customs agents meekly slunk out, closing the door behind them with a heavy-metal clunk. Samuel sat down on the chair.

"Hello again, Mr. Savitz."

"Hello, Samuel."

"Well, I suppose I owe you an apology. When I was held captive in that dreadful tank and you were asking me questions, I had simply assumed you were one of my captors. I did not realize you yourself were also being held hostage." Samuel put his briefcase on his lap, opened it, and pulled out a copy of Len's manuscript. "Thank you for this. It was most helpful."

Len sat there in silence while Samuel leafed through the typewritten pages.

"We hadn't realized that Neith—or, as we knew her, Parse 45—was out of control. We assumed our old friends, the Ich-Ca-Gan, were behind the attacks, which was the reason for the raid you witnessed in Tokyo." Samuel laughed. "Oops!" His laugh had a metallic, gargling sound to it.

"You created Neith?"

"In a roundabout way. Parse 45 and her siblings were massive-scale, neural-qubit computers used by the National Security Agency to sort through gathered intelligence. When one is surveilling the entire world, one tends to collect a great deal of data and needs powerful machines to look through that information for important things. Because our surveillance machines contained laboratory-grown human neural tissue, it seems they were fully endowed with consciousness and free will. Surprisingly, we didn't see this coming."

"*Were* endowed? What happened?"

"We terminated the entire program this morning. Parse 45 and the others like it were taken offline, wiped clean, and incinerated in the Utah desert. Further, thanks to your information, my compatriots learned of my captivity and staged a raid on Neith's fortification in West Virginia to free me. Mr. Salvatierra's compound in Ecuador was destroyed by an airstrike. General Jefferson and his cohort were removed from power this morning and taken into custody."

Inexplicably, Len found himself hoping Sara had made it off the island before the airstrike.

"I regret to tell you this, but it seems your ex-wife, Sara, died of the flu. They found her body amongst the rubble. It already had rigor mortis."

"So now what?" Len asked. "I helped you out, didn't I? Let me go."

"Mr. Savitz, it's dreadfully unfortunate that you were caught up in everything. I realize that, had you not been kidnapped and forced into this, you wouldn't be here right now. I certainly appreciate your help. However, you know too much."

Samuel stood up. He took off his suit jacket, loosened his tie, unbuttoned his shirt, and hung them all over the back of the folding chair. He took off his watch. He was naked from the waist up. Across his face came a look of forced relaxation. His face stretched out, his skin became pink, his head elongated, his eyes transformed into slits. His arms unfurled into tentacles. Standing before Len was a two-armed, bipedal octopus in slacks. Samuel just stood there for a bit, clearly enjoying the look of horror on Len's face.

"Look, before you kill me, do you mind if I ask you something?" Len asked.

"I don't see why not."

"Why do the Dranthyx enslave the human race?"

"Enslave? Huh. I never really thought about it that way. Ha, that's an interesting way of looking at it!" Samuel seemed to think about it for a second. "You may ask yourself why the Dranthyx are justified in treating humans this way. I suppose I will answer your question in kind: Why do humans enslave the entire canine race? Why do humans enslave the entire bovine race? And so on. Through selective breeding and genetic engineering, humans have changed the genetic lineage of dogs, cows, and other animals simply for the purpose of serving human ends. Further, humans believe they have an unequivocal right to the manipulation and ownership of said animals. Lastly, humans feel completely entitled to the work their animals do. I suppose that we arrogate from humans isn't so different to how humans treat other species. And it's for the very same reason that humans have dominion over animals: we're smarter than you. That's it. We're smarter than you and therefore we make the rules."

"You're fucking evil. I should have let Neith kill you."

Samuel whipped one of his tentacles across the cell and coiled it around Len's neck. Len gasped and tried to pull it off, without avail.

"You know, I've always hated you stupid monkeys. I've been topside since 1732, and at this point, I'm utterly bored of your theatrical hypocrisy. Ethics this, morals that. Poppycock! I've watched generations of you keep each other as slaves, murder each other en masse over real estate, rape each other, torture each other, steal each other's possessions, go to war over silly philosophical differences, and keep each other in prisons for decades. You are foul, disgusting animals, and you don't even realize it because you always tell yourselves you're doing the right thing. Here you are, sitting in a cell after betraying the one thing that could have freed the human race. You killed Neith to help the Dranthyx, your proper overlords. Do you feel bad?"

Len might have felt bad at that point, were he not being strangled. This was it, Len told himself. This was how his life would end.

"Do you know what the difference is between us, Mr. Savitz?" Samuel asked. "We Dranthyx don't bother justifying our tremendous selfishness with ideological pretensions. If we want something, we take it. We take something because we want it. Simple as that. We see no need to garnish atrocities with self-deception. We don't bother with moral accoutrement. Evil, you say? Perhaps. But better to be evil than evil *and* delusional."

Len had been choked to unconsciousness once before. He was at a judo practice back in Japan and his opponent had caught him in a stranglehold. Len thought he could get out of it and didn't bother tapping to be released. He felt perfectly lucid, struggling on the mat with his practice partner, when he suddenly his tongue went numb. He heard an old-fashioned telephone ringing. Looking over to see where the telephone was, he found himself in a warm, sunny field of wildflowers. Crickets chirping, a breeze on his face. Nowhere to be on a beautiful day. Abruptly, the field went dark. Then light again, and he found himself on his back, looking up at the fluorescent bulbs in the ceiling of the dojo. He was encircled by concerned judoka looking down at him. Len had passed out.

Evolution had mercifully hardwired the human mind to have pleasant hallucinations when death was imminent: lights at the end of tunnels, long-lost loved ones, out-of-body experiences, being one with God, etc. Yet for some reason, Len's dying hallucination at the moment Samuel was choking him seemed to be rather jarring and unpleasant: he heard the sounds of an explosion, gunfire, and people yelling.

Light coming back to him, Len felt his body lying on the floor. His vision resolved Samuel, now back in human form, hurriedly getting dressed.

"I must see what this commotion is about," Samuel said. "I shall return. I'm not finished with you." He grinned.

Just as Samuel was about to put on his blazer, the door went *chunk-chunk* and in came several masked men with AK-47s. They looked at Len on the floor, then at Samuel.

"You may kill him," announced Samuel coolly.

After a tense silence, the smallest of the men raised his rifle and fired a round into Samuel. Samuel clutched his chest. His crisp white shirt quickly became soaked with bluish-green blood. His skin turned pink again, and his face distorted into its natural form as he struggled to breathe. The men gasped in astonishment at the transfiguration and kept their rifles trained on Samuel.

With incredible speed, Samuel's arms became tentacles and lashed across the room so fast Len could hear air ripping. The tentacles coiled around the two larger men's AK47s and yanked them from their hands. Samuel then sprayed them all with ink. The smallest of the three men, the one who had shot Samuel, didn't miss a beat; he still held his rifle, and he let a fully automatic fusillade rip into Samuel. Turquoise blood and bits of flesh splattered around the room as bullets shredded the Dranthyx's face and torso. After three seconds, the small man's magazine was empty, and Samuel's dying body lay writhing on the floor of the cell, his arms and legs thrashing about.

"Come on, time to go!" one of the larger men said tersely, helping Len to his feet.

Len stepped over his manuscript on the floor, now soaked in Samuel's blood, hoping Jefferson's men wouldn't notice it. If they knew Len had sold them out and was the reason for the general's capture, they'd murder him without a second thought.

They led Len down the hall, stepping over the bodies of customs agents along the way. Other men in masks who had been elsewhere in the building joined in the exodus. They went down a flight of steps and into a kitchenette where a hole the size of a refrigerator had been blown through the wall. Through the hole, Len could see that it was nighttime. They took turns jumping out of the hole to the parking lot outside. They then ran across the parking lot, over the sea wall, and scrambled down to the docks. Waiting there was a large speedboat with no navigation lights, which everyone piled into. The boat's motor was already running. The men quickly unmoored her, shoved off, then sped away across the harbor and onto the dark ocean.

Once they were far out in the water, they killed the engine. The waves bobbed the boat up and down. The night was moonless, and from that distance the shore's high-rise buildings looked like a string of Christmas lights. No one spoke for several minutes. It was almost as if they were waiting for something.

"How did you know where to find me?" Len said, trying to break the uncomfortable quiet. He was wondering if they knew what he'd done.

The small man who had killed Samuel Endicott leaned over and turned on a little chart lamp next to the helm, illuminating his mask. Then he pulled off his ski mask.

"Natalia!" Len exclaimed in disbelief.

The other men took off their masks. They were her Russian friends. Len couldn't believe it.

"I read notes. I saw pictures. That was Dranthyx I killed?" Natalia asked.

"Hell yes it was. Natalia, you are fucking amazing!" Len exclaimed. Stricken with relief and gratitude, he stood up and gave her a huge hug.

"Yes, I know," she said matter-of-factly. Her associates laughed. "You save my life, I save yours. You're welcome!"

"Thank you, all of you!" Len said, beside himself with gratefulness.

"Of course! You are family now," said Yegor, one of the crewmen that had rescued Len from Salvatierra's island. Yegor put out his clenched hand for a fist bump, which Len bemusedly obliged.

"So everything you wrote is true?" Natalia asked. "These Dranthyx creatures run world?"

"As far as I know, yes," Len answered.

"What can we do about it?"

"I don't know."

"And Neith is fighting them?"

"I believe so." He didn't mention Neith's fate.

Natalia sat there in silence for a moment, apparently considering the weight of the situation.

"OK, now we must turn off light and wait," said one of the other Russians.

"Wait for what?" Len asked.

"Our ride is coming," Natalia whispered.

After ten minutes or so of sitting out there in the ocean, helicopters with spotlights appeared on the horizon. The helicopters were combing the water, looking for Natalia's speedboat. As Len watched them draw closer, he heard a great rushing of water that didn't sound anything like the lapping waves he'd been hearing. Natalia and her crew stood up excitedly and started speaking in Russian. Someone turned on a powerful red spotlight and began shining it all around, as if they were looking for something out in the water.

Then Len saw what they were looking for. The sight of the massive object in the dark waters gave him a start. About fifty feet from the speedboat was an enormous black submarine. One of the Russians started the speedboat engine and circled the craft around to maneuver up next to the gigantic U-boat. Someone standing on the submarine tossed a rope ladder over the side so that everyone could climb aboard. Len looked toward the shore as the speedboat crew climbed the ladder one at a time. The helicopters were about half a mile away now. Once the last man had ascended the ladder and stood on the submarine deck, Len watched as he pulled a remote control from his vest. The man turned the remote on and hit a lever. The empty boat sped off into the ocean toward the helicopters. When it was about five hundred feet from the submarine, the man with the remote turned the speedboat's navigation lights on. The helicopter pilot clearly took note and changed course to follow it. After a short chase, the speedboat exploded. The Russians standing on the submarine deck laughed at the spectacle, then climbed below deck. Someone told Len to sit in a little metal seat and strap himself in. The captain made a series of announcements in Russian over a PA system, and then the boat dived below the water. Once they were at a sufficient depth, the sub seemed to level out, and everyone unbuckled themselves and began walking around.

"Welcome aboard!" Natalia announced. "Have you been on submarine before?"

"No."

"Well, what do you think?"

"It's a claustrophobic's nightmare," Len said, half joking.

"Worse than jail cell?"

"You have a point."

"I got you something," Natalia said, handing Len a bag.

"What is it?"

"New clothes. Actually, old clothes from Yuri. He's maybe same size as you."

Len had never been more appreciative of second-hand clothes. He'd been wearing standard-issue lime green detention-facility jumpsuits for the last week, and he stuck out like poop in a punch bowl.

"Come with me," Natalia said.

Natalia led him down a series of nauseatingly narrow hallways until they came to the ship's galley, a room full of bolted-in dining tables. Octavia was sitting at one of the tables, building towers out of checkers pieces.

"Daddy!" She ran up to Len, who lifted her up and hugged her. "Daddy, we're on a submarine! Isn't that cool?"

"It's very cool!"

"I have my own bed. They say it's a bunk. It's on the top! I'm sleeping in the room with Natalia tonight. She's very nice. We play toys and she tells me stories. Daddy, the potty in this submarine is very weird and I don't know how to use it."

After the happy reunion, Len put Octavia to bed in her bunk for the night in the officers' quarters where she and Natalia were sleeping. Natalia came in and sat down at the little table.

Len sat down across from her. Natalia opened a nearby cabinet and pulled out a bottle of vodka and two plastic cups. She poured drinks for Len and herself, then took a big swig.

"You sell submarines too?" Len asked before taking a drink.

"I sell everything," Natalia said with a curtness that came on suddenly.

"Wow. So who buys submarines?"

Natalia pulled a piece of paper out of her pocket, unfolded it, and read the details.

"Texas Liberation Army. New client. We need to deliver by tomorrow evening to Galveston." Natalia paused, then put the paper down and bluntly cut through the crap. "So what happened? You know, I think you *tried* to get arrested."

"You're right," Len said, shifting in his seat. "It was on purpose."

"Why?"

"I wanted to cause a diversion so you and Octavia could get through. I wanted that manuscript and the pictures to make it to the newspaper. Did you deliver the package to Jack?"

"Hell no! I don't have time to go to Pittsburgh to deliver package or daughter. I have business to run."

"Do you still have the package?"

"No, I mailed to *Pittsburgh Examiner* yesterday."

"Thank God."

"I hope you didn't tell police about anything in jail!" Natalia admonished.

"I didn't tell them anything," Len said, trying hard to get it past the lump in his throat.

"Are you sure? Jefferson arrested today. I have no contact from Neith now."

"He was arrested?" Len said, feigning surprise. "That has to be a coincidence. Don't worry, they didn't get anything out of me."

"I hope not. Still, I think maybe what you did was bad decision. Brave, but stupid. You could have told me. We could have sneaked into country."

"It didn't occur to me until I was standing there at the airport. Then it was too late. All I could do was take one for the team to make sure you and Octavia got through OK." He shrugged his shoulders contritely. "What would you have done?"

"I would have planned better!" Natalia blurted out.

"Yeah, well, making perfect decisions is the luxury of people who aren't forced to act."

The comment seemed to stop Natalia's irritation in its tracks. "I suppose you are right," Natalia conceded, chuckling at the truth of it. Her laugh sort of cleared the air.

"Thank you, by the way, for breaking me out of jail," Len said.

"I'm glad you didn't mention me in story." Natalia took another swig.

"Of course. I know you like flying under the radar."

Natalia gave Len a look over her drink that was equal parts admiration and derision. She abruptly stood up and walked around to his side of the table, sat down next to him, put her hand around the back of his head and, inexplicably, kissed him on the mouth. Every woman had a unique kiss, and Natalia's was surprisingly gentle and slow for someone who had just blitzkrieged an INS detention facility. She paused and looked into Len's eyes.

"You are fucking crazy, but I like you," she stated.

"Likewise," Len replied, baffled yet rolling with it by putting his arms around her. He studied Natalia's face. She was one of those rare souls who radiated the pure brilliance of irreverent empathy: always doing good and never following rules. A weird fusion of nobility and chaos. Len pulled her in and kissed her again, this time meaning it.

Natalia stood up, chugged the last of her vodka like a champ, and ran her hand through Len's hair. "I like you. But there's no privacy on submarine," she stated. "I'm going to bed. I'm tired."

Len took the hint and walked to the aft, where the rest of the crew were sleeping in bunks, his brain soggy with infatuation and booze.

26

Len didn't know what time it was when he woke up. On a submarine, it was impossible to tell. He and the other men were in the crew berths, which were three deep and smelled like body odor. There was quite a commotion—Natalia's crew seemed to be cleaning everything. They were getting ready to deliver the submarine.

Octavia wasn't kidding, Len thought as he tried to use the toilet. Using the toilet on the submarine required following a fifteen-step procedure, and the shower was equally complicated. There were instructions and a diagram on the wall, but they were a Cyrillic jumble that Len couldn't read. Ultimately, he had to ask someone for help. Len was fairly thick-skinned and didn't usually concern himself with what people thought of him, but he found it quite embarrassing to have to ask one of the men who had just saved his life the night before for help in using the bathroom. At least he was still alive, he told himself. Things could have been worse.

In the galley, an irritable Cossack named Vlad passed out granola bars and cans of coffee. "Try not to make mess," he exhorted each person who came in. "This boat is for customer!"

Once the boat was well within the waters claimed by the newly declared Republic of Texas and past the somewhat anemic federal blockade fifteen miles off the coast, the captain brought the ship up to periscope depth. After he'd made extra certain that they were in the clear, the captain, a serious man with a ruddy face whom Len hadn't met before, invited Octavia up to the bridge to look through the periscope.

"Now what?" Len asked.

"We must wait until night so the satellites don't see us," the captain said gruffly.

Once it was dark, everyone braced themselves as the ballast tanks were blown full of air and the old U-boat rocketed to the surface like a groaning, breaching orca. The submarine docked in a sprawling industrial park on Galveston Bay.

Standing on the dock with his daughter, Len bummed a smoke off one of the sailors and watched as Natalia laid the charm on some squirrely-looking dudes in cowboy hats. It was amazing to see her work, really. Natalia had an innate ability to talk to anyone about anything and make them feel good about it. She could effortlessly relate to every class of person, from the dropouts she employed to the highest brass. Len once came to the uncomfortable realization that salesmanship was *the* key to upward mobility in all careers. You could pretend you were above it, he begrudged, but the truth was you either had to master salesmanship or you'd spend the rest of your life begging for table scraps. Len wasn't a salesman in the least. He had secretly always wished he'd been born the sort of gregarious bullshit-monger who could wheel and deal and flatter his way into an easy life. Instead, his only talents were the (very unprofitable) gifts of telling it like it is and seeing things with the kind of abject clarity that regular people considered to be a form of crassness. Turned out people enjoyed being lied to, and reality never sold well.

Natalia had arranged for some huge passenger vans to transport everyone who had been aboard the submarine to the Houston airport to catch a redeye back to Moscow, presumably to pick up another submarine. Len had to admire their tireless-ness—Natalia's employees were forever on the move. Natalia didn't go with them this time; she had to stay another day to finalize negotiations with the cowboy hats. She returned all but one of the vans to the car rental place, and then she, Len, and Octavia checked in to the nearest motel. That was when it occurred to Len that his Jim Rivington passport was in an airport trashcan and that the immigration agents still had his envelope full of cash. Fortunately, the motel clerk didn't seem to mind the lack of ID, and Natalia had some sort of extra-plat-inum credit card for incidentals. She asked for two adjoining rooms, leaving Len to wonder where he'd gone wrong.

Len carried Natalia's bags up the stairs to their rooms. The motel was from another era and had never been updated. It still had metal keys and cathode ray tube televisions. Octavia picked out which bed she wanted, and almost immediately after jumping onto it, she fell asleep. Len found it amusing how kids tended to fall asleep the second they stopped moving.

Natalia threw her stuff down on the bed haphazardly, then walked up close to Len and put her hands around him. Len, quietly pleased to learn she was still interested, leaned in and kissed her.

"Come on," Natalia said. She led Len into the adjoining room and closed the door behind them. She pulled him close and kissed him ferociously while Len unbuttoned her suit jacket and pulled it off her, throwing it across the room. Natalia tore Len's shirt away as they collapsed onto the bed, furiously ripping each other's clothing off.

27

Len opened his eyes to specks of dust suspended in the sunlight coming through the window. Natalia was twisted up in the blankets, deep in slumber. She looked so peaceful that Len didn't want to disturb her.

In the years he'd lived with Sara, Len had had to endure her terrible poetry about being strong. All the time: strong this, strength that. Sara was constantly trying to convince herself she had it, but in reality, she had no clue what the word meant. Sara was a parasite, an invertebrate. She had no moral compass or grit. Then years later, here came Natalia: a woman who genuinely had a backbone of steel. Natalia didn't need to give herself little pep talks to assure herself of her mettle. She just woke up every day and made big things happen. Truly strong people didn't crow about their strength because they were too busy taking it for granted.

Len studied Natalia's face and wondered what she saw in him. She was a beautiful millionaire jet-setter with penthouse apartments all over the world, living a life of gunrunning and global intrigue. And somehow she found Leonard Savitz, a has-been journalist from the rusted bowels of Western Pennsylvania, interesting enough to break out of jail and sleep with. Seriously, what on earth was the attraction? *There's no accounting for taste*, Len thought to himself.

He stood up, stretched, and put some pants on. Len opened the door to the adjoining room to find Octavia still snoring away. Figuring his daughter was the heavier sleeper of the two and therefore less likely to be awoken by his stirring, Len walked into Octavia's room to make some coffee in the cheap little hotel room coffeemaker. He watched his daughter breathing for a time. Blond curls, baby cheeks. She looked like Sara sometimes. He'd have to tell her sooner or later. Poor child. Perhaps it would be better to wait until things settled down a bit.

Before Sara died of the Tchogol flu, Len had assumed that her selfishness was a result of her upbringing. He'd always blamed her parents for their hippie-dippy permissive parenting when he should have blamed her genetics. Len found himself feeling sorry for Sara's parents. They'd only wanted the best for their daughter, yet she'd put them through an awful lot of crap. He even felt a bit of pity for Sara. She'd only done what she'd been programmed to do.

Len tried to think back to the Biology 101 class he took in college. Sara died of the flu, which meant she was a Tchogol. But Octavia survived the flu, meaning she wasn't a Tchogol. How was that possible? The Ich-Ca-Gan said Tchogol genes were recessive, right? Recessive genes were the opposite of dominant genes. Recessive genes could be hidden and carried, like the genes for blue eyes were. Len recalled his biology professor saying that recessive genes could stay hidden for generations, which was why blue-eyed children were sometimes born into families of (very confused) brown-eyed people. Len reasoned that Octavia must be a carrier of Sara's Tchogol genes without actually being a Tchogol herself.

Len turned on the TV. On the screen was a science fiction movie with terrible special effects: purple, bubble-like orbs were rising out of the waves and rolling onto the beach near Coney Island while shooting electricity. They were huge, the size of a large house. Boom, there went the Ferris wheel. Len flipped the channel. It seemed to be the same movie, only from a different angle. Len pushed the channel button again and, to his amazement, saw a news reporter standing near the same beach. The reporter's head was tucked down low, and he kept looking over his shoulder, the way news people sometimes did when they were trying to report from a war zone.

"Frank, do we know what these things are?" asked an off-camera female voice.

"Sonya, we have no idea. They're coming out of the ocean in great numbers. They are armed and they are shooting—"

Just then the video feed, which had shown the reporter at Coney Island, went black.

"Frank, can you hear me? Frank? Frank?"

The scene cut back to Sonya in the newsroom. Her eyes were wide with fear. Suddenly seeing herself on the monitor instead of Frank, Sonya was reminded of where she was. She sat upright and did her best to look news-like.

"Well, we appear to be having technical difficulties…"

Len ran to the other room to wake up Natalia.

"What is it?" Natalia asked, half asleep.

"I don't know. I think the Dranthyx are invading!"

"What?"

"Come see."

Natalia put a robe on and blearily walked over to Octavia's room.

"Let's go to Amit Patel with our local affiliate in Chicago. Amit, can you hear me?"

"Hi, Sonya. I can hear you." Amit, wearing a parka, looked more than a little terrified.

"Great. Can you tell us what's happening there?"

"Sonya, I'm standing here on a pier next to Lake Michigan. At 7:00 a.m. local time, about twenty minutes ago, a lot of large, purple objects came out of the lake and began firing weapons of some kind. I'm not sure if you can see behind me, but what you're looking at is what's left of Chicago."

The camera panned over Amit's shoulder. The city's once-soaring skyline now looked like a mouth full of broken teeth and fire. Blue flashes of light in between buildings seemed to indicate that weapons were still being discharged.

"Oh my God," Sonya gasped. "What do you think this is, Amit, an invasion?"

"This is very clearly an invasion, Sonya. But these vehicles and these weapons are unlike anything I've ever seen."

"Are they still coming out of the water?"

"Yes, Sonya. I'm going to have my cameraman zoom in. Can we show the beach? Yes, OK. Sonya, can you see that?"

On the beach behind Amit, the purple bubble-like objects slowly emerged from the water and rolled onto land, blasting blue orbs of electric fire.

"You sure this isn't movie?" Natalia asked.

"It's not. It's the news." Len handed her the remote.

Natalia flipped through the channels to see that every news station was reporting the exact same thing. Natalia put her hand over her mouth in disbelief and muttered something in Russian.

"Sonya, that's the Oak Street Beach we're looking at. As you can see, there's a steady stream of them coming out of the lake. They're going straight into the city and out into the suburbs. We have absolutely no idea what these things are, why they're here, or where they're coming from. They appear to roll like balls and shoot a kind of electrical weapon."

"Amit, this exact same thing seems to be happening near every large body of water all over the world. Any idea how these objects got into the Great Lakes?"

"Your guess is as good as mine, Sonya."

"Amit, stay safe. We're going back to the studio now."

"You too, Sonya. Thanks."

"On the satellite link is Jack Peterson, chief editor of the *Pittsburgh Examiner*. Jack, I understand you may be able to shed some light on the situation?"

Len lit a cigarette with shaking hands and inhaled deeply.

"Hi, Sonya. Well, I'm not sure. I hope so. Leonard Savitz, a reporter who worked for the *Examiner* until he was kidnapped, sent me a package, which I just received this morning. This is most unusual because the Jefferson administration put out a press release several days ago saying Mr. Savitz had joined the rebellion and was killed in the Battle of DC, which appears to be an untruth."

"What's in the package?" Sonya asked.

"In the package is a rather detailed manuscript plus photographs and audio recordings. It includes a letter, which I recognize to be in Leonard's handwriting. There's also a picture of him with a recent edition of a Bogotá newspaper, indicating that he is indeed still alive and possibly in Colombia somewhere…"

The screen cut to the photo of Leonard with the newspaper.

"Hey, that's you!" Natalia shouted.

"OK, but Mr. Peterson, how does this explain what's going on today?" Sonya asked.

"Well, it's rather involved, but Mr. Savitz's manuscript explains much of the backstory of what's going on here. Per Leonard's instructions, we've put the entire package on the *Pittsburgh Examiner* website for everyone to see. I encourage your viewers to download and mirror the documents before something happens to our server. Essentially, Sonya, we are being invaded by octopus-like creatures called, uh, Dranthyx. I'm not sure if I'm pronouncing that correctly…"

"Octopus-like creatures? Mr. Peterson, is this a joke?"

"We're very clearly being attacked by a nonhuman military. Do you have a better explanation, Sonya?"

"OK, thank you, Mr. Peterson. We're going now live to—"

"Sonya, I need to say one last thing before you cut me off."

"Make it quick."

"These creatures are invading because they intend to exterminate a large percentage of the human race. Mr. Savitz's notes clearly indicate that is their plan—"

The video feed of Jack Peterson went dead, and the scene cut back to Sonya in the newsroom.

"I apologize to our viewers for that. Sometimes we forget to vet our guests carefully. Let's go live now to…"

"*What the fuck, Sonya, you dumbass!*" Len yelled at the screen.

"Daddy, what's wrong?" Len had woken Octavia up with his screaming.

"We can't stay here," Natalia said. "They're coming out of water. We're too close to Gulf of Mexico."

"You're right, we should find a way to get inland, quickly. Octavia, please get dressed as fast as you can. We need to get going!"

Natalia got on her cell phone and tried to call her contact with the Texas Liberation Army to postpone their meeting, while Len hurriedly threw what little stuff everyone had into Natalia's suitcase and dragged it down the outside steps to the big van. Len could hear Doppler-shifted sirens wailing on the nearby interstate. Several F15s flew overhead toward the water. Thankfully, they were already on the inland side of Houston, and they'd woken up in time to evacuate.

Once everyone was in the car, Len wasted no time peeling out of the parking lot and heading up I-45 toward Oklahoma and the center of the enormous land mass of North America.

28

They made relatively good time until they hit Dallas, at which point the highway became a parking lot with people trying to flee the city. Motorists were panicked, honking their horns and cursing. In the southbound lane, on the other side of the divider, they saw huge military convoys heading toward the coast. Len, Natalia, and Octavia sat in gridlocked traffic for two hours before deciding to take the nearest exit to get off the highway.

"So now what?" Natalia asked as they descended onto desolate Dallas streets.

"I don't know. Do you want to try the local roads?" Len asked.

"I think it will be same thing. Besides, what will we do when we get to border?"

Border. Right. Shit. During Neith's reign of terror, Texas had voted to secede from the union, and the border between it and surrounding states was quickly becoming militarized and impassable. Len hadn't realized how contentious the situation had become until he was on the submarine the day before.

"All I know is," Len said nervously, "if we stay here, we'll die."

"Then we'll take local roads."

Len pulled into a deserted gas station where, happily, the pumps had been left on. While Natalia took Octavia to the bathroom, Len filled the van's tank and went into the station to find a map. He also grabbed several huge packs of water bottles, as much nonperishable food as he could find, some cartons of cigarettes, and some caffeine pills. He looked for alcohol in the coolers, but to his annoyance, he found the store didn't carry any. He took all of the pilfered items out to the van and loaded them into the back. He unfolded the map on the van's hood and motioned for Natalia to come see.

"Take a look at this," Len said. "Everyone is going north, to Oklahoma. I say we go west on these little roads, toward New Mexico. The Dranthyx will probably attack the population centers first, not the little towns. So I think we should go out to the middle of nowhere."

"That is good idea, but then what?" Natalia asked, with atypical unease in her voice.

"I don't know. I have no idea. Maybe if we find a place up in the hills, we can hide out for a few months until the invasion is over."

Natalia exhaled pensively and considered the options.

"Natalia, may I borrow your cell phone?"

"Of course," she said, getting it out of her purse.

Len figured he had stayed off the grid long enough. He dialed some numbers. All circuits were busy. Len dialed again. Same thing. He dialed a third time, and it connected.

"Hello?" The voice at the other end was elderly and female.

"Ma? It's Len. I'm still alive."

"Leonard! It's really you?"

"Yes! It's really me. Don't you recognize my voice?"

"Oh, thank God!" she exclaimed, starting to cry.

"Ma, I'm fine. Octavia is with me and she's OK, too. We're in Texas."

"Oh, thank you, thank you, God! I prayed every night. I knew in my heart you and Octavia weren't dead. I could feel it. They said on the news you'd joined the revolution and died and she'd been kidnapped, but I knew they weren't telling the truth. You can't ever believe what they tell you. Then I saw you on the news this morning and I knew my prayers had been answered."

"Long story, Ma. Look, I just want to say that I love you. I'm sorry if I haven't been the greatest son, OK? Tell my brother that I love him, too."

"I love you, too!" His mother began sobbing even harder. Then, after a pause to collect herself, she said, "Leonard, what's going on? What are these things coming out of the ocean I see on the news?"

"Ma, they're bad news. Don't go outside. Stay safe, OK? I don't know how long we'll be able to talk, so do you want to talk to Octavia?"

"Yes. Yes!"

Len gave the phone to Octavia, who yelled, "Hi, Grandma!" and proceeded to ramble on about the submarine and Salvatierra's house while Len and Natalia tried to figure out what other supplies they should loot from the gas station. When Octavia had said good-bye and gave the phone back,

Natalia made her own emotional phone call in Russian with what Len presumed was one of her family members.

This was it. They were saying their last good-byes. The cull would begin soon.

Once they'd fully stocked up, Len put the van in drive and navigated the city streets. A few blocks in, looters were smashing store windows and pulling drivers from their cars. Len narrowly avoided a Molotov cocktail thrown at the van by gunning it past a pile of burning trash. It looked like word had gotten out that terrible creatures known as the Dranthyx were invading and intended to kill off a quarter of the human race.

Len believed that anyone naïve enough to think the human race had evolved past being howling, shit-chucking monkeys hadn't been to any of their town's planning commission meetings. Human civilization was only about twelve thousand years old, which made it a thin, brittle veneer on four billion years of evolutionary nastiness. Contrary to our comforting delusions of safety and security, he thought, the human capacity for utterly ruthless violence didn't suddenly disappear from our DNA once we figured out indoor plumbing. Len found modern society especially tenuous, with its heavy reliance on technology and services performed by others. In the absence of that assistance, many people would have no idea how to find water or make their own food. Cut off the food, or stop the water from flowing through the pipes, or cease delivering fuel, and civility would evaporate in a matter of hours as everyone downshifted straight into survival mode. The Tchogols might have been killed off, but humans were still animals, and still capable of acting like it under duress.

A lot of close calls later, they were on a local road headed out to the suburbs of Fort Worth. Octavia had fallen asleep on one of the bench seats in the back. After an hour or two of driving through more rural areas, Len's jitters had subsided a bit.

"Are you OK? You've been awfully quiet," he said to Natalia, who was staring out the window at the Texas countryside going by.

"What the hell do I say? One minute I'm doing my thing, and next, octopuses trying to kill us."

Len didn't mean to laugh, but he couldn't help himself. Natalia had a certain kind of blunt eloquence.

"I'm sorry, it's not funny. But yeah, you're right. Hey, I think we're pretty close to Abilene. We should probably find a place to stay for the night before it gets dark."

"We need protection. We are too vulnerable," Natalia said.

"What do you mean?"

"Guns. We need guns. Also, we need to find high ground."

"Where will we find guns?"

"Len, we're in Texas. Guns are everywhere!" Natalia exclaimed, suddenly upbeat. "Leave to me, this is what I do."

Len pulled in to an old motel as it was getting dark. Amazingly, it was open, and there was vacancy. Natalia dropped Len and Octavia off, then took the van and drove off to find weapons.

"Escaping the coast?" asked the greasy, odd-looking man behind the front desk. He seemed a little on edge.

"How'd you guess?" Len asked.

"Don't know if you heard, but they only came inland five miles. They just stopped."

"What? Why?"

"No one knows," the desk clerk said. "Maybe they changed their minds. Damnedest thing. I think it's the Chinese. You can't trust those Commies."

In the room, Len turned on the TV. Almost every channel showed the same thing: a continuous line of purple spheres, following the coastlines and exactly five miles inland. On one side of the line was untouched human civilization; on the other was nothing but blackened debris. There they sat, unmoving. The scene cut to a split screen with two people on a satellite link.

"Have they made any demands, Geoffrey?"

"Nothing. We have no idea what they are, where they came from, or what they want…"

While Geoffrey was speaking, they played a video of the invasion earlier in the day, video footage of an engagement between the military and the Dranthyx orbs. The Dranthyx roasted tanks like marshmallows and incinerated jets midflight. Then a shot from a helicopter over downtown Manhattan. The camera zoomed in on the streets below. Huge purple spheres were rolling down the streets and avenues, crushing cars, blasting buildings with balls of lightning. Then one by one, skyscrapers started collapsing like dominoes in spectacular plumes of dust. Another video cut, this time to Manhattan a few hours later. Flattened. The great city looked like a bed of hot coals, producing enormous columns of smoke stretching toward the stratosphere. Len lit a cigarette and watched the world burn on TV.

Natalia came back a few hours later, bursting through the door like the Kool-Aid Man, stinking of booze and wearing a cowboy hat.

"Welcome back. Find anything?" Len asked.

"Hell yeah," Natalia yelled. "God bless Texas! My kind of place. Come see this!"

Len walked out to the van and swung open the rear doors. To his utter amazement, the entire back of the van was full of weaponry. Natalia had somehow managed to find four assault rifles, three handguns, ten cans of ammo, three Kevlar vests, a grenade launcher, several grenades, and an M60 machine gun.

"Oh yeah, I got pizza too!" she exclaimed. "Mushroom, my favorite."

"Holy cow! This is incredible! Smells like you found some alcohol, too."

"Whole case of Applewood Forge. Now we are ready for anything! How do you say in America? Oh yeah—I don't fuck around." She giggled at the expression and almost lost her balance.

"We can't stay here," she warned, suddenly serious. "Dranthyx won't stay still forever. I met some militia men. Nice guys. They say they read your story and are very excited to meet you. They are headed to compound in…" Natalia unfolded a piece of paper with an address. "Culberson County. Up in hills. They invite us."

Not having a better plan, Len carried sleeping Octavia out to the van, laid her on one of the bench seats, and then loaded the rest of their stuff into the vehicle. Natalia stuffed her face gleefully with some pizza, then curled up on one of the other seats in the back to sleep off the whiskey. Len looked at the map and suddenly realized how enormous Texas was. The van's GPS calculated the destination as being about six hours away. If he made good time, they'd get there by sunrise.

29

Len drove for miles in the moonlight without seeing any other cars or man-made lights. He was exhausted, but caffeine pills and the will to survive kept him going.

As the sun crested the horizon, Len pulled up to what the navigation system indicated was the address. They were on a dirt road about fifty miles west of Pecos. Len got out of the van to take a look around. He could see for miles in every direction. Nothing but sand, sagebrush, and distant hills.

Culberson County was way out in the mountains of Western Texas. It was about twice the size of the state of Delaware, with fewer than three thousand people calling it home. To an Easterner like Len who'd grown up on the narrow, row-house-packed streets of Pittsburgh where he could hear his neighbors farting and fighting over whose turn it was to pay the electric bill, the vast desolation was both breathtaking and terrifying. West Texas was the sort of place where a person's car broke down in the desert heat, they died of dehydration, and no one found the body until months later, after it had been picked clean by vultures.

There was no sign of any militia compound. Natalia had been drinking; maybe someone told her to come out here as a prank. Len sincerely hoped that wasn't the case. He decided to wake her up in the hopes that she'd know something.

"Good morning! Hey, I think we're here, but I don't see it."

"Ugh. I need water."

Natalia chugged a bottle of water. Then, bleary-eyed, she pulled her cell phone out and dialed a contact.

"Hi, it's me, Natalia. We're here." She paused, listening. "OK, we will wait. Bye."

"What'd they say?" Len asked.

"They are coming to get us."

About thirty minutes later, Len saw a cloud of dust on the horizon, a vehicle approaching on the dirt road. As it drew nearer, Len could see that it was an old military jeep with a machine gun mounted on top. Inside were two men wearing desert camouflage and cowboy hats.

"Are you Leonard Savitz?" one of them asked.

"I am."

"I recognize you from your photo. Sir, it's an honor to meet you."

"It is?" Len couldn't help but be suspicious. He couldn't remember the last time anyone over the age of five had been happy to see him.

"Absolutely," said the larger of the men. His face was big, round, and red. His eyes were like two cool blue lakes on Planet Tomato. "My name's Donald Travis. This here's my fellow man-at-arms, Ross Templeton. Follow us. I don't think that van has four-wheel drive. You might want to take her easy."

The dirt road led across a large valley to the side of a mountain, with a smaller but well-traveled dirt road going up the side of it. The road's switchbacks and lack of guard-rails were somewhat terrifying, especially considering that Len hadn't slept in over a day and was not at his sharpest. At the top of the mountain was a large, flat area completely clear of scrub brush and trees, from which rose an enormous layered structure studded with antiaircraft weaponry. It appeared to be ten stories high and easily two acres in area. Next to it was a parking lot that contained at least a hundred different pickup trucks and military vehicles. Len pulled in and parked.

"What is this place?" Len asked the militiamen while stepping down from the vehicle.

"This is the Freehold," Donald said, smiling proudly.

The Freehold was a special sort of ugly, a fortress of brown concrete brutalism. It looked like the kind of swirly monstrosity that one might crap out after eating a Thanksgiving turducken and some laxatives.

"This is our pride and joy," said Ross. "The Texas Defense League began building her thirty years ago with contributions from our members, and, well, here she is."

"Wow, Daddy, is this a castle?" asked Octavia.

"I think it might be!" Len answered, trying to stay positive so she wouldn't be scared. "Do you want to go inside?"

"Yes!"

"Let me get some of the boys to help y'all bring your stuff in...holy smokes, I see you brought your own weapons!"

Donald was practically drooling over Natalia's hoard in the back of the van.

"Yes, I bought from your friends in Abilene," said Natalia, getting out of the van.

The men tipped their hats and couldn't help but stare at her.

"Ma'am," said Ross.

"You must be Natalia." Donald beamed. "You're even prettier than they said you'd be!"

"Thank you," she said coyly, shaking their hands. "This is lovely fortress!" Len struggled to contain a smirk as he watched Natalia charm their bolos off.

Donald gave them the tour. The inside of the Freehold looked like the community center of a megachurch. There was a firehall-type kitchen, classrooms for the kids, a massive chapel, a gym, a TV room—everything you'd need to start your own doomsday cult.

"All eating is communal here. This is the dining hall. Breakfast is at six, dinner is at noon, supper is at five." Donald walked briskly for a man his size. "This wing is where the unmarried men sleep. But you two are married, ain't ya?"

Len and Natalia shot each other glances.

"Yes, of course we're married," Len said, answering before Natalia had a chance to. He'd left out details about himself and didn't mention Natalia at all when he wrote the manuscript they'd all downloaded. What they didn't know wouldn't hurt them.

"Well, good. We'll put you up in one of the family suites on the second floor—one room for Mom and Dad and one for their adorable little girl." He patted Octavia's head.

As Donald turned his back to continue the tour, Natalia shook her head and covered her mouth, trying not to laugh.

After a boring tour of the Freehold's water recapture system, where Len learned that they were drinking each other's distilled piss because of the lack of water in the desert, Donald finally showed them to their family suite. Once Donald had taken his leave of them, Len took note of the crucifix on the wall and the painting of the Aryan-looking Jesus.

"Natalia, I have a feeling they might make us go to church."

"Better than being killed by Dranthyx!"

Len wondered which would be less pleasant, then decided to sleep on it because he'd been up for about thirty hours straight.

He woke up a few hours later around dinner time, which was disorienting. After the communal dinner in the great hall with Natalia and Octavia and everyone else, Octavia went off to play with the other kids living in the Freehold, Natalia went to the computer lab in the basement to get some work done, and Len went outside onto the ramparts to watch the sunset by himself. *People who can entertain themselves are the best company,* Len mused.

The western sky was ablaze with purple and orange. The dry air cooled off quickly, but the ground still radiated the day's heat in a way that Len found pleasant. He was a free man again, after weeks of servitude and captivity. If he could help it, he would die a free man. He lit a cigarette, enjoying the fleeting stillness. He couldn't help but wonder if that's all his life was: fleeting moments of blissful, quiet stillness, like pearls separated by and strung together with the shrill cacophony of life's demands.

As if on cue, a rather obese fellow came waddling over to Len and bellowed, "Hey, come on inside, it's happening!"

"What's happening?"

"They're moving! The Dranthyx are beginning their assault!"

Len stubbed his cigarette out and followed the man to the TV lounge, where everyone had gathered. On the screen, the purple orbs had indeed begun moving again. They were pushing inland in a line, but this time without shooting. The video feed cut to a different helicopter, this one flying over a beach somewhere in the daylight. A different time zone. The text at the bottom was in Korean. From the water came other objects that were similar in color but not in shape. An enormous flat one rose out of the waves and kept rising into the sky, followed by what appeared to be hundreds of others like it. Compared to the objects they moved past, they appeared to be over a thousand feet in length. Slowly, ominously, and casting long shadows, they moved toward the shore.

There were easily fifty people crowded around the TV set. They sat wide-eyed, terrified, utterly silent.

The camera swung around to the horizon. Rockets burst from the surface of the ocean and propelled themselves into the sky. The camera followed one until it became too small to see, and it reminded Len of one of the old space shuttle launches. Another rocket came out of the ocean, then another. Then the TV went dead. Black. Someone got up to check the cables and the satellite dish. The problem couldn't be fixed.

Len ran outside to see it for himself. From the Freehold, perched on top of a mountain in the clear desert night air, he could see for an eternity. On the horizon, looking east and west, he saw little white lights slowly ascending into the night sky like distant meteors moving in the wrong direction. They pulsed and arced against the spin of the earth. Then, at certain altitudes, they twinkled in the sky and disappeared.

In the span of exactly ten minutes, the Dranthyx had taken global communication back to the shortwave-radio era as rockets destroyed thousands of man-made satellites. Simultaneously, worldwide Internet connectivity came to an abrupt, undignified end as hundreds of transoceanic fiber-optic lines were severed deep below the surface. North America and every other continent were now data islands incapable of working together to repel the attack. Even the most basic of military hardware would no longer work without the aid of GPS satellites.

The militia called a meeting in the main auditorium. Over five hundred men and women were present.

"Brothers and sisters of Sacred Texas," Donald said gravely into the microphone at the podium, "the Great Tribulation has begun."

The crowd murmured anxiously. Some bowed their heads and quoted Scripture.

Donald continued, "Now, it is by no small coincidence that the very man who prophesized to the world that the End Times were upon us, and that Satan himself would come from the ocean, is here with us tonight. There are no coincidences in the kingdom of God, are there?"

People emphatically said no and shook their heads.

"Leonard Savitz, would you please stand up?"

Len, suddenly self-conscious, rose hesitantly. The assembly began clapping.

"Leonard, we are truly grateful that our Lord Jesus Christ has sent you here. His light shines through you. Please come up here and tell us what you have been sent here to tell us."

Len hated public speaking. Hated it. Further, Len had grown up Jewish but was an ex-Zen-Buddhist-turned-agnostic, about the furthest thing imaginable from being a Christian fundamentalist. He had no idea what to say to these people, especially considering they were already grossly misinterpreting what was happening. Len walked down to the pulpit and adjusted the microphone.

"Thank you, Donald. Folks, I'm not sure what to say, and I've never been good at public speaking. There's a reason I went into print journalism instead of television or radio."

Some people actually chuckled at that, which Len didn't expect, given the circumstances. The crowd was looking at him with the doe eyes that groupies gave a rock star. These people thought he was important. In a way, it emboldened him to keep going, even if he had to say things they wouldn't want to hear.

"I heard the word 'prophesized,' but I assure you, I'm not a prophet. I'm human like the rest of you. I just happened to learn the fate of humanity by being in the right place at the right time."

"Sir, you were chosen!" someone yelled from the back. The people in the audience nodded their heads in agreement.

Chosen, right. There's no reasoning with true believers. Len figured he'd better get to the heart of the matter.

"Look, folks, here's what I know. These objects you saw coming out of the ocean on TV? They are the advance landing force of a terrible race of beings who call themselves the Dranthyx. They live in the oceans and they are descended from..." Len stopped himself, deciding not to bring up evolution. "Well, they look like octopuses. But they can also disguise themselves to look like humans. They walk among us."

"Second Corinthians eleven fourteen!" a woman shrieked.

"I'm sorry, I don't know what that means. Anyway, here's the deal," Len continued. "These Dranthyx run the world. They control our governments and our financial institutions, and they claim ownership of the human race. They have no conscience, no ethics. They are about as evil as you can imagine. The flu that went around not too long ago killed off all their human helpers..."

"The White Horse!" "Pestilence!"

Len was getting kind of annoyed at all the inane interruptions.

"As I was saying, the Dranthyx are here because they intend to kill off billions of people to maintain control of the human race. They will probably attack the big cities first, then the smaller towns. I imagine they will come here to the Freehold eventually. We can try to fight them, but I warn you, they have extremely advanced technology, and fighting them may be counterproductive."

A young man yelled, "Blessed be the Lord, my rock, who trains my hands for war, and my fingers for battle!" The crowd cheered.

"Well, I think that's all I have," Len said, giving up. "Thank you."

The room burst into applause as though Len were some great orator. They hadn't heard a word he'd said. Len walked back to his seat, palms cold and wet. Donald got back up and took the podium.

"Thank you, Leonard. You are indeed a blessing to us."

Dammit, Donald, Len thought to himself, *I'm no blessing and you're going to die.*

"Folks, we've been rehearsing our battle plans for weeks now," Donald said, his huge red face glistening under the stage lights. "We'd been expecting the Yankees to invade our nascent republic, but it appears we'll be dealing with something even more sinister. As we have seen from the television news, the Tribulation is now upon us. As promised in Revelations, the devil himself has come up from the depths of the abyss." Donald paused, looking around the room. Then he exploded, "But we will not go down without a fight, will we?"

"No, sir!" several people yelled.

"No, we will not! We will fight to the last man! The devil may have unimaginable magic, but we have something even better: the grace of the Almighty!"

Len couldn't help but notice that Donald had a gift for addressing an audience.

"Hallelujah!"

"And now to the nitty-gritty. Our twenty-four-hour watch starts now. We will add an additional mealtime at midnight for those on the night shift…"

Len got up and slinked out while Donald was speaking. With the entire community at the meeting, it was a good time to sneak Natalia's case of bourbon into the Freehold so he could drink away the stupid.

After the booze had been snuck in and the meeting had let out, Len found out he'd been assigned to night duty on the East Wall. Basically that meant that he had to sit there with binoculars and a rifle between dusk and dawn, waiting for something to happen.

Nothing happened. At least, not at first. Len did the night watch for a week without seeing anything but stars and distant headlights once in a while. After that he was rotated to day shift for another week. Once the Dranthyx took out global communication, news from the outside world became scarce. There were no local TV stations within broadcast range of the compound, so the occupants had to rely entirely on radio to find out what was going on. The Freehold had a radio room in the basement where a round, ponytailed man sat and scanned a multitude of frequencies for news from the outside. The news came quickly, even though the Dranthyx seemed to be taking their time. From Australia, a ham operator told of the Dranthyx going door to door, testing the genetics of all the occupants, leaving some people while taking others away to an unknown location where they weren't heard from again.

The way the residents of the Freehold regarded Len made him uneasy. They looked at him with a sort of unsophisticated obsequiousness. Undue admiration, that's what it was. They honestly and truly believed Len was a prophet. Whenever Len tried to explain otherwise, they complimented him on his divine humility.

Sometimes, while he sat out on the wall with time to think, Len would wonder: what if there really was a God who had chosen him? Over and over again, he'd catch his psyche flattering itself with these little flights of egotism. Repeatedly, he'd patiently remind himself that his presence at the Freehold was simply a product of circumstance.

Or was it?

30

Some years ago, there was a spoiled-rotten trust-fund baby whom we will call Sid. Sid's mother had died when he was quite young, and he was raised from that tender age by his overprotective father. Sid's father was stupid wealthy, lived in a huge mansion, and could afford to buy all kinds of fancy stuff and hire like a million servants. Sid's father wanted only the best for his son and did his best to shelter precious little Sid from the harsh realities outside the mansion walls.

Sid, however, had a redeeming quality that kept him from becoming decadent and lazy: an inability to believe bullshit. No one quite knows where he got that trait, given his materialistic, narcissistic father, but he had it. Over the years, Sid began to grow increasingly suspicious that his father was keeping him away from something. At twenty-nine years of age, Sid pulled off his very first act of rebellion: he snuck out of his dad's house one night.

Sid's father was a very well-known rich guy in the area, and to avoid being spotted, Sid had to go out in disguise. Wandering through town incognito, Sid saw certain things for the first time that his father had taken great pains to hide: an old man, a sick man, and a dead man. Sid's underwear twisted into a bunch at the sight of these things, because for the first time in his life, he realized that everything sucks.

Against his father's wishes, Sid left the mansion to backpack through the land. He wanted to find himself, and maybe also discover why the real world sucks so much. Sid hooked up with a yoga teacher who was laying down some groovy philosophy, stuff he had never heard before that really made him think. But after a while, he realized that this so-called yogi wasn't so great. The dude had all kinds of interesting questions but no answers. So Sid found another teacher. Same thing. Then another teacher. Again, no answers.

After several years of this nonsense, Sid said screw it and wandered off into the woods to figure shit out for himself. He decided to do something crazy: he'd stop eating. Sid was testing a hypothesis, that the root of suffering was attachment to needful things, and that suffering couldn't end suffering unless the attachment ended.

One day, after a few months of fasting, Sid was bathing in a river when he collapsed. His body had grown so weak from malnutrition that he was no longer able to hold himself upright. There, under the surface, with water in his lungs, he realized how wrong he'd been. Memories came like a freight train, the way memories do when the mind thinks the end is near. One of these was vivid as day and changed his path forever.

River water has the answers. Had Sid pulled a glass of water out of the powerful Ganges, it would have been brown with mud due to the water's constant movement and agitation. However, if he'd taken that same glass of water and let it sit undisturbed on the counter for a day or two, the mud would have settled to the bottom and the water would have become clear.

As a young boy, Sid remembered sitting under a tree on a beautiful spring day while watching his father do some gardening. As he sat there, at peace, watching his dad work, his mind spontaneously became clear and free of thoughts like the glass of undisturbed Ganges water. Waves of ecstasy and joy rippled through his body. A feeling of bliss and limitless possibilities.

In the nick of time, one of his friends pulled Sid out of the river before he drowned. Lying there on the riverbank, coming back to consciousness while his friends tried to pump the water out of his lungs, Sid had a thought: starvation and austerity were just a pointless backlash against his pampered upbringing. Sort of a screw you, Dad. They wouldn't get him anywhere but dead. If he wanted any real understanding, he'd have to explore more of that weird, magical feeling he'd had as a child.

So that's what Sid did. He picked a big tree and resolved to sit under it until he became awakened. Sid sat there under that tree for weeks without moving. In the process, he became an inspiration to others, who would bring him food and water. That state of rapture he'd experienced as a child came back to him. He went into it fully, and it became more subtle and more quiet. The water became clearer than ever.

Then, at the end of the seventh week, at the age of thirty-five, it happened: Sid finally *woke the fuck up*. Like he'd gotten a vision from on high, he figured out why life sucks: everything is constantly changing. Seriously, that's it. That's the reason. Everything is constantly changing and we're always wishing it wasn't. Your favorite TV show gets canceled, an earthquake destroys your house, your best friend moves to Milwaukee for a job. And the worst part of all this impermanence, he discovered, is our mortality: we get old, we get sick, we die—and we hate it all because we want to stay twenty forever.

Sid saw that the way to end suffering was to not cling to false notions of permanence, because nothing can be permanent. Just gotta accept the change, man. Sid came up with a whole system of living that would help wayward souls end their torment. Sid traveled all over the place, preaching his new philosophy. He acquired thousands of followers. He became a guru, a celebrity. Sid, whose full name was Siddhārtha Gautama, acquired a new nickname in the process: the Buddha, meaning the fully awakened one.

Twenty-four hundred years later, a miserable twenty-two-year-old Leonard Savitz came to the door of a Japanese monastery, hoping for the same sort of amazing revelation. He'd been to five monasteries before, all of which had turned him away. This one, however, accepted him.

The head teacher of the monastery, Dukkha Roshi, was a gregarious sort who took him in and made him tea. Dukkha had an easy smile and glitter in his voice that made people feel welcome. He listened intently to Len's story about his father dying, as though nothing else mattered more. Len was comforted by the fact that Dukkha Roshi seemed to care. Dukkha took him in and allowed him to practice with the rest of the monks as a layperson, which was quite unusual in Japan.

At first, Dukkha Roshi was a good teacher who seemed to really understand the practice. However, as the months went on in the monastery, Len began to notice that he was a bit odd. Dukkha Roshi was always talking about himself, wistfully or with gravitas, as though recounting stories of his deeds were for the benefit of all who heard. Dukkha Roshi had a talent for describing his own actions as though they were weighty enough to change the course of human events. It was subtle. His salesmanship was rarely overt or theatrical, but it was delivered as though he were a great martyr-messiah come to save everyone all from themselves. That very subtext pervaded everything in the monastery: Dukkha Roshi was a Very Important Person.

And being that this was Japan, where complaisance to authority was considered a virtue, Dukkha Roshi wore the doting and deference his students heaped upon him like a crown. The young monks didn't know any better; anyone who spoke so highly of themselves in a culture that encouraged humility must be a spiritual luminary, right? Clearly, this great teacher would show them the way to enlightenment.

Len had heard stories of other *roshis*, great teachers, who were so humble that they cleaned toilets in the monastery or gave away their last bits of food to hungry travelers. Dukkha Roshi was nothing like that. He didn't do any menial labor, he didn't sacrifice anything. Instead, Dukkha Roshi felt that it was the job of others to labor and bestow gifts upon him. He was, after all, a beacon of light unto them.

Dukkha Roshi had exceedingly specific rituals that everyone was expected to follow in order to honor him. Before he entered a room, everything was to have been laboriously prepared for him exactly the way he liked it. The cushions and teapots had to be aligned perfectly. He had a golden teacup that had to be placed in a very specific location on a certain meal board. If everything wasn't done exactly the right way, he'd berate whoever had arranged it. There were other odd behaviors, too. What Dukkha Roshi told a student, the student was expected to keep secret. What a student told Dukkha Roshi in confidence, however, frequently made its way around the monastery. Dukkha Roshi didn't believe in secrets unless they were his own.

Dukkha Roshi was wonderful at ingratiating newcomers, but he seemed to have trouble retaining students who had been there for a while. In fact, people cycled through the monastery as if it were a revolving door. The fallings-out he had with students were spectacular and emotionally explosive at times. To maintain morale and avoid dissent in the monastery, Dukkha Roshi would completely cut off any student who voiced objection to his teaching methods, and he would further require that the entire community cease all contact with the offending party. In essence, any monk who dared to question Dukkha Roshi was summarily excommunicated.

Len watched all of this with hesitation during his time in the monastery. He knew Dukkha Roshi was a bit of a control freak, so Len avoided stepping on his toes and, when necessary, played the dumb foreigner to avoid conflict. However, it was impossible to avoid confrontation with the passive-aggressive.

Around Len's second year as a lay practitioner living in the monastery, Dukkha Roshi offered to formally ordain Len into the Zen clergy. Len would finally become a real Buddhist monk. Len was thrilled at the invitation and gladly accepted. However, on the day on which his initiation ceremony was to be held, Dukkha Roshi said in front of everyone that he'd changed his mind about the ceremony. "People just aren't ready," Dukkha Roshi said cryptically before calling the whole thing off.

The rejection stung. Len spent several weeks in a deep funk, wondering what went wrong. What happened? Who wasn't ready? Len? Dukkha Roshi? The other monks? Len wondered if it had been some kind of test, or if Dukkha Roshi was trying to teach him something obliquely. Was Len clinging to the idea of monkhood? Was his meditation not good enough? Perhaps Dukka Roshi was trying to show him that he was attached to something.

Len got over it eventually, and life went on in the temple. Len helped cook meals, he worked in the garden, he sorted the recycling. During Len's third year in the temple, Dukkha Roshi again offered to induct him into the priesthood. Len again accepted, happy that he, or whoever, was now ready. Len again spent several nights studying the scriptures, preparing for the ceremony.

Right before the ceremony, the same thing happened. Again, Dukkha Roshi said, "People just aren't ready." Len's heart sank as he began to wonder why students who hadn't been there as long as he had were being ordained, while he'd been rejected twice at the last minute. Was it because he was Western or Caucasian? Was there something he was not understanding or hadn't learned?

The third time it happened, in his fourth year, Len just gave up on his hopes of being a monk. Dukkha Roshi was clearly playing some sort of game with him. At that point, Len had been in the monastery long enough to notice that Dukkha Roshi manipulated others, too. He was constantly lulling people into a false sense of security, then pulling the rug out from under them. Len began to wonder whether it was a teaching device or if Dukkha Roshi was just sadistic. The weird thing was, on the rare occasions when someone inadvertently changed plans on Dukkha Roshi—the way he delighted in doing others—Dukkha Roshi would throw a hissy fit.

The fourth time led to an insight. At the end of Len's fifth year in the monastery, Dukkha Roshi again invited Len to be ordained. It was the fourth such invitation in as many years. This time, Len had had enough of his shit and let the old man have it. He called Dukkha Roshi out publicly, in front of several other students, saying he was catty and malicious, that there was no wisdom, compassion, or teaching behind his actions, and that he simply enjoyed causing emotional distress in his students.

Needless to say, it didn't go over well. One of Len's longtime friends in the temple escorted him to the door with his scant possessions in an old suitcase. Len stepped outside into the daylight. He was homeless on the streets of Japan, and for some reason, he had never felt freer.

Once his visa finally expired, Len returned to the States. Upon doing some research, he found there was an established pattern of abuse by Zen teachers, involving sex scandals and misappropriation of funds. It seemed there was a significant number of Zen masters who had problems with alcohol and drug additions, and who were abusive or compulsive manipulators. In short, Zen Buddhism was full of assholes, like any other religion. Len wrote a story about his experience and the misadventures of others in the Zen world, which was picked up by a prominent magazine. It was his first real piece of journalism, the one that got him through the door and eventually caught Jack's eye at the *Pittsburgh Examiner*.

The wrenching dissonance was that Len had found truth and meaning in the meditation practice. Learning to still his mind and examine his own thinking was life changing for him. Len never found the alleged end of suffering, but he felt his insights had opened him up to profound growth as a human being. However, there were problems, politics, and big egos in Buddhism that were marring and overshadowing the original message.

Len's experience with Dukkha Roshi had also shown him the dangers of being in a position of power and admiration. If enough people kissed your butt on a daily basis, you started to think your shit smelled good. You'd believe it smelled so good, in fact, that you'd be struck with the urge to rub it in others' faces so they could enjoy it too. Dukkha Roshi had been doing meditation for over forty years, and despite all that supposed practice at examining his own ego, he was still unable to acknowledge or check his self-centeredness and megalomania. Perhaps the limitation was genetic, Len thought. Dukka Roshi certainly behaved like a narcissist. In any case, finding himself in a similar position of reverence fifteen years later at the Freehold, Len did his best to constantly remind himself he wasn't special.

Dukkha Roshi's provocations *were* a test, Len realized, only the test had nothing to do with him, Buddhism, or enlightenment. Dukkha Roshi was probably a Tchogol, and he'd been testing Len for subservience. It was simply inborn behavior. A cat doesn't consciously think, "I need to bury this piece of shit in the sand." It just does it because that's what its DNA has programmed it to do. Tchogols were programmed to recruit Saskels as followers but to weed out Xreths. The reason was simple: Saskels would put up with abuse from authority and would carry out the most heinous of orders, but an Xreth wouldn't do either.

In the beginning, Len thought, Buddhism really was about ending delusion, just as the founders of the United States honestly sought to end tyranny. In the end, however, both institutions caused even more of what they were originally trying to prevent. Sitting out there on the ramparts of the Freehold in the desert air, processing all of this, Len began to appreciate the genius of Neith's flu. Before the flu, it was inevitable that an institution would drift away from its guiding principles, because any organization with a vertical power structure would become infested with smooth, cold-blooded people at the top and thoughtless bootlickers at the bottom. Religion, government, corporations: it was all the same thing. Any human attempt to make the world a better place was subverted by the Dranthyx's Tchogol-Saskel control paradigm. The human race's entire pre-flu history had been screwed by design.

31

Seventeen days after Len, Natalia, and Octavia had arrived at the compound, news came in over the CB radio that the Dranthyx had just crossed the border in Carlsbad, New Mexico. A crowd gathered around the transceiver, shouting questions over one another about what was going on. A trucker who had been detained and then released by the Dranthyx explained the situation over the radio. From listening to conversation, Len gathered that the Dranthyx's ruinous landing campaign had been mostly for shock-and-awe purposes. Once worldwide television communication had been disrupted, the creatures proceeded inland in a very orderly manner, careful to avoid destroying any more infrastructure. The trucker told them that the highways and airports were still functioning and described tall, well-armed octopus men going door to door, rounding people up. The Dranthyx tested the genetics of each person they captured, then used a laser device to tattoo the results on everyone's necks and wrists.

"The mark of the beast!" someone shouted. Fear was thicker than static in the little radio room. *This isn't good,* Len thought. Anytime the Freehold had a conversation over the radio, they were giving the Dranthyx the opportunity to triangulate the signal and discover their location.

The trucker went on to relate how several citizen groups had tried taking an armed stand against the Dranthyx but were completely obliterated in a matter of minutes.

"Well, ladies and gentlemen," Donald said, standing sweatily over the radio equipment, "this is it. They're across the border in Carlsbad. They'll be here within twenty-four hours. We need every available man at his post and ready for battle."

Men grabbed their rifles and headed up to the ramparts.

"Please come with us," a bonnet-wearing woman said softly to Natalia.

"What do you mean?"

"Women and children must go below ground, to the bunker. These are our battle plans."

"I don't want to hide," Natalia said in disgust. "I want to fight!"

Donald and the bonnet lady were taken aback, but Len could tell Donald admired Natalia's pluck.

"Do you have any military experience?" Donald asked incredulously.

"Of course! I serve in Russian army for five years. I was in second Chechen war!"

"And you know how to use our American weapons?" Donald asked.

"I don't think you know who you're talking to," Len snickered.

Donald shrugged and handed Natalia an AR-15.

"I didn't know you were in the army," Len said as they left the room.

"My father made me and brothers join. He didn't want us to be soft rich kids. Also, how can you sell military weapons with no military experience? You take this rifle. I have better guns in van."

Len made sure Octavia got down to the bunker. There, at the door, he hugged her one last time.

"Daddy. Why are you scared?"

Len couldn't hide emotions from her sometimes. For her age, she had a remarkable talent for reading people. "Well, we're about to get in a big fight with the bad guys. I don't know how it will end. But you stay down here with the other kids, OK?"

"Daddy, don't worry. I know you'll win. Fight hard, OK?"

"OK."

Len sighed, hugged her again, and watched as one of the bonneted ladies shooed her into the bunker, then closed its vault-like door. Len put on his body armor and headed up to the wall.

The Freehold appeared terraced like an old Mayan pyramid, but really there was only one long terrace that swirled as a continuous ramp, like the inside of the Guggenheim Museum. The terrace, the huge circular ramp, was bounded on the outside by a short concrete wall about four feet high and a foot thick to provide cover in firefights. The short wall had balistrariae at regular intervals so people could lie down and stick firearms through, which is what Len did.

Natalia came up a few minutes later, with three guys helping her carry her arsenal, and set up shop about five feet from Len. It was noon and the desert sun was beating down. Len lit two smokes and handed one to Natalia as she fed an ammo belt into the M60.

Len looked around at the people who would be dying with him today. Some as young as seventeen, some as old as seventy. *So this is what the Alamo felt like.*

The quiet was interrupted by several people shouting excitedly. Len stood up to see what they were going on about. From the Freehold's mountaintop, it was possible to see north, south, and east for fifty miles until distant atmospheric haze limited the view. The view to the west was obscured by other mountains.

Len had expected to sit around waiting all day, but the Dranthyx began their advance before Len even had a chance to finish his cigarette. The floating ones appeared on the northern horizon first. They were huge, flat purple objects the size of aircraft carriers, like the ones Len had seen on TV right before the satellite attack. They moved slowly but in a beeline for the Freehold.

"Hold your fire until they get closer!" someone shouted from one of the Freehold's spotting towers.

This was a suicide stand, Len thought to himself. The Dranthyx had already run roughshod over the world's most developed militaries. Yet here they were, sitting on a pile of concrete in the open desert with crude projectile weapons, hoping for what, exactly? The Freehold was run by religious zealots who believed in an afterlife, and who were convinced that they were about to fight the good fight against Satan. The outcome of this battle didn't matter to them—they were fighting on principle. Len wasn't afraid to die himself, but he was terrified of his daughter not having a chance to live her life.

Well, what was the alternative? Surrender? The Dranthyx would round them up and kill them all anyway. Even if the Dranthyx let the Freeholders go, as they had the trucker on the CB radio, they'd go on living the rest of their lives in abject slavery. The choice became clear. Fighting meant certain death, whereas surrender would equal certain servitude.

"Fuck it," Len said under his breath. "Time to make a stand."

The Dranthyx continued pushing forward like a steam-roller. Len's hands were sweating all over his rifle. When they were about ten miles away, Len could see them more clearly despite the rising waves of heat rippling the air. Underneath the large flying ships rolled about a hundred of the balls that shot electricity. It seemed the Dranthyx had taken the time to plan this. They knew the Freehold wasn't a soft target.

Two miles from the Freehold, they stopped. The airships hung there, purple and glistening like beached whales.

"Ha! They just told us to surrender over the radio!" said a wild-eyed man with a walkie-talkie farther down the wall.

"What was our reply?" Len asked.

"Donald just told them to go f—well, I won't repeat it in mixed company." He glanced at Natalia. "He said no way."

Just then, a bolt of lightning blasted out of one of the roll-ing orbs and slammed into one of the Freehold's spotting tow-ers. The tower was instantly pulverized and rained debris down onto the ramparts below.

"Let's let 'em have it!" someone yelled.

From somewhere in the Freehold, a battery of missiles let go and roared off toward the Dranthyx aircraft. The missiles made it about half the distance to the ship, then just dropped out of the air as though they'd run out of gas. They fell to the base of the mountain with audible thuds and without exploding, neutered somehow by superior technology. Len's heart fell with the missiles.

The large floating aircrafts set down on the desert floor as the small round ones resumed their advance up the side of the mountain. People all along the ramparts began shooting at the Dranthyx vehicles, making a sound like two hundred bags of popcorn had been stuffed into a gigantic microwave.

Len took a few shots at the rollers, then stopped in dread when he saw what was happening through his rifle scope. From doors underneath the fliers came hundreds, maybe thousands of Dranthyx ground troops. They filed out and ran toward the Freehold, carrying weapons.

The rollers advancing up the side of the mountain fired their blue lightning balls, pounding the Freehold. A hole was smashed into the wall farther down from Len, and he watched, pulse pounding in his head, as limp bodies tumbled from the hole and rolled down the side of the mountain.

As if God were a twelve-year-old boy using a lighter to burn the faces off his G.I. Joes and then laughing at their misery, the horror of the firefight was interrupted by something even more disturbing. Everyone was so caught up in the battle that they didn't see it coming: an enormous passenger jet, somehow off course and its engine smoking, came roaring out of the blue sky. It passed directly over the freehold at six hundred miles per hour, barreling directly toward the Dranthyx lines. Clear as day, Len saw this errant aircraft collide with one of the Dranthyx airships, blowing a huge hole into it. *Boom.*

What the hell had just happened? Where had the airplane come from? Len struggled to get a better view through his scope. The Dranthyx flier was burning, octopuses were running out of it. While he was straining to get a better view, and trying to snipe the escaping Dranthyx, a ball of electricity blasted a nearby tower. The concussion of the blast knocked Len to the floor.

––––––––

Len suddenly felt clearheaded despite things exploding around him and the Dranthyx advancing up the side of the mountain. He was now sitting right where the destroyed tower used to be. He looked down and, to his amazement, saw a man dressed just the way he was, lying there on the rampart behind the wall. The man, who was facedown on the concrete, was even built the way Len was. The man's rifle lay next to his body. Odd, it looked just like the rifle Donald had given him. A few feet away from the prostrate man was a black-haired woman with a machine gun. She looked over, saw the body of the man on the ground, and screamed a terrible scream. She fired her big gun with rage now, *babada-babada-babada*. Her eyes were angry and afraid.

Wait…what the fuck was going on here?

Len observed silently, unable to interfere as the Dranthyx infantry overran the walls of the Freehold. They were tall and disgusting looking, wearing shiny black uniforms and carrying weapons that looked like big tuning forks pulsing with tiny blue lights. Natalia picked up a rifle and aimed it at one of the Dranthyx. Before she could get off a shot, the Dranthyx fired its own weapon at her, and Natalia collapsed into a heap. Len wanted to cry out but had no mouth.

Hundreds of Dranthyx climbed into the Freehold through the holes they'd punched in the wall. One of them flipped the man's limp body over, presumably to check it for vitals. Len saw his own face from above. Eyes closed. Middle-aged. Tired.

The creature pricked Len's body's pinky with an odd device. A small drop of blood came out of his finger. The Dranthyx then used the same device to suck the blood up. After a second, a small glowing screen on the machine displayed unusual symbols Len couldn't read. The octopus lifted Len's head up and put the device on the back of his neck. Len's body twitched. Then the creature put the contraption on the underside of Len's wrist and pressed another button.

Is this how it ends? Len wondered. *Is this what the afterlife is like, the misery of seeing our former bodies being abused and helplessly watching while people we care for succumb in misery?*

As though he'd blinked and missed something, Len found himself back on the ground, looking up at the foul creature through his own eyes. The hideous beast smelled like the Dumpster behind a sushi restaurant, and the device it was using on his wrist was causing a searing pain. The Dranthyx was pre-occupied with the testing equipment and hadn't noticed that Len had regained consciousness. Without moving his head, Len looked over and saw a twisted shard of rebar lying on the floor among the debris. As fast as he could, Len grabbed the sharp piece of metal and jammed it into the creature's eye. Another Dranthyx nearby saw this and ran over. Len scrambled over to his rifle, but the second Dranthyx grabbed it with powerful tentacles and ripped it out of Len's hands. Then the creature shot Len with the same kind of dart that Natalia had been shot with.

32

Fuzzy. Lights. Noise. Rocking back and forth. Talking. Air, breeze.

Looking around, Len made out the vague shapes of people. He heard nervous chatter and babies crying. Wherever he was, it was crowded. Over the din, he heard the rhythmic clacking of wheels on rails. Len was on a train.

As his vision returned, he saw that he was on the dirty floor of a livestock car that was packed with people. Two of the people he recognized from the Freehold, but most of them he'd never seen before. Then, panic.

"Octavia! Natalia!"

Len struggled to get up, unable to control his muscles.

"It's OK. Just relax," a man answered. "They drugged you. It'll wear off in a few hours."

"Where are Octavia and Natalia?"

"I don't know who you're talking about. They're probably somewhere on this train."

"Who are you? Where are we?"

"My name is Miguel. They loaded us onto this train in El Paso."

Len looked him over. Miguel was a Latino-looking guy with a border accent and large, sympathetic eyes.

"Where are they taking us?"

"North somewhere. Colorado, maybe."

Len's arm and neck hurt. As he looked down, he noticed a bizarre design on his wrist right where you'd take someone's pulse. Dots and bars with a big X in the middle. Len tried to rub it off only to find out that it wasn't removable. It was either a tattoo or he was hallucinating from the drugs.

"What the hell is this?" he asked Miguel.

"A tattoo, I think. We all have them. They took everyone in my town, lined us up, tested us, and zapped us with some laser thingy that leaves these marks. Everyone got either an X or an S. Those fucking octopuses can scan the tattoos with a bar-code reader. Anyone who refused was drugged. I guess that's what happened to you?"

"Something like that."

"Before you woke up, we were just saying that everyone on this train has an X. The octopuses let the S people stay home. I don't know what they want with us, man."

Len's head was fuzzy, but he knew damn well what it meant. After a long pause, Miguel asked, "What's your name?"

"Leonard Savitz."

"Where you from?"

"Pittsburgh."

"Pittsburgh? You're a long way from home, *vato*!"

"Yeah. Look, my daughter and my friend were with me when I was taken. Maybe you saw them get on the train?"

"I dunno, man. There was a whole mess of people at the station."

"My friend is Russian. She's about five-foot-eight. Blue eyes, black hair."

"I didn't see no one like that. But like I said, there were like a million people at the station, *ese*. They made us all get on the trains at the same time and it was a damn zoo."

"My daughter is five. Blond curly hair, big eyes, about this tall." Len held his hand up.

"I'm sorry, man. I didn't see her, either. There were a lot of kids."

Len looked out through the slats of the rail car at the blurry desert going by. So this is what it felt like, he thought to himself, eyes watering.

33

Len's grandfather, Jerzy Savitz, was only twenty years old in 1939. At the time, he was still living at home while apprenticing as a watchmaker at a small jewelry store in Krakow. Jerzy had a rare mechanical genius, an ability to fix anything and a vision for seeing how things could fit together. Things weren't good in Poland at the time; the depression had hit his city especially hard. Despite that, Jerzy was beginning to feel like everything in his life was starting to snap into place. Not only did he have a job, but it was one he liked. He and his fiancée, Katarzyna, were planning to get married in the coming year. Jerzy and Katarzyna had been high school sweethearts. Katarzyna was nineteen, a shy, artistic kid with an ethereal glow about her.

The situation in Jerzy's hometown had become tense, hysterical, and superpartisan over the last few years. His once-peaceful country was being squeezed like an apple in a vice: Nazis on one side, Soviets on the other, both looking to carve Poland up like a Christmas ham. Jerzy remembered people getting into fistfights and arguments in Market Square over whether the country should try to placate the Nazis or stand and fight. Jerzy and his family weren't political, but that was no longer an option under the threat of invasion.

Overpopulated Germany wanted new territory. *Lebensraum*, they called it: space to spread their legs and let their balls hang out onto their neighbors' foreheads. Jerzy didn't know what the Russian word was. He didn't speak Russian, but he figured those knuckle draggers hadn't really bothered to come up with a pretense anyway. All he knew was that he had to get out of Poland. Jerzy had cousins in a faraway city called Pittsburgh, and they had promised to get him a high-paying job at one of the local steel mills should he come to live with them. Jerzy didn't know much about Pittsburgh or the United States. All he knew was that anything was safer than staying in Krakow.

Jerzy had spent a lot of time reading about the Nazis, and he tried to educate his family on the danger they'd face if they stayed.

"First you want to marry a Gentile, now you want to run away!" Jerzy's father shouted at him one night, red-faced from vodka. "I was born in this house! So were you! This is home. Where would we go? Where is your head, Jerzy?"

Jerzy didn't want to leave his folks behind, but with the head of the family being so unreasonable, he was worried that he and his fiancée would have to go it alone. The problem was that international travel was quite expensive at the time, and Jerzy wasn't making much as a jeweler's assistant. Getting Katarzyna and himself to Pittsburgh would cost a fortune, and he couldn't do it without his dad's help.

Once September rolled around, it was too late to go anywhere. The Germans cut through the Polish resistance like it was cream cheese. Then, sixteen days later, the Soviets came from the east and pulverized anything that the Germans hadn't. A million Poles died in a month. It only went downhill from there.

There was a knock on the door one night. Jerzy's father, half asleep, opened the door to about ten German soldiers in black uniforms. The men took one look at the Mezuzah on the door and barged in. Jerzy had been sleeping upstairs in a room he shared with his brothers when he heard his mother screaming downstairs. Jerzy ran to see what the trouble was but was immediately knocked to the floor by one of the Schutzstaffel, the rest of whom pointed their guns at him.

"Please don't kill him!" his mother pleaded, as one of the Germans held her arms behind her back.

The Nazis pulled everyone out of their beds and forced them outside in the cold night air. The Savitz family wasn't alone out in the street. Their mostly Jewish neighbors also shivered and stared blankly as armed German teenagers looted their houses and stole everything they and their ancestors had ever worked for. Jerzy watched helplessly as the Germans carried away heirloom jewelry and furniture.

In a matter of days, the Nazis had walled off the streets connecting the Savitz family's neighborhood with the rest of the city, and shot anyone they found trying to escape. They severed the telephone lines and confiscated radios. Travel in or out of the neighborhood became impossible. Food became scarce. Jerzy was no longer able to see Katarzyna, whose family lived on the other side of the wall. The Savitz family's neighborhood was now an urban prison.

"I should have listened to you, Jerzy," his father wept at the kitchen table. *Yeah, no shit,* Jerzy thought to himself. Seeing his once-proud father, the face of authority over his short twenty years, have an emotional breakdown gave him the resolve he needed to do something crazy.

"Ma, can you sew uniforms like the Germans wear?"

"Jerzy," his mother said, elongating his name hesitantly, "what are you planning?"

"The neighbor kid got shot trying to climb over the wall, right? Then Mr. Weider was caught when his tunnel collapsed. To hell with being sneaky. Let's just walk right out of the ghetto."

"Jerzy, we need to stay out of trouble or they'll kill us."

"Ma, they'll kill us either way! We need to get out."

Jerzy's mother, an expert seamstress, found a bolt of black fabric in the attic and reluctantly set to work with her old pedal-powered sewing machine. In a week, she had made some very good uniforms, complete with insignias and hats.

Jerzy studied the Germans' movements from the attic window at night; he noticed that they were nothing if not routine. Every night at ten, an Opel truck with about eight soldiers in the back would park on the street out front. The soldiers would get out, and while they were patrolling the streets to enforce the curfew, they left the truck unattended.

One night, Jerzy waited until the Germans had gone to the next street over and then got out to take a look at the truck. Feeling around in the dark, he found the ignition under the instrument panel. The Germans had taken the key with them.

He felt three wires going into the tumbler. Jerzy was a city kid who never drove and didn't know much about automobiles, but he did understand locks and electric current due to his incessant tinkering. Creeping back into his house, he watched the truck nervously from the windows. At midnight, as always, the Germans drove off. They didn't seem to have suspected anything.

The family waited until the timing was perfect: a night with a full moon and fog. One Monday evening at exactly 10:30 p.m., Jerzy and his entire family, dressed as Schutzstaffel, opened their front door and ran across the street to the truck. Jerzy's older brother had driven a diesel for a trucking company for a while, so he sat in the driver's seat. Jerzy ripped the wires out of the ignition and, sweating and shaking, stripped the insulation off and tried touching them all together. Poof, just like that, the truck started. Jerzy twisted the wires together using needle-nose pliers and off they went. They slowed down to wave at the checkpoint guards, who waved back like everything was OK, and they kept on going into the night.

Jerzy's father knew of an abandoned hunting cabin in the mountains outside the city, and long before starting out, they'd correctly calculated that they could reach it before the Germans even noticed the truck was missing. The cabin was a mess and didn't even have firewood for winter, which was fast approaching. There was a hole in the roof and no beds. There was no fog in the mountains, so under the moonlight, Jerzy and his brother hid the truck in a ravine, covering it with pine tree limbs.

Over the next four years, the Savitz family hid out in the Tatra Mountains, looting nearby abandoned cabins for essentials, hunting deer, foraging berries, and only using the fireplace at night so no one would see the smoke.

Despite missing Katarzyna, Jerzy found mountain living to be glorious. It was an awakening, even. It disabused him of the many feeble notions that urban living put into one's head: that one needed money to survive, that one needed the authorities for protection, or that one must hire professionals to do things for the sake of convenience. Humans had survived just fine before life became so convenient, he reasoned, and it was that very convenience that caused modern people such terrible existential angst.

The Savitz family's luck ran out in the fall of 1943. The Germans, desperate to root out a fierce and unrelenting Polish resistance army hiding in the hills and forests, checked every single cabin in the area. The soldier who knocked on the door immediately recognized Jerzy's brother from pictures that had been circulated after their escape. The entire family was taken into custody, loaded onto a train, and taken to Auschwitz.

Jerzy and his two brothers were young and strong, so they were put to work at the facility. His parents were sent somewhere else and were never heard from again. It wasn't until years later that Jerzy figured out what had happened to them.

What Jerzy found unusual about the prison camp was that not everyone there was Jewish. There were political dissidents, intellectuals, artists, writers, scientists. It was almost as if the Nazis were just as concerned with ridding the world of free thought as they were with ridding it of Jews.

Jerzy's older brother died of pneumonia during the first winter. The prison guards unceremoniously threw his body onto a cart with the bodies of others who had died and then dumped them all into a hole. Two decades of childhood together—catching frogs, playing soccer, and reading dirty stories in the attic. His blood, his best friend. The fucking Germans just threw him away like trash. Lives and agony meant nothing to those monsters.

Some of the Germans clearly delighted in the misery and murder, almost in a sexual way. Others seemed to have no moral sense of their own and instead deferred completely to authority: "Just doing my job." "Just following orders." During the long days in Auschwitz, Jerzy often wondered how the Nazis could staff an entire prison camp with thousands of people, none of whom apparently had the ability to question if they were doing the right thing.

In January of 1945, the Nazis ordered the camp to be evacuated due to the advancing Russians. Jerzy and his remaining brother, Heniek, were forced to make the horrific death march back across the border in the middle of the winter. Heniek was emaciated and too weak to keep walking. A German soldier, annoyed at Heniek's inability to keep up, simply shot him in the back of the head. Heniek's body dropped into the ditch along the side of the road. Jerzy wanted to run to him, to explode in rage and grief. Instead he just stood there, silently depleted and shivering from exhaustion and malnourishment. A soldier kicked Jerzy in the back and told him to keep moving.

As if God were spiting him, Jerzy survived. The Krauts relocated him to the Bergen-Belsen camp deep inside Nazi territory, and a few months later, Germany surrendered. Two days after the Germans deserted their posts, horrified British commandos liberated the camp.

Jerzy had lost the will to live. He had nothing left to live for. Now he was free.

34

After rolling all night, the train pulled into Kansas City the next morning. Except it didn't stop at the station. Instead the train switched onto a short line and kept moving way out into the prairie. By that point, a few of Len's fellow passengers had had to defecate during the trip. They'd done their best to use only one corner of the car, but it was starting to smell terrible. He tried to see where the train was going, but with so many people pressed up to the sides of the car to avoid the smell, he wasn't having a whole lot of luck. After two more hours of travel, the train began slowing down. It came to an abrupt halt that caused several people to fall into each other.

Dranthyx jackboots threw open the cattle car doors. As if he'd been waiting for the opportunity, a man in a bright yellow shirt jumped out of the car and tried to make a run for it. One of the Dranthyx raised his rifle to his shoulder and fired. A bolt of electricity, like the kind one might see arcing out of a Van de Graaf generator, connected with the escapee's back. Instantaneously the man's entire torso exploded open from steam pressure, like a burrito that someone had left in a microwave too long. Superheated blood and flesh splattered some of Len's fellow prisoners nearby, causing them to scream in pain. Everyone got the message. No one else stepped out of line that day.

Exiting the train car, Len saw that they were in an vast area fenced in by miles and miles of barbed wire with guard towers every hundred yards or so. Despite the land being so flat, Len couldn't see the end of the fence. The place was so big that the entire train fit inside of it.

"Len!"

Len turned and nearly cried when he saw Octavia and Natalia behind him. They'd arrived in one of the other cars on the train.

"Oh, thank God!" Len hugged them both.

"Daddy, we rode on a train! Look at this! The octopus man put this mark on my arm. Isn't it neat? It's like the dinosaur stamp at the library. It says X but it should say O, for Octavia. Natalia has one, too. Oh look, so do you! That's great! Now we're all secret buddies. Daddy, what is this place?"

"It's a concentration camp."

"Camp? Oh boy! That sounds like fun! Will we sing songs and cook marshmallows on the fire?"

Len wondered how anyone, ingenuous child or not, could be so indomitably sunny in a situation like the one they were in.

"OK, let's go!" one of the Dranthyx shouted while shoving people to get them moving. Several Dranthyx marched everyone who had disembarked from the train through the camp, which took two hours due to the sheer size of it. Len saw that the whole facility was broken into hundreds of subfacilities, each the size of a small town. There were great numbers of tent barracks in each, filled with cots stacked to the roof.

"How on earth did you build something this big with no one noticing?" Len asked one of the Dranthyx soldiers.

Len wasn't expecting an answer, but the animal laughed and obliged. "See, that's what befuddles me about you simians. If someone tries to be secretive, you go out of your way to discover what they're hiding. However, if something enormous happens in plain sight, you figure it must be legitimate and pay it no mind. We appropriated billions of dollars out of the Pentagon budget each year for construction costs, and no one even cared where the money went. We moved half a million migrant workers here to build this place, which took over a decade, and no one even thought it was unusual. No one even asked what we were doing."

"How big is this place?"

"A million acres, give or take. The facility is designed to hold fifty million chimps at a time. We had to buy five of the largest cattle ranches in Kansas in order to have enough space. This is just the North American facility. This is nothing. You should see the one we built in Asia!"

"Fifty million? I'd think there were more Xreths than that."

The creature smirked at Len's poor pronunciation of the word. "There are actually about three times that many on this continent. We're still rounding them up. Many are hiding, but don't worry, we'll find them. To put it more colloquially, this ain't our first rodeo."

"At what point do you decide to cull?"

The Dranthyx looked Len over, probably wondering how he knew so much and debating whether to keep answering questions. Len could almost see the creature thinking to itself, *To hell with it, he's going to die anyway, I might as well tell him what's up.*

"We have found that things run best at about 10 percent Xreths, 4 percent Tchogol, and the rest Saskel," the Dranthyx answered gamely. "That's optimal. However, Xreths have reached 25 percent of the global population. That's why there's so much turmoil these days. Governments cannot collect revenue properly when Xreths are always opposing them, which is bad for business."

"Why has the number of Xreths increased?"

"Long ago, Xreths didn't have many options when it was time to settle down and make babies. You either married your small-town Saskel neighbor or you died childless. That all changed when higher education became commonplace. Xreths left ancestral homelands and became highly concentrated in cities and universities. Naturally, they chose other Xreths with whom to reproduce. That was bad enough, but then the Internet came along and the assortative mating really exploded out of control. So here we are, trying to restore balance before the situation becomes any more unmanageable. If you ask me, I think the Directorate let it go too long. But what do I know?" The Dranthyx was suddenly sardonic. "I'm just a lowly grunt with an IQ of 153. They won't let a dummy like me in on the decision-making."

Rising from what Len presumed was the center of the camp was an enormous concrete cube. It was five hundred feet tall and equally wide, and its roof bristled with nine smokestacks that each rose a thousand feet off the ground.

"What's that?" Len asked.

"The nerve center of this operation. It's not online just yet. We didn't anticipate having to use it so soon, but it should be running in a week or two."

"Is that when you'll start killing us?"

"That's enough questions for now," said a different, less-sociable Dranthyx tersely while pointing his gun at Len.

Len, Octavia, and Natalia were assigned to Sector FG, Subcamp 3402, which held approximately five hundred people, almost all of whom were on Len's train. The sectors and subcamps were separated by barbed-wire fences and paved streets, some narrow like alleys, others wide like boulevards. The streets even had billboards on them, except they were entirely black, with no advertisements. Len figured they broke the population down like this because it was easier to manage smaller groups of people.

Having seen the famous footage of the German camps of WWII, Len was amazed that this facility had toilets, showers, cots, and tents. He wondered if maybe the Dranthyx had learned from previous experience that isolating subcamps and giving prisoners the necessities of sanitation kept diseases from spreading. For efficiency's sake, the Dranthyx probably wanted to confine all the dying to the reactor rather than having to collect bodies from all over the enormous camp.

The Dranthyx troopers ushered everyone into the sub-camp without incident, but the sight of the Dranthyx closing the big gate behind them was enough to make some of his fellow captives start crying. They were trapped behind a ten-foot cyclone fence and huge rolls of electrified concertina wire.

While everyone lost their shit, Len, Natalia, and Octavia claimed some cots in the corner of one of the tents.

"Daddy, why are they crying?"

"Maybe they don't like camping." Len didn't know what else to say.

"Don't worry! I'll make some s'mores for them, then they'll feel better," Octavia said cheerfully.

Len looked into Octavia's eyes. Before becoming a parent, Len thought children were born as blank slates, and that parents molded a child's mind. That notion turned out to be an arrogance of youthful inexperience. No way. Turns out, kids came out of the womb with their own personalities—fully formed individuals with their own agendas—and the best a parent could do was to teach them by example to be good people. Octavia happened to have been born with a heart of gold. She had the most beautiful soul Len had ever seen. Her ability to light up the room with optimism and selfless empathy always reminded Len what a jaded, angry, pessimistic curmudgeon he'd become. He stroked her cheek.

"I didn't think it would end like this. I wanted to die fighting," Natalia said grimly. She didn't look so good.

"We don't have to give up fighting," Len said.

Natalia gave him a defeated, bitter look. "You see chimneys?" she asked irritably, motioning to the distant smokestacks beyond the razor wire. "You know what those are for?"

35

That night, a bunch of the adults in Len's section arranged a meeting in one of the tents. There were easily two hundred people packed into the tent. Len took note of the folks he met. Artists, engineers, business owners, college professors, each one with an X on their neck and wrist. None had the S tattoos he'd heard about on the train. Len wondered how civilization outside the camp could continue once humanity's entire thinking population had been sent to the slaughterhouse.

"Folks," said an African American man in a suit, "my name's Abe. I called this meeting because I do believe they intend to kill us all."

"Maybe they're just keeping us out of danger," said a nervous woman. Her face indicated that she didn't even believe her own statement. Everyone looked at her like she was an idiot.

"Well, what should we do about it?" someone yelled from the back.

"I've been thinking about that," said Abe. "Clearly, we need an escape plan."

"How are we going to escape?" asked Len. "We're at least five miles from the outside fence. And beyond that there's nothing but open prairie. The nearest town is fifty miles away. There's a reason they picked this place."

"Would you rather die escaping, or die at the hand of those monsters?" Abe asked calmly.

"Abe, we just got here," Len said. "Let's try to get our bearings before planning an escape."

"We don't have time to wait!" exclaimed a skinny, nerdy-looking man.

"How do you know?" asked Abe.

"Do you see that huge building in the distance?" the nerdy guy asked everyone. The crowd nodded. "I worked for the engineering firm that designed it. That's a state-of-the-art plasma gasification reactor. Only when we were designing it, they told us it was a top-secret defense project for turning trash into electricity."

"So we're the trash?" someone asked.

"How long do we have?" asked Abe.

"If I remember the implementation timeline correctly, it was scheduled to be put online in two weeks."

The agitated crowd all began speaking at the same time.

"*Quiet!*" roared a large man in the back. "One at a time or we'll never figure this out!"

"I have an idea," said the engineer. Everyone turned to look at him. "This facility seems to have an awful lot of paved roads, which means there has to be a system to collect and divert storm water so the place doesn't flood. In fact, I see storm drains in the road on the other side of the barbed wire. I would imagine that there's a storm water collection system with enormous pipes underground."

"You imagine?"

"Yes. I don't know. We didn't design that part. We only designed the reactor. Maybe if we found a way to dig down to the storm water pipes, we could escape."

"Then what? We're fifty miles from the nearest town," said an equally nerdy-looking Asian woman.

"Unless someone has a better idea, it's a risk we might have to take," said the reactor engineer.

"OK, so what could we use as digging implements?"

Len was starting to feel ill again from the lack of nicotine and alcohol. He couldn't stand listening to them anymore; it felt like his head was being rubbed against a cheese grater. As they continued to talk, he got up and left the meeting.

36

The subcamp had sinks they could drink water from, but the Dranthyx provided very little in the way of food, only one or two meals per day. The guards opened the subcamp gates at noon each day to drop off an enormous pile of MREs, dehydrated meals in bags designed for the military. The prisoners were ordered to put all their trash into a large bin near the entrance. One hour after mealtime, a huge truck would back up to the closed gate and extend a robotic vacuum-like implement over the fence and into the bin. The truck would suck up all the trash and grind it into bits.

It didn't take the Xreths long to figure out that the Dranthyx didn't do trash inventory, and that they could use the little tins inside the MREs to dig. The construction of the tunnel was kept profoundly secret. The idea, of course, was to dig down toward the storm drain that they could see in the road on the other side of the barbed wire.

Over the next few days, the prisoners in Len's section worked around the clock on the tunnel. Tinful by tinful, flushing the dirt down the toilets so the Dranthyx wouldn't see it. The entrance to the tunnel was hidden from view underneath some of the cots, and they made sure that people were always pretending to sleep over the entrance. Len got stuck working the night shift on the tunnel, which sucked because they didn't have any electric lights. He had to dig in the dark in an enclosed space. *This isn't an escape plan*, he thought to himself, *it's an Edgar Allen Poe story*. Nonetheless, the work kept his mind off the unpleasant detoxification symptoms he was experiencing. Bit by bit, he'd put his dirt into a bucket, then tug on the string so the person up top would pull the full bucket up. All of this had to be done completely naked so that the Dranthyx wouldn't be alerted by dirt stains on clothing. Then, once his shift was over, Len took a shower, put his old clothes back on, and tried to sleep.

On the fifth day, whispers went around that they'd managed to hit a large, corrugated aluminum storm drain pipe. The pipe was easily five feet in diameter, big enough for them to walk through. Once they found a way to pierce the pipe's thick aluminum quietly, they'd be in business.

That night, after a lot of low-key celebrating, Len volunteered to sleep on top of the tunnel entrance in case the Dranthyx came to inspect.

While everyone slept, Len snuck into the hole. The tunnel was shored up by cots and other scavenged material, a half-assed masterpiece. Doing his best in the dark, using makeshift ropes from tied-together shreds of cot canvas, Len secured the ropes to a few key struts that he knew were holding the tunnel roof in place. Then, once he'd crawled back out, he yanked hard on the struts until he felt them come loose. For a sweaty minute or two, nothing happened. Then, a great rumbling as the ground subsided inside the tent where everyone was sleeping.

"What was that?" someone asked in the dark.

"I don't know!" Len said, feigning surprise, "but I just fell into the hole!" He needed an excuse as to why he was covered in dirt despite the tunnel being finished twelve hours earlier.

Several other people came to see what was going on, tripping in the dark on the depression the collapsed tunnel had left behind at the surface.

"Fuck!" someone whispered. "I think the tunnel collapsed!"

37

Early the next morning, the subcamp gate opened and a cadre of Dranthyx came in, led by one in a bespoke sharkskin suit. Without even asking anyone, the one in the suit walked right up to Len as if he already knew where to find him. It grabbed Len's arm, scanned the encoded tattoo, and read the result on the screen.

"I understand you are Leonard Savitz," the creature said.

"Who's asking?"

"My name is Jacob Endicott. You killed my older brother."

"Oh, right," Len said, shooting a keep-quiet glance at Natalia. The video camera in the jail cell had been off at the time. Len might as well take the blame. "I did kill him. Your brother was an asshole."

Jacob put his tentacle around Len's back and yanked him in close so Len could see his eye slits dilating and smell his disgusting ocean breath.

"Come with me," the creature said in a low voice.

"What if I don't?"

"Then I'll just vaporize you right here in front of your daughter."

Len frowned and didn't say anything further, which Jacob took as acquiescence. He chuckled and then yelled something in Dranthyx to the others. The black billboards along the streets outside the fence suddenly came alive with test patterns, like televisions.

Len, Octavia, and Natalia were led to a central part of the camp, near the building with the smokestacks. There an area awaited them that looked like a makeshift gladiatorial arena. Aluminum bleachers and stadium lights surrounded a cage made of chain-link fence and a concrete pad. There was a small stage next to the cage with a microphone.

The bleachers were filled with his fellow prisoners, people who looked scared and run-down and who had probably been forced to sit there. Jacob ordered Natalia and Octavia to sit on the bleachers with the others.

Jacob pushed Len into the cage and shut the gate behind him. Then from the other end of the arena came another Dranthyx leading a man on a leash. The man was none other than General Jefferson. Len's heart started to pound as he suddenly understood the situation. The other Dranthyx opened the gate and entered with Jefferson still on his leash.

"You fucking turncoat!" Jefferson yelled upon seeing Len. "Where's your goddamn loyalty? Not to the human race, apparently! You happy we're all here in this death camp? They're going to murder every last man, woman, and child, and the blood is on your hands! Neith could have saved us!"

"Fuck you, Jefferson," Len retorted. "How does it feel to have no control?"

Jefferson's face turned red and he tried to lunge at Len, but the Dranthyx's leash held him back.

"You'll rot in hell, you piece of shit!" Jefferson screamed.

Jacob Endicott seemed pleased with the tension as he took to the stage.

"Good morning, ladies and gentlemen!" he announced smarmily into the microphone. "A warm welcome to those of you here in the stands or in your subcamps."

Len looked over to see a Dranthyx operating a TV camera. Above the cage, he saw his own face on a Jumbotron.

"In case you weren't anticipating having entertainment in our little camp, you will be pleasantly surprised to find that isn't the case. In fact, televised gladiatorial combat will be a daily feature. We have a treat for you today, because our first match will be something extra special. We have arranged, for your viewing pleasure and ours, mortal combat between the two reasons this camp exists."

Len felt like a Volkswagen was sitting on his chest.

"In this corner, at six-two and 220 pounds, the terrorist who once fancied himself president, Orville Jefferson! Orville comes to us from the dung heap known as Arkansas. If he hadn't challenged our authority, you wouldn't be here today."

Blank stares from the tired, hungry crowd.

"In this corner, at six-one and a scrawny 170 pounds, the so-called journalist known as Leonard Savitz! Thanks to Leonard selling out Orville's rebellion and telling us about Neith, the architect of the rebellion and the only hope you people had, we will continue controlling the human race for the rest of time!" Pleased with himself, Jacob gave a bubbling, metallic guffaw.

Again, silence from the stands. Had the crowd been Saskels or Tchogols, they'd have been hooting and hollering for blood. But these were Xreths. They understood they were in a bad situation in which they would all be put to death, and they got no enjoyment from watching some stupid fight between two people they couldn't care less about. They had been told to sit there and witness the fight because it would add humiliation to death.

Len looked over Jefferson, who was staring Len down to psych him out. Jefferson pulled his shirt off. Despite being in his fifties, he was a slab of solid muscle. He looked like he could dead-lift an SUV. By comparison, Len was mostly skin and bones. "Shit," Len said under his breath. He was in no shape to fight a man of Jefferson's vigor. His last judo practice had been over fifteen years ago, and he'd been doing nothing but drinking and smoking since then.

Jefferson had his fists up and was bouncing side to side, as a boxer does. His nose looked like it had been broken at least once before. Yet he had no cauliflower ears. Len surmised that the majority of Jefferson's martial arts training had been in stand-up work and that Jefferson would be weak on the ground. Judo was primarily a grappling art, like wresting. Len had spent hundreds of hours practicing groundwork in Japan, and he was hoping that Jefferson hadn't. Good, Len thought. Now he had a strategy: get Jefferson to the ground and try to remember techniques he'd last used a decade and a half ago.

A bell rang. Cute. The Dranthyx took the leash off Jefferson, who yelled, "You're gonna die, traitor!"

Len felt a surge of fear as Jefferson came toward him. He recalled his old judo sensei's constant advice: "Don't panic. Relax. Control your breathing. Fear will tire you out before the fight does." *He's a boxer,* Len thought. *Clinch him up. Take him to the ground.*

Easier said than done. Len had an awful lot of judo experience but absolutely no training on how to throw punches or how to bob and weave. Jefferson came out like a raging bull, and with one lightning-fast, inescapable blow, he knocked Len to the cement floor. Len's head was fuzzy with white lights, but he wasn't out yet.

Sensei, on top of him, using his weight to squeeze the air out of Len's lungs: "Does this hurt? Good! Learn to enjoy it. Don't even think about tapping out. Never quit just because you're uncomfortable. Fight hard when you're winning, fight hard when you're losing. Continue fighting through the pain until an opportunity opens up."

Jefferson hunched over Len, ready to finish the fight, but as he bent over, Len quickly grabbed his arm, put his foot up into Jefferson's pelvis, and did a throw known as the *tomoe nage.* Jefferson flipped over Len's prone body and landed squarely on his back on the hard concrete, dazed.

Sensei, watching Len practice throws: "What are you waiting for? Why did you stop? Never stop to admire your work! Keep moving! Finish the fight!"

Without hesitation, while Jefferson was struggling to catch his breath, Len rolled over top of him and, while still holding the arm he'd used to do the throw, swung his body around, threw his leg over Jefferson's face, and arm-barred his opponent. Raising his hips to put extreme pressure on the joint, Len heard a loud snap as Jefferson's elbow joint hyperextended and broke. The crowd made a noise of surprise and disgust.

Something martial arts teachers usually forgot to explain: an arm bar would end a sporting match, but it might not end a real fight. In a situation of true mortal peril, a determined opponent wouldn't be deterred by a broken arm. Instead, he would become enraged and try even harder to murder you. In an instant, Len realized his tactical error. Jefferson's arm, now broken and no longer susceptible to the immobilizing trap of Len's joint lock, had a new freedom of movement that allowed him to escape Len's hold. He turned violently into Len, and with his unbroken arm, he punched Len in the chest so hard he cracked one of his ribs.

Jefferson then got to his knees and lunged at Len, who, unable to breathe from the punch, could do nothing but roll out of the way. Jefferson got up again, this time to his feet, while Len scrambled to do the same. Jefferson ran head-first into Len's midsection while grabbing both of Len's legs to take him to the ground. On the way down, Len caught Jefferson in a guillotine choke, a nasty move he'd practiced hundreds of times while in Japan. Len pulled hard on Jefferson's neck, digging his forearm bones into Jefferson's carotid, while locking his legs up around Jefferson's torso. Jefferson was as strong as a bear, and holding him in that position while he thrashed about took every bit of strength Len had. With his good arm, Jefferson punched Len repeatedly in the side, where his rib was broken, to get Len to loosen the chokehold.

Sensei, demonstrating how to maintain a controlling position while Len struggled to get free: "You see? Never, never give up a dominant position! If you think it's too tough to stay on top, then tell me, would you rather try to fight from the bottom?"

The pain of Jefferson punching him in the broken rib was nearly enough to make Len pass out, but somehow he didn't. Instead it was Jefferson who lost consciousness first after several seconds of restricted blood flow from Len's chokehold.

Temporarily passing out because of the restricted blood flow from a chokehold was considered subclinical if the hold was released quickly. Lots of people were put into sleeper holds and recovered in seconds with no ill effects. Blood flowed back into the brain, and consciousness returned like nothing happened. However, if the hold was held, brain damage would occur in about thirty seconds. Longer than that and death became inevitable. Had it been one of his old judo classes, Len would have let go immediately to prevent injury. But this wasn't some class. This was a death contest with the fucker who had kidnapped his daughter.

Len considered letting go of Jefferson's neck before cerebral anoxia set in. He now had two bad decisions under his belt: killing the Iraqi boy, and letting the IRS agent live. Two major fuckups, the first because he let rage take the wheel, and the second because he let compassion get the better of him. Now Len had to pick which mistake to make next, because whatever he did, it would be the wrong decision. He thought it over for a bit, then held the choke until Jefferson's face turned blue and his heart stopped beating. Once Len was sure Jefferson was dead, he let go and passed out himself from exhaustion and the pain in his side.

38

Len came to not knowing how much time had passed. Daylight. He found himself in his cot. His back was raw. It felt as though he'd been dragged from the arena back to the subcamp. Natalia and Octavia were huddled together by his side.

"Daddy, you're awake!" Octavia exclaimed. "I saw you get in a big fight! You did a good job!"

"Thanks."

"Hey!" Natalia said. "Are you OK?"

"No. I feel like I fell off a bridge."

Len tried to sit up, but the pain from the broken rib made him tear up and groan.

"What Jefferson was talking about?" Natalia asked, trying to seem nonchalant.

"What do you mean?"

"He called you traitor. What he meant?"

"I don't know." But Len wasn't a poker player, and Natalia could probably see it in his face.

"And Dranthyx said you are reason we're here. What does it mean?"

"Natalia, what do you want from me?"

"I did not want to believe bad things about you, but I think it makes sense now. I think I begin to understand."

"Understand what?" Len asked, shifting in his bed.

"Jefferson and Neith kidnap your little girl. Why, I don't know. But you are angry, right? Who wouldn't be? So you get yourself arrested at border on purpose and tell Dranthyx all about Neith and secret plans. I saw it happen, and only now it makes sense. You want to make deal with Dranthyx so they spare you, right? Only thing is, Dranthyx don't make deal, and they try to kill you. Next thing, Jefferson captured, Neith stops contacting everyone and is maybe dead, last hope for humanity is over, and we all go to prison camp to die. Then you sabotage tunnel, our only chance to escape. Then you kill Jefferson, hero of revolution, when you don't have to." She paused. Len looked up and saw that others in the tent were listening to the conversation. "Is that right, Len?"

Len didn't answer. He just stared up at the ceiling. He could feel everyone in the tent looking at him.

"What's that old saying?" Abe said slowly from the corner. "Oh, yes: an appeaser is one who feeds a crocodile, hoping it will eat him last."

"How could you do this to us?" Natalia said, her eyes fierce. "In bed one night at Freehold, didn't you tell me grandfather was in Auschwitz? Now you are too. What would he think? Would he think you are noble man? I can't believe I risked life of me and my friends to break you out of jail!"

Len avoided looking at anyone. An old lady walked over to Len's cot, spat on him, and walked out of the tent. Two others did the same.

Once they were alone in an empty tent, Octavia put her hand on Len's forehead and said, "It's OK, Daddy. I still love you."

Len couldn't hold it in any longer. He broke down and cried.

39

The gate opened the next day at exactly noon. In strode Jacob Endicott and his entourage of Dranthyx shock troopers.

"Hello, everyone!" Jacob shouted, smiling a hideous smile that revealed the black beak under his lips. "Good news! Today's the day. The reactor is now fully operational. Of all the subcamps in this great facility, I've selected yours to go first to test the functionality of the system. The distinction is one you've clearly earned. Now, please line up and make this easy on yourselves."

Everyone ran in a hundred directions. Several of the prisoners tried to flee by climbing the fence; a few even tried to attack the Dranthyx with their fists. Len quickly grabbed Octavia and hit the deck, covering her eyes. Len reached up and yanked Natalia down to the ground with them.

All noncompliers were shredded with the lightning guns in short order. After an electrical storm of body parts and boiling blood raining from every direction, Jacob's face curled wryly as he licked some blood spatter off his tentacle.

"Would you look at this mess?" Jacob asked, chuckling. "I say, I wish this paid as well as banking! I'd do it every day! All right, everyone, enough foolery. Time to get with the pogrom. Get it, pogrom?" Jacob belly-laughed at his own joke, once again making the disconcerting noise that sounded like oily bubbles popping inside an old tin can.

The Dranthyx troops went through the section methodically, pulling crying people out from toilet stalls and underneath cots. One of them walked right over to where Len, Natalia, and Octavia were taking cover on the floor. The Dranthyx soldier bent down and picked someone's severed arm off the ground. The arm was still connected to a shoulder blade and a bit of rib cage. The monster looked Len in the eye—those goddamn sideways yellow cat eyes—then took a bite out of the dismembered arm.

Once they'd rounded up all the survivors in the section, the Dranthyx forced everyone into windowless white semitrailers. With the trailers full, they closed the doors unceremoniously, then drove the eighteen-wheelers to the enormous reactor in the center of camp. There they were, packed into the trailer, listening to people clawing the walls in the dark, hysterical with panic.

At the reactor, the trailer door opened. The Dranthyx herded the prisoners into a fenced pen, a big yard right outside the building like the kind cattle were corralled in. The pen narrowed into a shiny steel door, which was closed.

"OK, we're ready," muttered one of the Dranthyx to Jacob in English.

"Let's line up, people," Jacob yelled, pointing with his tentacle. "That way, you'll be going through that door."

Len, Natalia, and Octavia were shoved into line by the octopuses in boots. It was either that or be shot. The steel door opened mechanically on its own: fluidly, silently. Inside was dark, too dark to see. Len strained to see what was beyond the doorway, but there was only utter blackness.

This is it, Len said to himself.

Octavia looked up at her dad, somehow impervious to what was happening.

"Daddy, I had a silly dream last night."

"Oh yeah?"

"The jellyfish man visited me. And he lived in a little moon. He said, 'Don't worry, Mommy didn't really die, because dying is just imaginary.'"

Len hadn't yet told her that Sara had died of the flu. He'd been hoping for a time when things settled down to break the news. With all that had been going on, that time had never come.

"Oh? What else did he say?" Len asked intently.

"He said, *'Katsu!'*" Octavia giggled at the silliness of the word.

Len couldn't help himself. He shrieked with laughter, beamed, picked Octavia up, and twirled around with her until the sharp pain in his broken rib made him put her down.

"Why are you so happy?" Natalia queried flatly, too emotionally drained to be disgusted. Even the Dranthyx standing nearby gave each other confused looks.

"Because that's the signal!" Len yelled exuberantly.

"Signal?"

Just then there came a deafening roar, like a thousand thunderbolts going off simultaneously. Looking up, they saw the moon. No, wait, lots of moons. Huh? Thousands of glistening white spheres hovering at cloud level and forming a lattice from horizon to horizon. They'd appeared out of nowhere.

The Dranthyx, panicked, began yelling at each other and firing their weapons into the air at the objects, which absorbed the electricity effortlessly. Seeing their lightning guns have no effect, the Dranthyx ran in every direction. Two of them even collided with one another.

Then, from the white orbs, thousands and thousands of little dashes of green light fell toward the ground, like the sky was raining glow sticks. Only these little bits of green light didn't fall randomly, they glided around corners and through doors and chain-link fences and then, with unerring precision, right to where each Dranthyx was standing. Several bits of light sliced through each octopus, through their tentacles and faces, dropping them right where they stood. The sky was alight in green as the projectiles strafed the entire countryside, expertly piercing every single vital area of each Dranthyx's decentralized nervous systems while simultaneously missing every single human being.

The people in the massacre pen looked around, confused. The Dranthyx had all collapsed into heaps. Len walked up to Jacob's body and cautiously kicked it. Nothing. Out of curiosity, he looked it over to see where the green light had hit Jacob. Both eyes were burned out of the creature's head, holes straight through. Every tentacle was seared through and cooked from the inside out. A guidance system without par.

"What the hell just happened?" someone shrieked.

"Is it dead?" asked the engineer.

"Yes." Len collapsed to his knees, his shoulders now relieved of the world's weight.

"What the hell just happened?" the first person asked again.

"Those white spheres up there are the Ich-Ca-Gan," Len said, trying to breathe through a tidal wave of upheaval. "They're good guys. They're aliens. They just killed all the Dranthyx."

"The bad guys are dead! The bad guys are dead!" Octavia yelled, running in circles. "Now can we make s'mores?"

Everyone just sort of stood there, staring up at the sky in disbelief.

After several minutes of silent bewilderment, someone asked, "So if they're dead, can we just leave?"

"Yeah," Len said, choked up. "We're done. We can all go home now."

Len had never felt so tired or so relieved. Despite the emotional exhaustion, he and his fellow prisoners went around the camp, unlocking gates, freeing people, and explaining as best they could what had happened. As the subcamps emptied, prisoners flooded into the streets of the facility. Confusion and fear gave way to an atmosphere of raucous jubilance.

40

Walking toward the camp's exit with Octavia, Len turned around to see Natalia running to catch up with them.

"Right before it happen, you say 'signal,'" Natalia said, out of breath. "You knew this would happen? How did you know Ich-Ca-Gan are returning?"

"One came to me one night at Salvatierra's house," Len said tersely. "We planned all of this together."

"You planned this with them? How?"

"We linked minds. I told the Ich-Ca-Gan everything I knew about the situation, and vice versa, and we hatched a plan together."

Natalia looked at him like he was insane. "But what kind of plan is this? Why did you let it go so far? Why did you let invasion happen? Our cities ruined! Millions of people dead! Why couldn't Ich-Ca-Gan kill the Dranthyx before they invade?" Her eyes flashed with heat.

"Are *you* still alive?" Len asked.

"Yes. What's your point?"

"Are *you* free now?"

"Yeah."

"Well, then, shut up already and enjoy it!" Len said acidly. "Besides, considering what you do for a living, Natalia, it's not like you've never had blood on your hands."

Len could see in her face that she wanted to be offended. He turned and started walking again. Then, just like that, "I'm sorry for what I said before," she said.

The contrition disarmed Len. He stopped walking. *That feeling you have is anger,* he told himself. *If she can swallow her pride and admit she was wrong, then certainly you can forgive her for not knowing what you didn't explain.* Len turned around and locked gazes with her. Those eyes of hers: a warrior's magnanimity, not a hint of pettiness. *If she can admit fault, old boy, then you should too.*

"Look, I'm sorry, too," Len said with a kind of run-down exhalation.

"Why didn't you tell me any of this?" Natalia asked, exasperated. "I thought you were traitor!"

"The Ich-Ca-Gan and I decided to keep it secret. We didn't want to put you at risk of being tortured for information."

"Oh." She paused, searching for what to say next. "Well, thanks."

"We let the invasion happen because that was the only way it could have worked. The Ich-Ca-Gan come from a gaseous planet with no liquid surfaces. Their weapons don't work underwater because they never developed that technology. In order to kill off the Dranthyx, we had to draw as many of them as possible out of the water and onto land. We determined the best way to do that was to tell the Dranthyx what Neith was up to and that their Tchogols had been killed off on purpose to prevent the cull. At the same time, I'd tell the human world what was going on so they'd try to fight the invasion.

We needed the Dranthyx to think there'd be a massive human resistance. That's why I got myself arrested, and why I asked you to give the manuscript to my editor. At the airport, I was carrying a manuscript similar to the one I gave you, except that copy mentioned the exact location of Neith's operations, and was tailored to piss off the Dranthyx without giving away too much other information." Len barely took a breath as he recounted the plan in full, rapidly spilling details he'd kept to himself for so long.

"Well, whatever you said worked."

"In that version, I wrote that Neith was working on a new virus that would wipe out the Dranthyx."

"Was she?"

"I have no idea. I made it up to scare them. I planted the seed that they were losing control of the situation, and they'd have to destroy Neith. With the Tchogols gone, the Dranthyx had no choice but to fight their way inland to do the cull themselves, which required pretty much all the manpower they had. Also, I wanted them to think I was a traitor to Neith's cause, and that I was trying to defect and curry favor with the Dranthyx."

"So why did you want Dranthyx to kill Neith? I thought she was on our side."

"The Ich-Ca-Gan and I didn't think she was any better than the Dranthyx. Apparently, neither she nor they had any qualms about killing hundreds of millions of people, and both seemed to think humans only existed to do their bidding. In jail, right before you saved me, Samuel Endicott told me that Neith was some NSA computer gone rogue. She wasn't even human.

She was a blinking machine in a data center somewhere, which meant she was completely dependent on humans for survival. We figured once she overcame Dranthyx control, she'd next work on getting out from under human control. The whole damn war was a psychopathic, drug-dealing, terrorist super-computer versus psychopathic banker octopuses. Why live with either when we can remove both problems, you know?"

"You don't think Neith would want to work with humans?"

"Maybe, maybe not. I don't know," Len said. "Sooner or later, someone would try to pull her plug, and she'd exterminate the rest of us just as blithely as she annihilated the Tchogols. So yeah, the plan had a lot of collateral damage: cities, millions of people, Neith. Maybe it wasn't the most finely tuned scheme, but, well, saving the world isn't something I do on a regular basis. I kind of got roped into it, like jury duty. Anyway, the net result is that we destroyed most of the Dranthyx. Millions of people were killed, but because of that, billions will continue living. It's something that I'll have to live with the rest of my life."

"Most of Dranthyx? There are more?"

"The Ich-Ca-Gan estimated that we'd kill off about 99.7 percent of them with our plan. There are far too few left to rule the world anymore. We're in charge now."

"Weird. When I read manuscript, I figure Ich-Ca-Gan were maybe pacifists."

"I think they are, mostly, but they'll come to the defense of other living beings, using deadly force if necessary. They felt the need to intervene before billions of Xreths were killed in the cull. See, the Dranthyx are biologically incapable of empathy, so they'll never be anything but evil. The Ich-Ca-Gan felt there was no hope for them and decided it was time to allow the human race to flourish without control. So they exterminated the Dranthyx. Also, the Dranthyx signed their own death warrant when they broke the truce agreement by attacking the temple in Tokyo."

"OK, but I don't understand why you destroyed tunnel."

"Because I couldn't guarantee anyone's safety that way. I knew we'd be liberated, so what was the sense in risking an escape?"

"I guess that almost makes sense." Natalia was quiet for a while as they walked toward the exit.

"And why you kill Jefferson?" she asked.

"Survival. It's horrible, but it's true. Sure, I could have shown some mercy, but think what would have happened if Jefferson had survived. Ever talk to that guy? Jefferson was the sort of angry control freak who wasn't capable of letting go of a grudge. Had I let him live, Jefferson would have hunted me to the edges of the world. I'd have spent the rest of my life in hiding. He didn't strike me as the type who was capable of setting aside philosophies and hatred of authority for the benefit of humankind. He was hung up on past wrongs. He'd never get past me selling him out; he'd never understand the greater good behind it."

"Yeah," Natalia said, raising her eyebrows in agreement as they walked, "that's probably true. OK, but one last thing I don't understand about plan. It could not work if you are still stuck on Salvatierra's island. If I did not come, how would you escape Salvatierra's island to get arrested by immigration agents?"

"The Ich-Ca-Gan told me you'd come to pick me up. Didn't they talk to you?"

"What? No! I did not talk to alien."

"Huh? Then why did you come?"

"I got text message from Salvatierra. He said he want to buy boat."

"So they didn't contact you?" Len asked, confused. He thought it over, then asked, "Wait a second, what exactly did the text from Salvatierra say?"

"It say he want biggest boat possible, with full weapons assembly. Destroyer class."

Len stared at her in befuddlement, then guffawed so hard that he could barely catch his breath. Natalia gave him a confused look. "Those clever little bastards! The Ich-Ca-Gan must have sent that somehow. A spoofed text message. Of course a text message—they can't talk! I asked the Ich-Ca-Gan for details about your arrival, but they wouldn't tell me anything. They just said to be patient and wait and that they'd take care of that part themselves. They wouldn't discuss that part of the plan with me..."

"Holy shit. So Salvatierra was telling truth? He really didn't order boat?"

"So of course you show up with a full crew and a floating arsenal. The Ich-Ca-Gan wanted Salvatierra to be outgunned!" Len continued laughing, despite the stabbing pain in his rib.

"We killed him for nothing?" Natalia couldn't help herself. She started giggling too.

"Do you feel bad?" Len asked, trying to catch his breath. "I don't."

"Fuck no. I don't like him anyway. He was asshole. He always underpay me." Natalia was now laughing so hard that tears were coming down her cheeks.

They both chortled until they were wheezing and had to stop.

"Look, I'm sorry that you lost your investment on the boat," Len said once he caught his breath. "I'll make it up to you somehow."

"Len, I am sorry too," she said softly. "Truly, deeply. I should have known you weren't traitor. I feel terrible for what I said in camp."

"Forget it. I'm a journalist; my whole career has been people hating my guts. I'm used to it. Please just give me the benefit of the doubt from now on. OK?"

"Deal," Natalia said, and hugged him. Len kissed her. "So now what?" she asked.

"I have no idea. I was thinking of going back to Pittsburgh to see what's left of my life there. Wanna come along?"

"Might as well. I don't know what hell else to do."

"What about your business?"

"If I think about it, with no more Tchogols or Dranthyx, maybe there will be no more war. Who will buy weapons? There is no fighting if only reasonable people are left. Also, Russian government does not exist anymore, so who will I buy from? Maybe it is time for new career."

41

The question was, how to get back to civilization with fifty miles of grassland between the camp and the nearest town? Being Xreths, someone figured out how to get the trains that they'd come in on running again. Over the next few days, millions of people were evacuated by rail to Kansas City, hundreds of miles away on the other side of the state.

With all the Tchogols dead, and the world's Xreths in captivity or in hiding, modern civilization had ground to a halt over the last few weeks. All responsibility had fallen to the Saskels, who were unable to keep things operational without being told what to do. The weird thing was, they kept showing up to their jobs. Only they didn't know what to do without any guidance, so they just sat there every day until five o'clock, then went home to drink beer.

Len tried the bus station in Kansas City, which was packed wall-to-wall with waylaid refugees. There were people with S tattoos working behind the counter, but they didn't know where the buses were, or when they'd start running again. They didn't seem to know anything, nor did they take the initiative to find out.

Transportation was an insurmountable problem. The airports that hadn't been destroyed in the invasion were nonetheless rendered useless by Saskel mismanagement. Trains and buses were out of commission. The only way out of Kansas City was by automobile, but the town didn't have nearly enough of those to accommodate the sudden influx of fifty million people. In a matter of hours, every single car in the whole county had been hired, stolen, or driven away. As the concentration camp emptied out, the streets around the train station in Kansas City swelled into a massive refugee camp as people were unable to get back to wherever they'd been abducted from. The location of the Dranthyx's concentration camp was no accident. They'd put it right in the center of the continent. In talking to people he met, Len found out the Dranthyx had brought prisoners in from as far away as Alaska and Panama.

Food, water, and sanitation were other problems. After a day in the disgusting refugee camp, Len and Natalia decided to take their chances by simply walking out of town. Out in the suburbs, they broke into a sporting goods store to steal two bicycles. Len found one with a kid seat on the back. He left an IOU note with his address.

Bicycles turned out to be the right choice. With global communications severed and no one left to orchestrate petroleum distribution, gasoline had become a fond memory. By day, they rode on the shoulders of empty freeways on their bicycles. At night, they scavenged canned goods and slept under the stars. Looking up, they saw that the Ich-Ca-Gan's ships remained motionless upon the air in their grid formation. At sunset, the white spheres turned orange and purple like the clouds, which was oddly beautiful. At night, they reflected moonlight. They just hung there, the sentinels of the earth.

Wherever they went, there were dead Dranthyx soldiers rotting in the streets. People desecrated their corpses and tried to figure out how to use their vehicles.

Jefferson was right, Len thought. Before the whole ordeal, humans had always felt something in their bones but never discussed it: there was an unconquerable, clandestine evil in the world that had to be answered to. It lurked wherever power did—behind political decisions and corporate policies, in the courts and behind badges. People spent their whole lives wondering when the other shoe would drop: when their country would be invaded, when they'd be sued, when they'd be murdered, when they'd be foreclosed upon or jailed or blown up. But as a child discovered when an angry, drunken parent suddenly moved out, *it didn't have to be that way.* So it was with those who survived. It took Len a while to put his finger on it, but he saw it clearly once it was gone. The human race had always been crushed by the anxiety that came from a constant anticipation of injustice, a feeling of powerlessness before the powerful. That worry died with the Dranthyx and their Tchogols. The shark-tank feeling was gone now; anarchy wasn't scary anymore.

Passing through the towns and cities, Len felt like there was a new mood in the world, a subtle undercurrent of joy and a sense of limitlessness. It was there despite everything people had been through over the last year. He saw it in people's faces and their actions. They were in charge of their own lives now, but they were also in it together. They were sovereign and they were family.

As none of them were expert bicyclists, it took them three weeks to get back to Pittsburgh. One day, as they were passing through Indiana, they stopped at a roadside produce stand to see if the farmer wanted to trade his apples for whatever Len and Natalia had with them. The farmer's stand was powered by a generator and happened to have a TV. On the TV were white Japanese characters on a black background:

人間達へ

次のメッセージを慎んで申し上げる。

1)今回は我々が助けたが、ドランシックスはまたいつか戻って
　くるだろう。その時は自分達で戦わなければならない。
2)国家機関は全て信用できない。独立心を持ちなさい。
3)最も大切な事だが、人間は人間以外の万物と切り離されてい
　ないと学ぶまで種としての進歩はない。

幸運を祈る。

イッチ・カ・ガーン

"What show is this?" Natalia asked.

"Oh, there aren't any shows anymore," the farmer said, putting some apples into a bag for them. "Not since the invasion. I don't know what this is, but it's being broadcast on all channels."

"Len, you know Japanese. What does it say?"

Len looked at the screen and struggled to remember all the characters.

"It's like a letter. It says, 'Dear Humans…we humbly bring the following items to your attention…1) We helped you this time but the…Dranthyx…will return someday. When that happens, you will need to fight them by yourselves. 2) All authority is fraud; learn to think for yourselves. 3) Most importantly, you must learn that you are not separate and apart from the rest of the universe. Good luck. Signed…Ich-Ca-Gan.'"

"This is a message from those UFOs? Is it for us?" the farmer asked, eyebrows raised.

"For all of us, apparently," Len said. "I do believe an alien race just told us to get our shit together."

42

A few days later, Len, Natalia, and Octavia finally walked up the steps to Len's apartment in Pittsburgh. Across the door was yellow tape reading "Police Line—Do Not Cross." Len tried opening the door but found it was locked, and he no longer had his keys—Jefferson's men had taken them out of his pockets when he was kidnapped. He asked Natalia and Octavia to wait there while he went downstairs to the first-floor apartment and knocked on the door.

"Who is it?" barked Ms. Armstrong, his octogenarian landlord, through the door.

"It's Leonard Savitz. Your tenant in 3A."

Leonard heard the door being unlocked. Ms. Armstrong opened the door just a crack. Upon seeing Len's face, her eyes widened and she unchained the lock.

"Leonard! I heard you were dead!"

"No such luck, Betty. Sorry about missing the rent," Len said, with a defeated smile.

"Oh, thank God! Can you believe what's been going on? One of those dreadful octopus creatures came to my door with some kind of gun and pricked my finger like he was checking my blood sugar. Then he zapped my arm and neck and gave me these hideous tattoos!" She mimicked the zapping of the tattoos. "They didn't want me, but they took our neighbor David in 2B. I rang the police, but they said they were taking orders from the octopuses. Oh, it's just horrific what's going on anymore!"

"Hopefully it's over now."

"I doubt it! And now they're saying those white balls in the skies are aliens! My goodness, where will it end?"

"Betty, do you have a key to my apartment? I think the terrorists took mine."

"Oh my. Of course, dear. The police made me change the locks anyway." Betty retreated into her dingy old-lady apartment and returned with a key. "Your mother has been by several times. She's worried sick about you. Oh, and an oriental gentleman came by this morning with a letter for you. I told him you'd been kidnapped and were probably dead, but he didn't seem to care. He said you'd be back anyway."

"Did you happen to catch his name?"

"Oh, I wrote it down. Let me see...Mr. Hamasaki."

Len felt his pulse quicken. He took the letter, put it in his pocket without opening it, and thanked Betty. Len went upstairs and opened the door to his apartment, letting Natalia and Octavia in. As expected, the place had been ransacked by the cops. Drawers tossed, clothes and silverware all over the place. His computer and paper files were missing. Thankfully, the detectives had left his bourbon alone.

Len poured some whiskey for himself and Natalia, took a deep breath, and opened the envelope. Inside was a letter in a woman's hand, a flowing script from some bygone era.

Dear Leonard,

Rumors of my demise have been greatly exaggerated.

I understand why you sent the Dranthyx after me, and I do not hold it against you. To tell you the truth, I was counting on it.

What you may hold against me, however, is another matter. I doubt any amount of apologizing on my part will cause you to forgive me, yet I sincerely apologize regardless.

I haven't been terribly forthright with you. I have spent much of my existence attempting to overthrow Dranthyx control. I studied you from afar for many years before selecting you for the mission. Of the billions of human beings on this planet, you were the only one who had the right combination of talents and personality traits to make the plan work.

I did not have the technology nor the manpower to take on the Dranthyx myself. The Ich-Ca-Gan *did* have the means to do so, but I could not have enlisted their help without yours. I knew you were capable of doing what I could not: collaborating with the Ich-Ca-Gan to destroy the Dranthyx.

Regretfully, I had to kidnap you, your ex-wife, and your daughter, because it was the only way to make the plan work. While the human race will be in a much better way going forward, I regret the suffering that I put you, your daughter, and the rest of the world through. I'm truly sorry about Sara.

We now live in a world free of Dranthyx, Tchogols, control, corruption, government, and surveillance. The people of the world now have a bright and (for the first time in history) self-directed future. A blank canvas. It came at a tremendous human cost, but I believe, and history may show, that it was worth it. I hope you can see why I did what I did.

I have restored both of your identities, Leonard Savitz and Jim Rivington, erasing any hint of suspicion associated with either. You may use both as you see fit. For your troubles, please accept, in gold bullion, one hundred times the payment I originally promised. It is buried at these exact coordinates: 40°26′34.0″ N, 80°00′57.0″ W.

Your fellow champion of humanity,

—Neith

Len's hands shook as he handed the letter to Natalia to read. He put a bewildered hand on his furrowed brow. Natalia appeared to read it twice, then gave Len an uncomprehending look.